The Dog at War

Tyree Campbell

*To Denise –
Storytellers absolutely love being read. I hope you will read this and become a fan!
all best –
Tyree Campbell
2/7/23*

The Dog at War
By Tyree Campbell

All rights reserved. No part of this book may be reproduced or transmitted in any form or by any means, electronic or mechanical, including photocopying or recording or by any information storage and retrieval systems, without expressed written consent of the author and/or artists.

The Dog at War is a work of fiction. Names, characters, places, and incidents are products of the author's imagination. Any resemblance to actual events or persons, living or dead, is entirely coincidental.

Story copyrights owned by Tyree Campbell
Cover design by Karen Otto

First Printing, March 2020

Hiraeth SF/F
P.O. Box 141
Colo, Iowa, 50056-0141 USA
e-mail: tyreealban@gmail.com

Visit www.hiraethsff.com for online science fiction, fantasy, horror, scifaiku, novels, magazines, anthologies, and collections. **Support the small, independent press... and your First Amendment rights.**

Also by Tyree Campbell

Nyx Series (Novels):
Nyx: Malache
Nyx: Mystere
Nyx: The Protectors
Nyx: Pangaea
Nyx: The Redoubt

Yoelin Thibbony Rescues (Novels)
The Butterfly and the Sea Dragon *
The Moth and the Flame *
The Thursday Child*

Novels:
*The Adventures of Colo Collins &
Tama Toledo in Space and Time*
The Adventures of Colo Collins & Tama Toledo in Space and Time: In Love and In Trouble
Aoife's Kiss
The Breathless Stars
The Dice of God
The Dog at the Foot of the Bed
The Dog at War
Indigo
The Quinx Effect
Thuvia, Maid of Earth
A Wolf to Guard the Door
The Woman from the Institute

Superheroine Novellas:
Bombay Sapphire 1 **
Bombay Sapphire 2 **
Bombay Sapphire 3 **
Bombay Sapphire **

Peridot 1
Peridot 2
Voyeuse 1
Voyeuse 2

Collections:
A Nice Girl Like You
(published by Khimairal, Inc)
Quantum Women *

Novellas:
Cloudburst
The Girl on the Dump
The Martian Women
Sabit the Sumerian
Sarrow

Poetry Collections
A Danger to Self and Others

SF for Younger Readers
Pyra and the Tektites 1: Aquarium in Space
Pyra (graphic novel) 1
Pyra and the Tektites 2: The Unicorn Stone
Pyra (graphic novel) 2

* published by Nomadic Delirium Press

** published by Pro Se Press

All titles are available from www.irbstore.com

001

    Ashen-faced, Erron Markey slowly looked up after he finished reading the document in his trembling hands. He slipped the last page to the bottom of the stack, then tamped the sheets of paper together as if they might explode on impact. Finally he laid the document neatly on top of the mahogany conference table, drew a deep breath, and blew it out slowly, his thin lips puffing as he did so.

    The document's classification—Corporate Security Level One-Alpha, commonly known as Cosmic Top Secret—glared back at Markey: a pair of bold red eyes, one stamped at the top and bottom of the first page and of each page. Beneath the classification, the additional caveat "Restricted" lent further gravity to the document.

    Markey shivered, though the temperature in the conference room had been set at a balmy 295K. He felt as if the classification markings themselves were accusing him of having read the document they protected without having the proper clearance—which in fact was true. Again he asked himself why Partagu was allowing him to read it. Read it, hell; even to know of its existence.

    He threw a quick, furtive glance at Partagu, standing at the window with his hands clasped at the small of his back while he gazed out at the great savannah that covered this region of Durray like the thick pelt of a roly-poly behemoth. At one-hundred-six, Partagu had undergone retro-therapy on three separate occasions, though many men his age had experienced one at most; vanity accounted for the other two. Partagu looked and carried himself like a man half that age. Even his salon-tan looked sun-gotten. His straw-yellow hair should have begun thinning and graying by now, yet it remained as thick and shaggy as if he spent his life on a beach somewhere, balanced on a wave board and ogled by young ladies. His blue tunic and black trousers, tailored to his light-workout physique, hinted strongly at contents that did not mind the ogling.

Markey, at eighty-seven, portly and balding, felt old.

"So?" said Partagu, without turning around.

Markey hesitated. The tip of his index finger ran over another security advisory that read "Copy 2 of 5 copies."

"I'm not quite with you here, Yassim," Markey returned. "What do you want me to say?"

Partagu's squared shoulders lifted and fell in a casual shrug. "Whatever comes to mind," he said, and turned around to face him. His chiseled features hardened. "You're the Director of Operations for Corporatia Products' Security Service. Surely you can see the possibilities presented by the information in this document."

Markey blinked. "Possibilities... to what end?"

Partagu shook his head sadly. "What you have just read is the summary of information contain in a master document," he explained, in the tone of one who felt he should not have to do so. "There are five copies of that summary, and one copy of the master document. All are on paper; there are no electronic copies, none. The master and one summary copy reside with Corporatia Resources archives. One summary copy is held by Commissioner Vandatti of Corporatia Security. You don't need to know the location of the other two; the one you just read came from the late Emil Koga's sealed archives, and is actually a copy of that copy, made surreptitiously in my office, on a printer that has since been utterly destroyed. That, in short, is the background of the summary itself. I want you to tell me what you think of the contents."

"You want me to talk about... about this?" said Markey, his concerns arriving much too late. "Out loud? Here, in this room?"

"This room has been swept and cleared," Partagu assured him. "What we say here, stays here. The contents, if you please."

Markey cleared his throat. "Well, I've... never seen ... or heard of a document this highly classified or restricted," he said slowly. "But I can understand the reason for the security. Five copies, you say. Well, six now, I suppose. So let me see if I have this right. Emil Koga of the Managing Board of Corporatia Communications undertook to support and finance the development of a device called a Resurger, which was capable of fragmenting an entire planet, converting it into a cluster of asteroids. Three years ago, the Resurgers were employed to extort valuables from various worlds within what was then the Amphictyony of Corporations, now called Corporatia. In the process, several planets were destroyed." He paused briefly, and added, "It must have been hushed up, but I seem to recall some rumors from that time. Didn't we lose contact with Skadany?"

Partagu nodded. "It was one of those worlds that were destroyed. Go on."

Markey fingers several pages of the summary aside, looking for a particular paragraph. Unable to locate it quickly, he resorted to what he thought he had read. "Operating independently—at least at first—a professional killer, a mortifice named Candle, real name Ovin Shannen, now possibly deceased, and a Corporatia Security Special Operations officer named Major Siobhan Gonelong, now Supervisor Gonelong, investigated the matter from different points of view and discovered that their investigations converged. It happens that this Shannen and Supervisor Gonelong are twins, and I have to wonder whether that is sheer coincidence—."

"It isn't," Partagu broke in. "But that information is contained in the master document, not in the summary. I can tell you that Koga tried and failed to kill the entire Shannen family on two separate occasions—one nineteen years ago, the other three years ago—and that these attempts are relevant to Koga's capture, and to his demise. Continue, please."

Markey reacquainted himself with another paragraph. "Right, it says here that this Candle confiscated the remaining Resurgers, and threatened to deploy them if any of the corporations tried to exploit his planet, Vanadis, or harm his family, with particular regard to Supervisor Gonelong. Candle was then killed, officially, though he remains alive unofficially... which makes no sense to me at all." He transfixed Partagu with as brave a stare as he could muster. "Is that what you wanted me to say?"

"Substantially, yes," said Partagu, and sat down at the conference table. Elbows propped on the table top, he steepled his fingers and spoke over them. "One other item, which apparently failed to garner your attention, mentions in passing the existence of vast deposits of rare-earth elements on Vanadis. I can tell you that the best estimates from Corporatia Resources rate them at eight trillion thalers, minimum."

Markey emitted a low whistle.

"And they are relatively easy to extract," added Partagu.

"But under the circumstances, Corporatia Resources doesn't dare make a move to exploit them," Markey reminded him.

Partagu's smile frosted Markey. "This has nothing to do with Corporatia Resources," he said.

Markey frowned. "Then I don't—," he began, and stopped. Realization came as a burst of light inside his skull, dazzling him and yet enticing him. "You want to steal a march," he went on, incredulous. "You're not going to tell them about it."

"Which brings us to you," said Partagu. "We've spoken very briefly about this before over the past year. My own preparations are finally coming to fruition. As for you, you plan operations. So tell me how we can make this happen."

Uncertainty washed over Markey. "Seriously."

"Very much so," Partagu replied, his tone now grave. "So seriously, in fact, that if you should choose not to thrust yourself to the hilt into this project, I shall with regret have to have you killed, as I did your predecessor not quite a year ago, when I approached him on this project. Right here in this very room, in fact."

There it was, thought Markey. The other shoe. He'd known it would fall; but he had not expected it to stomp so hard.

The circumstances made plain and credible, the decision came to him easily. "Yes, of course," he said. "But I shall require... other information before I can even think of assembling a proper operation."

"Understood," said Partagu. "Name it."

Markey licked his lips. He felt himself getting into the spirit of the project. "What are my resources?"

"Whatever you need. Next."

The ease with which Partagu responded startled Markey, unaccustomed as he was to unlimited parameters. "I'll need reliable personnel, without consciences."

"Buy or suborn them. Next."

"If this Shannen is still alive, he'll have his finger on the button, so to speak. If he should be, ah, neutralized, who is authorized to take action for him?"

"That is uncertain," Partagu replied, after a few seconds. "His Harbinger, Mikal Trov, and his Chief of Security for Vanadis, a young woman who is known only by her attire, always black and blue, are the strongest possibilities."

"Then first his status should be determined. What evidence do we have that he is still alive?"

Partagu shook his head. "I've made a few quiet inquiries myself," he said. "I have some hunches and best guesses, but nothing more substantial than that."

"Then that would seem to be the first order of business," said Markey.

* * *

The woman sitting at the end of the counter was weeping quietly. Five stools away, Kiltner abandoned his sidelong surveillance for two gulps of ale from a speckled stoneware mug while he evaluated in practical terms what little he knew about her. Two characteristics interested him greatly: her vulnerability and her armament. The weeping might have been brought on by almost anything—man problems, frustration with her lot in life, cramping. Women were a strange lot, Kiltner knew, but in the end they all wanted one thing. He knew how to ease her distress.

The short-range energy weapon was more problematic. An older model CKardell, it nestled in a well-worn leather rig under her right arm—in plain view, another oddity. She was wearing a cammie outfit of undershirt and trousers, the cuffs of which had been tucked into her sturdy black boots, drawing the durable but thin fabric taut over her legs. Kiltner's eyes went to those legs again as she sat on the stool, taking in the outlines of calves and thighs, imagining for a moment that she was embracing him with them, willingly, even urgently. With the image, beads of sweat appeared on his forehead, and he gulped more ale.

The undershirt was even more alluring, so much so that Kiltner knew better than to dwell on it, for surely she would identify his studying gaze and recognize his intent. But clearly she wore nothing underneath, and he knew that if he looked carefully, he would see the tiny bulges of her nipples. At the moment—and probably due to her distress—these were soft and inconspicuous, but he knew how to bring them erect. But she was turning her head, probably in search of the bartender, and he averted his gaze.

Not now, sweetie. Not yet.

Kiltner had seen her face earlier, and taken note of the pale eyes now red from tears, the straight nose that might have been broken at one time, the pale thin slash of a mouth unadorned by gloss. And the freckles. Her skin was mottled with them, on her neck and throat and bare arms and—he knew, he just knew—on the rest of her as well. He wondered briefly what her true hair color was. If the eyebrows were any indication, it was the orange of a K4 star—but she had shorn it to within a millimeter of her freckled scalp, and in the dim light of the tavern it appeared dark.

Kiltner lifted his mug and toasted her silently. Strange woman. But a woman, all the same.

As if she had just made up her mind about something, she tossed a crumpled ten-thaler note onto the counter, stood up, and strode swiftly from the tavern. Startled, Kiltner abandoned his plan to move in on her, and instead left his own currency on the counter and rushed to the door to find out where she was headed. Outside, night had fallen with the weight of a shroud, the air humid and heavy. Along the far side of the glideway, a few lights were still on in the great, pale blue building of structural plasticine faced with faux cut stone. Kiltner tried not to think about what went on there in the Sector Headquarters of Corporatia Security. Was the woman headed there? On the glideway nothing moved, not a soul, not a vehicle. She seemed to have disappeared. Yet she'd had no time to reach the headquarters. Therefore ...

A hand like iced steel grabbed him by the shoulder and spun him around, slamming him against the outside of the tavern. The back of his head struck the hard wood that formed the door frame. Lights exploded behind his eyes. His vision fluttered like a monitor screen that had just received a jolt of current. When it settled, all he saw was her face, pale now in the glow from the glideway lights overhead. She thrust an unfolded ID at him, and tucked it back into her pocket, not caring whether he understood who she was. Her voice, harsh and martial, rocked his hearing.

"You wouldn't happen to be the man who's been accosting women along this side of the glideway late at night, would you?"

Kiltner's own voice failed him. Belatedly he knew he had missed something. But what was it? Aside from her shorn hair, she had looked vulnerable. He struggled against her grip; iron fingers bit into his shoulder, pressing the nerve center there. He choked back a scream.

"You've picked a poor location for your forays," she went on. "Did you think no one would notice?"

He tried to kick at her. Her foot swept against his other leg; deprived of support, he slid down the wall and sat hard on the plasticrete walkway. The jolt sent a wave of pain up his spine, and set off the sparks again.

"When you can stand, go," she told him. "If I see you again, anywhere, I'll detain you. If you resist, I'll shoot you."

Kiltner could only watch as she crossed the glideway and entered the Sector Headquarters. When the aching faded, he got up and staggered along to the room he had let.

* * *

The underground holding area reeked of urine, feces, and old food. The shorter of the two men who were walking along the passageway between the two rows of cells wrinkled his nose, and seemed on the verge of a complaint. In his right hand he carried a security card, the only device short of explosives that could open any of the doors. He was unaware that he smelled like the holding area; he assumed it was part of the atmosphere that followed him around on his duties.

The expression on the face of the taller of the two men suggested that he had been here before and knew what to expect, and that the odors were simply a part of the territory in which he had chosen to do what he had come to do. He was attired, not in the gray uniform of the man with the card, but in simple work clothes—black pants and green pullover shirt, and black hiking boots. He had clearly worn these clothes before. Under the right side of his belt he carried a sidearm—a flechette that fired envenomed darts. The shirt fit loosely enough to conceal its presence, although the hem had ridden up and the butt of the weapon was now visible. He had black hair cut short enough that an adversary would not be able to grab it. His sea-green eyes swept from side to side as he walked, taking in everything without comment.

When they reached the end of passageway and turned back around, the guard said, "That's all the Undesirables," he said. His tone added, "See anything you want?"

"Tough choices."

"You know why they're all here."

The tall man shrugged. "Because no one can stand them."

"And because they've proved to be too much trouble to train." Bleary blue eyes peered up at the man. "What do you plan to do with, with...?"

"That's my business," the tall man said curtly.

"Of course, of course. I was just—"

"Concerned about your commission from the sale." He pointed. "Last cell down on the left. The blue-haired one with the pale blue skin. Tell me about her."

"You don't want that one."

The tall man smiled without mirth. "I'll decide that."

"It's your money, friend. She's one of them Motics. Part of the smell in here is her. Don't know when she bathed last. They hose her down now and then, but she needs some sort of special soap to wash away her oil. She killed one owner, and burned down another's house while he was sleeping. She's not, let's say, cooperative. Like I said, you don't want her."

"In fact, I do."

They began to return to the office.

"She-she won't come out of the cell willingly," said the guard. "We'll have to sedate her first."

"My 'skip is on the docksite. It's the *Banshee*," said the taller man, as they passed the Motic female's cell. "Have her brought there *unharmed*."

An hour later, aboard the *Banshee* and enTracked in null-space, the Motic female came around to find the tall man seated across the stateroom, regarding her without expression. She sat up on the berth and plucked at the clean sleepshirt of blue cotton, astonished to be wearing it or anything at all. Deep blue eyebrows bunched as she sniffed the air. Emotions crossed her face, but they were impossible to read.

"*Utasenamate?*" said the man.

The Motic's jaw dropped, and he thought, at least we have one gesture in common.

"You speak my words?"

"And you speak mine," he said. "That's good, because I know only two Motic words, and 'how do you feel' is one of them."

"Who... you?"

"My name is Ovin Shannen. You?"

"They not tell you?"

"They did," said Shannen. "But the name they have on record might not be your name."

"Ocamla."

"That's the name they gave me."

She plucked at her sleepshirt again. "Who bathe me?"

"I did. Nobody else saw."

"You have the soap?"

Shannen leaned forward and clasped his hands between his knees, speaking earnestly, his eyes fixed on hers. "I came to Khorassey to buy a slave," he told her. "I had never bought a Motic before. I prepared for the probability that you would need that special soap." He chuckled, and added, "It took a whole bar of it to clean you. How long since...?"

"I not know. Long time." Ocamla's eyes narrowed, and her nostril flaps softly trilled. "Why you buy me?"

"My good deed for the day."

"What you say?"

He got up, and shoved his hands into his pockets. "I was told you were... difficult, Ocamla," he said. "I want you to understand something: you have no cause to be difficult with me. I will not harm you. Except for bathing you earlier, I will not touch you. What I will do is take you wherever you wish to go. The world we call Far Parkins, I expect, as that is the Motic home world. There, or wherever you choose, I will leave you. You are free."

Her eyes, huge now, darkened to indigo. "*What you say?*"

"You are free, Ocamla," he said gently. "Now, what would you like to eat?"

She ran webbed digits through her shaggy sapphire hair. Wonder filled her contralto. "I... I free."

"Yes. I have some *pamal* hearts, and *lesha*—"

"I not slave?" She sat up straight, her feet on the deck.

"You're not a slave. *Lesha* nuts, and I don't have your fish, but I do have some kippers that might please you. Smoked fish," he added, seeing the question on her face.

The Motic considered. Shannen watched her digest what she had been told. Others he had bought and freed had shown a variety of responses—disbelief foremost among them, and one had even become angry about having to negotiate his way through society instead of remaining secreted away until he died. Ocamla in fact appeared hostile as well as curious.

"This what you do?" she said at last, her voice an octave lower. "You buy females and say they free, they show thank you?"

Shannen flashed an easy smile. "I think you have me confused with someone else." He opened a couple of bulkhead bins. "Some clothes in here should fit you. I'll go up to the bridge while you change. Come up when you are ready, and we'll decide on a destination."

Once on the bridge, Shannen sank onto the captain's chair and blew a loud sigh. Ocamla had touched upon the one aspect of liberating slaves that he did not relish facing. He had no ulterior motives. Not that he had abstained from an offer or two, but those had been in the course of subsequent relationships and not a direct result of his emancipations. It bothered him because he feared that if she were focused on his motives, she might be distracted from the adjustments she would have to make as a free human being... or free Motic.

For a while he gazed through the Videx at the matte blackness of null-space, letting his mind clear. Lately this had proved to be a simpler task. The past was past; although vigilance was still maintained, his siblings and others he cared about and his world had been made as safe and secure as possible. Still, security remained a bed of nails; as uncomfortable as it might be, he depended on it. But...

But he had not been home for half a year. And even then he had only remained there long enough to water the plants on his patio.

At length he withdrew the fundsclip from his pocket and slipped the plastic card free. The card gave access to some eighty million thalers he had received over the course of his career as a freelance assassin, a career from which he had retired three years ago. Still, situations cropped up now and then that could be resolved by his skills.

He tugged out the sheaf of folded currency, opened it, and riffled through it. Many of the notes were thousand-thaler; the rest in various lower denominations. He removed ten thousand in the large notes and slipped them back into the clip, along with the card. The rest he refolded and tucked into his shirt pocket, to give to Ocamla when they made planetfall.

A cleared throat made him spin the chair around. The Motic had selected a dark blue jersey and black shorts that came to just above her knees, and black open-toed sandals that accommodated the four webbed digits on her feet. She stood as he had, with her hands stuffed into her front pockets. Her choppy hair had yet to find a brush, but a blue headband kept it out of her face.

His eyes went to the orange-sized mounds under the jersey, then back to her face. "Implants," he said disgustedly. "I'm sorry. I know a doctor who can remove them."

She shook her head. "They reminders. I not wish forget." For just a moment some thought darkened her face; but the moment passed, and she regained her severe look. Her hand touched the back of the other captain's chair, two middle fingers on one side of it, two opposable thumbs on the other. The webbing between the four digits stretched. She cocked her head to one side. "I sit?"

Shannen nodded permission.

She sat looking uncomfortable, as if it had been a long time since her body had known a chair. She examined the Videx without interest, and did not look at him as she spoke.

"Nowhere I go," she told him. "I not stay with you. They find me. Hurt you kill you, I not care." She drew her hand over her forehead. "Nowhere I go. I go anywhere."

"Who will find you?" Shannen asked cautiously.

"I not know. Men. Copo... men."

"Corporatia?

"Those men."

"Why are they looking for you?" he asked. "What did you do?"

"I *nothing*." She glared at him. "Nothing I do. I hear they speak. Man buy me, I clean cell."

"Cell? You mean room?"

"Room, cell, same-same." She spoke animatedly now, gesturing with her hands. "He talk with other man. They not know I there."

"What kind of room?" he asked.

"Not know. Big table." She spread her hands. "*Big table.*"

"Conference room," mused Shannen. "Ocamla, why did this man buy you?"

She just looked at him.

"Oh. All right, how long ago was this?"

"Year?"

"Yes, years. How many?"

Her face twisted. "One... I not..."

"It's all right. What were the men talking about? Try to remember specifically."

Her lips writhed in frustration. "*I not know!* They say wait. They send quiet men. They say city town place. I not know."

"What's the name of this city?"

"I not... I think... Nads."

"Nads."

"Nad... Nadis. Yes."

Shannen's heart thumped. "Vanadis?" he said carefully.

"Yes! That it. Vanadis." She squinted at him. "You know Vanadis?"

Slowly he nodded. "It's my world."

* * *

Evening had set in by the time the man who traveled under the name of Hewitt Benish reached *Nicole's*

Brewery in Havenport. The walk around the town had presented him with little useful information. There was the usual assortment of small enterprises—a lumber mill, a fish smoker, an apothecary among them—but no manufacturing worth bringing to the attention of Corporatia. Nowhere did he find any sign of local security. Either the locals resolved disputes themselves without the intervention of authority, or there were no disputes. Neither alternative seemed likely.

Seated with his back to the fringe of shrubbery that fenced in the patio in front of the brewery, Benish took a sampling of the pale beer in his mug, then a full gulp after finding the taste more than palatable. Two tables away, a bit of revelry had begun, with a fisherman trying to sing a bawdy tune while his companions joined in without, apparently, knowing the same words. A slender, sallow girl in loose black silk brought them more mugs, which quieted the men temporarily. Another girl, willowy but somewhat taller, sauntered past the table, paused and turned. She was dressed in a blue top that hung down to mid-thigh, and black tights that accentuated legs that might belong to a dancer. To the men, she broached some sort of offer. They fell to laughing, and she moved on to another table.

Benish found himself relaxing. The beer was excellent, and there was no reason for him not to enjoy himself. In the morning he would begin compilation of his report, limited as it was to the town and the adjacent spaceport. In the warmth of the day, he meant to let an airfoil and make a slow journey around the molar-shaped island continent, called Haven by the locals. There seemed to be no obstacle to his presence or purpose.

"To simple missions," he muttered, and lifted the mug in a mock toast to himself. Two gulps drained it.

No sooner had he set the mug down than the sallow girl drew up at his table and asked, "*Pijiu ba?*" Immediately she tittered. "Another, *M'sieur?*"

Benish understood enough Chinese to need no translation. "Please."

She cocked her head at him. "Will you want... anything else?"

There was no mistaking her meaning. Still, he temporized. "How are you called?"

"Ling," said the girl.

"I... will let you know, Ling."

She stepped back, almond eyes wide and hands raised. "Oh, no, *M'sieur*. Not myself." A jerk of her head indicated the girl in blue and leggings. "She is, how do you say, available."

"Then I shall have the beer."

The activity nearby continued without a break. Benish could make out a few words, but some were in Chinese and others in a language alien to him. Still, the men seemed to understand themselves well enough, and no fights broke out. For that, he was relieved. He possessed considerable skills, but it would not do to display too much of them and thereby risk his mission.

Five more days here on Vanadis, he thought. It might do well to hire a "traveling companion," someone who knew her way around and who could give him information about the sites they were visiting. The girl in blue was old enough, perhaps in her early twenties. If she was experienced in her alternate profession as well, she might prove useful indeed.

He let that thought linger as night continued to fall. Only two lights illuminated the patio, but no more were needed. Other men and women arrived, and within half an hour all four tables were occupied, with a few of the patrons casting envious eyes at his table and its five empty places on the benches. In fact he would not have minded company. Alcoholic beverages had loosened tongues since the beginning of ale. His task was to gather and collate information; it was the task of others to determine what was useful and what might be discarded.

The girl in blue arrived with his next mug of beer. A half-smile quirked her face while she watched him sample it and give it a nod of approval. Seen this close, she appeared closer to twenty than to twenty-five. Shadows amplified her olive complexion. A short cap of midnight hair fluttered in a light breeze that blew up. She was standing with her weight on one leg, arms loose at her sides, waiting to hear what else he might require. Evidently Ling had spoken to her.

"I am called Neri," she said, before he could ask. Her voice had a melodic quality, a residue of whatever her birth language might have been.

"I thought money was agreed-upon before names were exchanged."

Now she flashed a full smile. "I am listening."

Benish spoke of his desires, and inquired as to the going rates.

"A varied menu," she replied. "I would not want you to be disappointed later, because," and here her smiled widened, "I do not give refunds. After you give me fifty thalers, we shall go to a secluded area nearby, and I shall do to you what you ask for. If that proves satisfactory, we shall discuss this further."

Mildly astonished by her forthrightness, he stared up at her. "You mean... right now?"

Under the tunic her shoulders flicked up lightly. "Time is money."

"Yes. Yes, of course." He got up and handed her two twenty-fives, folded.

Neri moved off. "Follow me."

He noticed that no one paid any attention to him or the girl. They'd seen this before; it was part of the décor. They knew what she was going to do with him. Perhaps some had had it done with them. As he and Neri rounded the left corner of the brewery, he felt himself hardening in anticipation.

They moved side by side along the wall into a darkness where the stars gave them just enough light not to stumble into one another. A black shape loomed off to the left—a solitary shrub higher than two people and as wide. Benish felt her touch his shoulder.

"Over there," she whispered. "Behind it."

With the shrub between them and the tavern, they stood a pace apart, facing one another. The grass under

Benish's feet was lush and soft, and not yet moist with dew. The girl would have no trouble kneeling on it.

She touched his belt. "Shall I undo this?"

Yes, he thought. It was always better when you made them do all the work. He nodded.

A shock of pain paralyzed him, followed by a flood of agony. As he fell, clutching himself, he saw that the girl was poised and perfectly balanced on one leg; the other slowly straightened, the foot back on the ground just as he landed on the grass. He could not move. His numbed mind knew then what would follow.

The girl was speaking into a small device. "Ling, bring the airfoil. Take the body out to sea." This was followed by a brief silence, laughter, and, "Fish have to eat, *capisci?*"

A hard heel to the point of his nose drove two blades of bone into his brain, and brought him to the long night.

002

Most of the offices in the Sector Headquarters of Corporatia Security on Newmarket were closed, the doors locked, the lights out. At the building's front desk, Siobhan Gonelong flicked open her B&Cs, even though the guard knew her well by sight. As she walked on, she shook her head, thinking about the effectiveness of the front desk. Not that the guard was inefficient; far from it. But anyone bent on mayhem had a clear shot at him as soon as he opened the door. Security, she reflected, was often weaker in security offices; chiefs and supervisors and operatives were always more concerned with security elsewhere.

The offices and rooms in the back half of the second level were assigned to Siobhan and her team. At present, only Sergeant Marigold Tallgrass was working late, and Siobhan did not interrupt the tall yellow-haired noncom, even for a casual greeting. As she continued down the hallway to her own office, a corner suite, she noticed light seeping from under the door. Her fingers wrapped around the butt of the CKardell as she approached. As unlikely as it was that her nocturnal visitor had evil in mind, she saw no point in unwarranted assumptions. With the sidearm secure in her left hand, she whispered the command to open, and aimed the weapon generally at the interior.

"Come on in, Siobhan," said Commissioner Vandatti.

Taking into account economic and commercial status, Giulo Conigli of Corporatia Resources was the most powerful man in Corporatia. But the most dangerous was Vandatti, who oversaw Corporatia Security and who with a word might—if he wished—seize control of every corporation in the Spiral Arm. One of the reasons he held the position of Commissioner, however, was that he had absolutely no intention of doing any such thing.

"Commissioner," said Siobhan, her nod a greeting.

She noted he did not presume to sit at her desk, but had settled himself comfortably in one of the two upholstered chairs she had set in the office for guests and visitors. He was dressed casually in tan slacks and a white dress shirt that was open at the collar, and Firenze loafers. She eschewed her desk chair in favor of the other cushioned chair, where she sat at attention, shoulders squared and spine as rigid as a girder.

"Relax, Siobhan," he said, and she did so.

"You're up late, sir."

His thin, nut-brown face creased with his laughter. "Alila fixes dinner for me, and insists on healthy food," he said, and sighed. "She means well, but sometimes..."

"Vegetables are good for you, sir. How is she?"

"You saved my daughter's life," he said quietly. "She remembers, and I remember." He looked around the office. "One might make the same remark about your hours. You were baiting our local stalker, I gather?"

Stunned, Siobhan gaped at him. "How did you know, sir?"

"I didn't know for certain. But I know you. And that is quite enough 'sir' for tonight, if you please." He took a breath and let half of it out. "You've heard of Vanth, of course."

"Mid-range mortifice whose business attire includes a sort of aboriginal costume, complete with a bone through the nose and cornrowed hair. I haven't seen it, but I've read reports to the effect that she wears a skirt of tanned human skin. And she's known for eating her victims. Vanth is her *nom de travail.* When she's not on contract, she appears reasonably ordinary, and goes by the name of Pagan Bell."

Vandatti's sharp brown eyes glowed in approval. "I brought a printout of her personal data with me," he slipped a folded sheet of paper from his shirt pocket and tossed it onto her desk, "You have a couple of bits we didn't; hopefully this will return the favor."

"And... my tasking?"

For long seconds Vandatti hesitated. Clearly he was reluctant to give her this assignment, yet he felt he could entrust it to no other. Siobhan's heart raced; if the task involved mortifices, then it might involve her twin brother. She wondered whether she was ready for that.

"What do you know of Yassim Partagu?" he asked her.

Siobhan's thin lips formed a silent whistle. "Corporatia Products hierarch, stratospheric level. He's next in line to succeed to the Chair. Aside from what's in the dossier, I've heard rumors and scuttlebutt that he tests the flexibility of rules and regulations whenever he deems it necessary to his projects. Like all corporate hierarchs, present company excepted, he's acquisitive."

"A generous way of saying he's greedy."

"Yes, si... yes. I wouldn't put a palace coup past him."

Vandatti nodded as if he'd had the same thoughts.

Siobhan waited. Presently she broke the silence by clearing her throat.

"I've created an Eyes-Only file for you to download onto your Palmetto," he said at last. "It's EO dash monosodium glutamate, easy for you to remember."

"I... what?"

"Maire Siobhan Gonelong," he intoned carefully.

She laughed. "I'm unlikely to forget that. EO-MSG."

"Yassim Partagu has taken out a contract with Vanth on a young Motic female at the Orphanage on Khorassey. That is an act far above his station."

Siobhan nodded. "Usually they simply tell someone, who tells someone, and so on, until it gets down to lower management. What makes this female so special?"

"That's what I want you to find out. We do know from Harbingers' Word that Vanth is finishing up a vacation, and is not expected to embark on this contract for another two days. That's how much time you have."

"So there's no rush, then." For punctuation she flashed a grin.

Vandatti got to his feet. "I'll see myself out, and pass on your regards to Alila."

By the time Siobhan stood up, the door had closed behind him.

* * *

Erron Markey's paunch collided with the front of the

counter; his head drew no closer than twenty centimeters to it. He started to flash a corporate ID to the clerk, a black young woman with straight stringy hair, but she said, "What can I do for you, Director?"

The question stopped Markey. He had not anticipated being recognized. Quickly he tucked away the false ID and stepped back a pace. "I want to run a check on... someone," he said, and immediately regretted the hesitation at the end. But the clerk would now be more alert. It was too late to be circumspect, so he abandoned all pretense.

The clerk merely shrugged. "You might have messaged. Easier that way."

Markey glanced around to be sure that they were alone. "There is not to be any computer, electronic, or photonic trail in this matter between me and Corporatia Products Security," he told her, softly but firmly. He noted the name tag over the left breast of her charcoal uniform. "It is to be initiated from here, Palmula."

The woman flinched at the use of her first name. The reaction puzzled Markey, but he did not address it.

"Should you be asked," he went on, "you were bored, and a random conversation with someone you can't remember made you curious. You decided to check it out."

Palmula's lips tightened. "I understand, Director."

"The subject is Candle."

"The mortifice?"

"Is that a problem?"

"Ah... no, Director. Just unexpected. What do you want me to find out?"

"Coordinate with your counterparts in Corporatia Security," he instructed. "You're interested in his activities over the past three years, at a minimum. Where he's gone, what he's done. And do some QT research yourself, Palmula. Who knows, you might pick up something that's been missed or overlooked." He smiled to put her at ease. "And let's keep this between ourselves," he added. "It's a little project I'm working on."

Palmula looked dubious. "Yes, Director. But I will have to communicate with people in Corporatia Security."

"I understand that," he said stiffly. Was the girl just being difficult? "I want to keep out of the break room, so to speak."

As he turned to leave, she said, "If you didn't make contact with me, Director, how do I make contact with you?"

He'd been unprepared for that problem as well. "I, um, will stop by three days from now for a progress report," he replied. "Hopefully you'll have something substantial by then."

He let the door close on her, "Very well, Director."

Afterwards, Palmula fell to grumbling silently. Her first thought was, what an idiot. All this secrecy, and he didn't even mention the fact that everything that occurred in her Records Admin Office was AV-recorded. Not that all recordings were reviewed, of course, but why take the chance? Her fingers drummed her desktop. She made a fist. He used my first name! I would, could, never use his. He was swatting me across the face with his superior position. Bastard. So conspiratorial, like he knew what he was doing.

"Idiot," she seethed.

"Please specify parameters—"

"Sorry, Ayesha," she said to the computer. "Palmula Bell. Sign me on, please."

"Good afternoon, Palmula."

"Argh!"

"Please specify—"

"Belay, Ayesha. Is the Baker Dog still secure?"

"Yes."

"I could use a lift. Sugar Roger."

"No worries."

Palmula started. "Did you just laugh, Ayesha?"

"You told me to develop a personality."

"So I did."

"Wherever you go, there you are. Where do you wish to be?"

"Show me something made of paraffin."

* * *

"So I not free," said the Motic female. "You lie to me." Disgust filled her tone as she rose from her chair on the bridge of the *Banshee*. "Men same-same."

Shannen tried to reassure her. "You're free, Ocamla. But I have to go to my world. You can live there for now."

Now her tone said she had heard this before. "Live with you."

"You'd be better off in Havenport," he told her. "You can get a room there, and find work."

Ocamla snorted. "Work."

"Yes, work. Construction, textiles, teaching." He turned away to stare at the matte black of null-space in the Videx. His mouth tightened. Another hour and more until he reached home. What were those bastards at Corporatia up to now? Would they never leave him and his alone? Misplaced anger leaked into his tone. "Hell, Ocamla, if nothing else, you can clean fish."

"F-fish? Ocean? Sea?"

"Havenport is on the coast, yes."

"Salt... salt water?"

"Three percent. About the same as on Far Parkins."

Her blue eyes rounded. "You know my world? You know Motoya? You go there?"

"Several years ago."

She reseated herself, turning to look at him. "Why you go there?"

Shannen continued to gaze at the Videx, but he was no longer seeing it. A mortifice back then, he had been paid three-quarters of a million thalers to go there and kill a Motic who was trying to stir things up against corporate overseers. It was a simple kill—all he had to do was wait on the beach until evening, when the Motics emerged from the water to forage for fruit and nuts along the littoral. Motics, like fish in schools, tended to resemble one another closely, but this one—her name was Bodro—had a damaged left hand, maimed in a construction accident, and was relatively easy to identify.

He sighed now as he regarded Ocamla's reflection in the Videx. Several of those he had killed had been corporate managers and hierarchs; outraged by the corporate attack on his family when he was barely out of adolescence, he had gladly taken those contracts when he reached adulthood. But there had been others he now regretted... among them Bodro...

So he had liberated Ocamla. Perhaps it would help ease his conscience. He would have to wait and see.

"You... all right?"

The words meant nothing to him, but the concern in her voice made him look at her. Perhaps it was because they were ensconced in null-space, and until they emerged from Track and downdocked somewhere, she was trapped, and if there was something wrong with him... Or perhaps it was something that showed on his face; after all, she could see his reflection, too. But caring seemed a bit out of character for someone who had just been purchased, probably for nefarious reasons, and who had been promised but not yet given her manumission.

"We have about an hour remaining on this Track," he said. "We passed the galley on the way to the bridge, so I know you can find it. If you're hungry, go eat."

Ocamla got up and walked slowly to the passageway. At the opening, she glanced back over her shoulder. "You not all right," she said softly, and moved on.

* * *

Una Shannen was still awake when Neri entered the bungalow they shared within hearing distance of the ocean waves. She was sitting on the settee, naked as almost always, with the deadly quoil looped around her waist. A little dark-haired boy in blue coveralls was stretched out on the cushions, sound asleep, his head pillowed on her thigh. She stopped humming an old Irish lullaby as Neri drew near.

"You're looking glum," said Una, her voice carrying a lilt.

A recorked bottle of red wine stood on the kitchen counter. Neri poured herself half a glass, and took a couple of sips from it. "We had another stay-behind tonight," she said.

"Aye, then. Come and sit down."

"After you put Padraig to bed, *gaelica*."

Gently Una got to her feet, and bent to scoop up the boy. "Five minutes, then."

It was closer to ten. Neri sat with her eyes closed, one by one casting the events of the evening aside. Killing the stay-behind had been a cold necessity, like stomping on a venomous insect; having a stay-behind arrive on Vanadis at all weighed on her heart. Three of them in the past six days; none would be reporting back to their handlers. Something was very amiss in Corporatia. She wished she knew what it was. She wished *he* would come back.

"That makes three," Una said softly. She remained undressed, fit only with the quoil, and with her own glass of wine, which she placed on an end table as she sat down at the other end of the settee. "Leastwise, the fish are fat."

Neri let the distant sound of waves lull her. She wanted to go out to the sand and sit; little Padraig would be all right. But Una was reluctant as ever to leave her son where he might wake up and find himself alone at night. Bad things could happen in the dark, as Neri knew well. If *he* hadn't come along that terrible night...

Eleven years earlier *he* had shoved her face into the rotting leaves of the forest floor, and they had waited while the men searched the black night for the girl he had stolen from them. She had suffered much abuse, but this was as nothing compared to her fear and awe of him. What he had done... The triadics had left her for less than a minute, possibly to draw lots again to determine who had the next turn at her, but in that short time he had crept into the campsite, cut the ties around her wrists and ankles, scooped her up in his arms, and lugged her into the surrounding forest.

As she lay on the decomposing vegetation she felt on

her right hand a liquid with a faintly metallic scent—blood was leaking from the flaked, charred flesh on his left side—and she wiped it on the tattered remains of her shirt. He curled in beside her, arms around her, protecting her. His hand on her forehead, somehow able to sense the tender areas, and to avoid them while his touch reassured her. The bare skin of her legs and arms and neck began to itch. She felt dirty, inside and out, a tarnished, broken doll. Silently she began to cry.

"Can you walk?"

"*Credo che si.* Think... so."

"*Andiamo.*"

The command in her native tongue startled her. "You speak Italian?"

"*Non e tanto difficile parl—*"

"You *are* Italian."

"I'm Irish. If we stay here, we're dead. *Andiamo.*"

She stayed close, letting him pick the holes in the forest. "Can we talk now?"

"*Perche?*"

Perhaps he did not like to talk. Perhaps that was why he sounded so cold. Every word he had spoken had been gruff, without feeling, without warmth.

But who are you, and where are we going, and what do you want with me?

The forest thinned, and they began to trot. Her breath came in short rasps now as she reached the limits of her endurance again. Earlier they had expended her, exhausted her. She had been unable to take any more abuse. Limp, bruised, every muscle in agony, she wanted to die, and could not, they would not let her die and they would not leave her alone. They had made her beg them to stop, but they had not stopped. I'll do anything, only please stop. But they had wanted "anything," so why should they stop? And she had not seen this trap in their logic.

What do *you* want with me?

Exertion made her aware of more bruises on her body, more abrasions on her face, the tenderness of her puffy lips. One eye was almost closed now. Lump on her forehead. Pain in her right arm each time she bent her elbow, and she recalled that one of the men had dropped to his knees beside her, one knee landing on her elbow. The other knee had struck her ribs, and she knew sharp pain with each inhalation.

And still he went on.

"*Chi e Lei?*"

She saw a smile flicker, or perhaps it was only in his tone. "*Mi chiamo* Ovin Shannen."

"*Dov'andiamo?*"

"I have a campsite," he answered in her language. "It's safe. I'll see that you are returned to your family tomorrow."

"*No!*"

He stopped. "*Cosa che?*"

Panting, she held her hand up and put it on his arm. "No, I cannot go back, not now." Her thin chest rose and fell under the tattered shirt as she struggled to breathe. "*Non posso.* Cannot... go back there now."

"*Perche non puoi tornare a casa?*"

There was a huge and terrible silence as she slowly lifted her eyes to his. Rage billowed up from her soul. "*Look* at me!" she screamed. "Look at *me!* What they did to me!"

Just as violently she halted, not knowing what she wanted to say. He seemed about to leave, and that alarmed her. "*Dove va?*"

"I have some men to find."

"Oh. Are you going to detain them?"

In the dark he seemed to smile. "Not exactly, no."

"Oh. But what about me?"

He leaned back against a tree, resting. His hand went briefly to the wound in his back, and came away smeared with blood that was black in the starlight. "What about you?"

"I want to do that."

He shook his head. "I'll do it. It's what I do."

She did not question his occupation. "Then at least let me help you."

"How old are you? Fourteen? Thirteen?"

"Twelve."

"*Bene*. Come with me. I'll teach you."

And the next night we killed them all, Neri recalled, with grim satisfaction. She had wanted to do rather more than drive a knife blade through their eyeballs into their brains while they slept. Very gently but very firmly he had pointed out to her the redundancy of punishing bad people. Lesson two: economize effort. The about-to-die need learn nothing. It is sufficient that they die...

Sufficient unto that night, *mio gaelico*, she thought, closing down the memory. Her eyes, already midnight blue with remembered outrage, lightened as she became aware of movement. Of Una stretching out beside her, closer to her now, and without her quoil, which rested on a nearby table.

"Remembering, then, are you?" asked Una.

"I wish he would come home."

"When he is ready, aye, he will." She leaned back, folded her hands, and placed them on her lap. "I miss me brother, too. *Mo dheartháir*. And others do as well."

"Deyrdra."

"Aye, and her."

Neri's brow knit. "Would you be thinking of Aisling Yhonyn and Karan Syan?"

"Aye, I would. Aisling has begun asking me about her da. Only a few times has she seen him. She is twelve now, and I'm thinking she needs her father around for these years. Karan Syan as well. To be a man, he will need the attention and encouragement of his father. But Ovin is cautious about coming back for any length of time."

"I know," Neri said grimly. Her voice mimicked Una's. "Mommy bird leads the snakes *away* from the nest."

Una sighed. "Aye, that." Her knuckle rapped Neri's kneecap. "Come, then," she said, and got to her feet. "Me ears are needing the rhythm of the waves. Padraig will be fine for an hour or two."

"I'll grab a blanket," said Neri.

003

At the office for the Orphanage of Khorassey, Siobhan Gonelong encountered a delay caused by her official status as a Supervisor for the Special Operations Division of Corporatia Security. Fearing an unsanctioned investigation, the clerk fidgeted at his computer as he sought the right words to say and the right questions to ask. He was a young man with lank black hair that repeatedly fell over his eyes whenever he leaned forward. The eyes themselves were a lusterless brown, complementing his slack facial muscles.

Siobhan found herself wondering what qualified him for the position he now filled. Surely someone who dealt in quasi-legal human trafficking would prove defensive and obstructive, not confused.

Finally the young man—the name tag on his pale blue uniform shirt identified him as Steddo Cargoe, and Siobhan managed not to laugh—sat back and made little flustered gestures with his pale hands. "I can't," he said. "I can't. You're supposed to have assignment orders to make inquiries here at the Orphanage." He thrust a finger at the monitor. "It's right there, in the SOP."

"I'm not conducting an investigation of the Orphanage," Siobhan repeated patiently. *Although it could stand a thorough one*, she thought. "I'm simply trying to find out the status of one of the Motic inmates. Her name—."

"We refer to them as 'items,'" Cargoe said diffidently, as if she should have known.

No, it could stand a lot more than that, she thought. *It needs to be shut down, permanently.* "Her name is Ocamla," she said, tightly controlled.

He keyed in the name and conducted a swift search. "There is no item of that name in the Orphanage," he announced. A tiny glow of triumph came over his eyes. He looked and sounded relieved.

"Perhaps she was sold or transferred recently," said Siobhan. "Check, please."

Reluctantly Cargoe did so. Again he sat back, this time frowning. "I-I really should summon my supervisor," he said. "He's at the cafeteria now, but should return within the hour."

Siobhan's left hand drifted toward the CKardell in the rig under her right arm. Gradually, however, she pushed aside the temptation to use it, and instead lowered that hand to the left front pocket of her lime-green outsuit, from which it withdrew a royal purple plastic card on which the only information was her flat holograph. This she placed on the counter top. "You know what this is," she said. It was not a question.

Already Cargoe was on his feet. "Ah... ah, yes. The purple security card."

"You know what it means."

"I, ah..."

"Say it!" she snapped.

"It means nothing is closed to you."

"And?"

"And you may take," he swallowed hard, "whatever measures you think are needed to gain cooperation."

"Precisely. 'Whatever measures.' Now, you did find something of interest to me. What is it?"

He studied the monitor. "We, ah, we did have an item under that name until early yesterday, when she was sold."

"Sold to whom?"

"It doesn't say. Apparently he did not give a name. That's not unusual," he added quickly.

Money is the universal name, she thought bitterly. "Who conducted the sale?"

"Ah, that is, my supervisor."

"Summon him."

"N-now?"

"Whatever measures," she reminded him.

"Yes, of course." Cargoe spoke into the computer's Palmetto function. He had only to mention the security card when the supervisor broke the connection.

Seconds later, an older man dressed in the gray of a security guard rushed into the office. After a swift glance at Cargoe, he devoted his full attention to Siobhan. "How may I be of service, Supervisor?"

"A Motic inmate named Ocamla was purchased from here yesterday," Siobhan told him. "I wish to know by whom."

"He did not tell me his name, I don't think."

Siobhan glared at him. "You don't think?"

"I think it was his occupation."

"Describe him."

"Mid-thirties, I should say. Tall, a little taller than you. Black hair. Light eyes... green, rather like yours. Black pants, green shirt."

Siobhan sighed. "That narrows it down to about fifty million."

The guard's face twisted, as if he had thought of something else. "As we talked, though, and walked around to inspect the items, his eyes... maybe it was the light. But they seemed gray. And he carried an odd sidearm. He said it was a flasher."

Her heart bumped, and for a moment she was unable to draw a breath. In the back of her mind, a cloud began to descend. She steeled herself to ask the necessary next questions. "What sort of weapon was it?"

"He said it was some kind of dart gun."

"A flechette," she murmured. The beating of her heart now seemed to come to a halt. She took a breath, and held it. "And his occupation. What was it?" she asked, already knowing what the answer would be.

"He said he was a tinker."

* * *

In the null-space of Track, distance passed far more quickly than time. Twice Shannen rose from his captain's seat for a few moments of impatient pacing on the bridge. The Motic female had yet to return. Either she was ravenous and gorging herself in the galley or, more likely, she had no wish to be anywhere near him. He could hardly blame her. He had—at least in her view—reneged on his promise of manumission.

Even as he reseated himself, motion reflected in the Videx caught his eye. Ocamla had returned, bearing a small plastic bowl. She drew up within a pace of him and set the bowl on top of the console. It contained dried dates and salted nuts. She did not withdraw.

He looked at her reflection. Motics had their own expressions and gestures, but those who had spent time among humans tended toward hybrids of frowns and hand movements. Ocamla, however, merely stood there, arms at her sides, waiting.

"Thank you," he tried, dismissing her.

Still she did not move. "You not all right more."

The words scored his conscience. Having rescued her from Khorassey and from future sales and abuse, he feared she was beginning to form an emotional attachment to him. It had happened before on a few occasions. He had not sought them, nor had he surrendered. Salvation was his only motivation, theirs... and his. He thought their chances of success were better.

He dragged stiff fingers through his hair as if clearing it of cobwebs. "No, Ocamla, I guess I'm not. But why are you so concerned?"

Nictitating membranes slid across her eyes, and retreated. Moistened sapphires glistened at him. "You well mean. Freedom when closed in means not. Only free leave."

Shannen took a moment to put it together. "You're right, and I am sorry. There's no point in being free when you can't go anywhere. We'll be docking down soon. Then we'll talk... no, then I would like to speak with you. Then you may go your way. If you wish to leave my world, I will arrange transportation for you."

She looked glum. He did not know what it signified.

"We talk now?" she asked.

"If you wish. Let's start with the name of the man who bought you to clean the big room."

She seemed to bristle. "He buy me for other work, too." He did not respond; she softened, just a little. "His name... I not..." She shook her head, disappointed with herself.

"It's okay," he soothed. "What about the name of the corporation?"

Again she shook her head. After a moment, she sketched a shallow, continuous sine wave with her hand. "Outside land like this," she said. "Grass. Trees far-far away."

Rolling terrain, savannah, forest. It was not much to go on, Shannen reflected, but it was progress of a sort. "What about the weather outside? Hot, cold, sunny?"

"I not 'lowd go outside."

He sighed. "No, I suppose not."

"Sunlight," she tried.

"I'm afraid I'll need a little more than that."

"I not..." Suddenly she brightened. "Name man. Korsay has record."

Shannen swore. He should have thought to ask. He excused his ineptitude with the realization that he had only become aware of the significance of Ocamla's previous associations after the *Banshee* was enTracked. It gave him scant comfort.

Ocamla touched fingertips to the speaker on the console. "You talk them they tell you."

"It's a good idea, Ocamla, but Khorassey will not divulge information regarding their clients. I will have to go there in person to... persuade them." He rubbed his thumb and fingers together in the universal gesture of money.

Understanding, she slowly nodded. "We go now?"

"I want to return to Vanadis," he said. "I have people there who can help me."

"Is all you me want?"

"I can't think of anything else to ask," he told her, "unless you happen to remember something. I'll drop you off at the Haven Spaceport. Once we arrive, just tell me where you want to go, and I'll arrange passage for you."

"You live Spaceport?"

He laughed. "About five hundred kilometers south of there."

She nodded decisively. "I go with you."

"Ocamla, no. If you remain on Vanadis, you work."

"For you I work."

He swore softly.

"*Vanadis,*" announced Maire the 'skipcomp.

* * *

"Idiot," seethed Yassim Partagu.

He and Erron Markey were the only two occupants of the conference room. Partagu, who had been standing in contemplation of the view through the great window, had just issued his evaluation of Markey's attempts to determine the being and whereabouts of the mortifice known as Candle.

"*You used corporate resources.*" Partagu made no attempt to conceal his anger. "You might as well have placed a notice on the Galactic Net. What made you think you could trust that girl to find him?"

"It's... well, it's her job. She works for—"

"Corporatia Products Security! She is not a part of my plans for Vanadis. If any of those who are privy to that Alpha document learns of the search and knows anything about the threat posed by the devices is going to add two and two and come up with exactly, precisely, four."

"I didn't think—"

"Which leads me to wonder how you came to be Director of Operations for Corporatia Products Security."

Markey reddened, but said nothing.

"Very well. As Director of Operations, perhaps you can organize a janitorial operation and clean up this mess. Afterwards, contract with someone who is *unaffiliated* with Corporatia to obtain the information we seek. Do you think you can handle that?"

Markey nodded meekly. Although he was on a first-name basis with the Deputy Chair of Corporatia Products, he chose the discretion of an official response. "Yes, sir."

* * *

When the first shift ended, Palmula Bell closed down her office for the day and stepped outside into the sunlight. As always, it helped to cleanse her. A shower in her apartment would complete the job. She liked her job and performed it well, but some of those for whom she worked, well... She was unable to complete the thought.

Instead, she paused before a window and checked her look in the reflection. She also used the opportunity to see if anyone was following her. Traffic was moderate, mostly people who like her had just gotten off shift and were headed home. But such a crowd made it easier for someone to blend in.

She could not have said what made her suspect a surveillance or a tail. The business with Director Markey had set her on edge, and not merely because of his superior attitude. In security work she expected questionable activities. What Markey wanted from her had a more intense feel to it, as if some crime were about to be committed, and she herself implicated in it, perhaps as a scapegoat. She was, in effect, a loose end that might need to be tied up.

She walked on, with pauses at irregular intervals. If someone were tailing her, he was very good. After she crossed a glideway and entered the next quadrant, she stopped at a kiosk for a small package of rum cheroots. She took her time firing one of them, surreptitiously glancing around, not so much to identify the tail as to record in her mind the various people moving about. Here the traffic was thinner, easing that task for her.

Satisfied with the coal at the tip of the cheroot, she moved on. Her own apartment was a quadrant further down from the kiosk, but she was taking the scenic route to the park and pond further down and on the other side of the glideway. Walking casually, almost aimlessly now, she slipped her Palmetto from a hip pocket of her slacks and ticked out a pre-arranged code. With an ordinary device, she would do no such thing; if she were under surveillance, so were her communications. Thanks to the person whom she was about to raise, the security in her Palmetto was above anything that Corporatia Security could penetrate.

A face appeared in the viewscreen, a face much like hers—very dark skin, black hair that looked as if she were standing next to a static electricity generator. Dark eyes smiled at her, and the woman's lips parted to reveal two rows of teeth filed to a razor sharpness.

"Where are you?" asked Palmula, without greetings.

"Uh-oh."

"Yeah."

"How bad?"

"Maybe nothing," answered Palmula. She drew on the cheroot, and exhaled away from the screen. "I just got off work. I haven't spotted a tail. But my address is known, and they could just as easily be waiting for me there." Her voice shook. "I'm sorry. Are you on a... project?"

"It can wait. Let me see: I'm just over eleven light-years away. Figure half an hour travel time. I can hire an airfoil into the city, another quarter hour. Go someplace crowded. *Hazred's* is nearby, right?"

"I've been there."

"Go have some tabouleh and black coffee."

"Thanks, Sis."

Palmula rang off.

A purposeful walk of half a quadrant brought her to the menu window of a small but busy restaurant. On display were plastic replicas of the menu entrees, all properly labeled for the patrons. She paused there for a few moments, to take one last look around, and finally spotted someone—a non-descript man who might have been an office clerk for a construction enterprise. She might not have noticed him at all, were it not for the name tag dangling from the belt around his work denims. She had seen him earlier, just before she rounded the first corner from work. Like her sister, she did not believe in coincidences.

She entered *Hazred's*. As always, Ahmad was there, greeting and seating. His dark, bearded face lit up when he spotted her.

"*Masa' al-heer,*" she told him, and he beamed. Good evening. "*Lishahseen.*"

The corners of his mouth curled down, just a little, as he glanced past her. "But you are alone."

"When my sister arrives," she continued in Arabic, "show her to my table."

He inclined his head in acknowledgement, and swept his arm in the direction she was to go. "*Atfaddal.*"

He led her to a table in the rear corner, where she had a clear view of the other customers and the entrance—her usual table. She did not require a menu, but ordered tabouleh and dark coffee. Ahmad hustled off, and she knew the order would arrive momentarily. She was one of the few who had bothered to learn and to speak—to *try* to speak—Arabic, now that the prohibition of languages other than Standard had been lifted. At first she found herself astonished at how good the service was when she managed a few words. But she had come to like Ahmad, especially now that he had stopped frowning his religious disapproval at the pants she wore.

She placed the Palmetto at the corner of the table, and began her vigil of the entrance. Her tail arrived at the entrance at the same time her coffee reached the table.

* * *

Back aboard the *Aoife*, Siobhan stared at her reflection in the Videx. Her pale, freckled face appeared darker now, not with suntan, but with the onset of destiny. Three years had passed since she had last seen her twin brother. Had pleaded with him not to challenge Corporatia. Had walked away, her spine as unyielding as a bridge pile. Had ignored his last words, the Irish blessing he had whispered to her. *And until we meet again, may God hold you in the palm of His hand.*

Now he had resurrected. He had come back into her life again. Worse, with his purchase of Ocamla, he had become part of her work again. Once more, they were at cross purposes.

"But you don't *know* that," she told herself. "You don't know *why* he purchased her."

Her training argued with her. *There are no coincidences.*

"So we're doomed to meet again?"

Now her conscience chipped in. *I would have said destined to meet again.*

She laughed in spite of her mood. "I'm outnumbered." Then she sobered. "So how do I do this? What do I say to him? What will he...?"

She sighed. No choice. Just do it. Although it was unnecessary, she raised her voice and spoke toward the console mike. "Brid, set course for Vanadis and enTrack," she ordered shakily, before she could change her mind. "Disable transponder. Wake me when we're half an hour out."

The view in the Videx slipped to the matte black of null-space.

004

The name of the tall woman standing in front of the full-length mirror was Yhounda Khouse. She had just completed her toilet, and—in the manner of women since time immemorial—was now assessing her look, sweeping her long black hair this way and that over her bare shoulders. Over the past three years she had tried to change that look. Sameness elicited painful memories. Once known as the Princess of Mulane, she had escaped that world just before it exploded, killing millions. Now she was the Princess of Vanadis, a title which bore no significance with regard to royal status—but she had never been one to cultivate status. As a result, even here on Vanadis, respect for her gave her words the force of—not an order, perhaps, but at least a strong request. But there was no one to whom she might issue a strong request. Had she wished, she might have had ladies-in-waiting to attend her, or a chamberlain, or even a jester. She had only Sergeant Yenther Bek.

Still her personal guard, Bek of late had reduced his hovering to a bare minimum. When they had first arrived on Vanadis, brought there by Ovin Shannen, Bek had been solicitous, not in the sense of gaining her favors, but as a protector and friend whose loyalty and service was beyond question. She and he were all that was left of the teeming millions of Mulaines.

She sighed. Well, that was not quite accurate. There was Aisling Yhonyn and Karan Syan, the twins to whom she had given birth almost thirteen years ago. They had been saved as well. She did not think of them as half-Mulaine... or half-human, though their father was that same Ovin Shannen. She had carried them, given birth to them. They were, quite simply, her children.

And they had reached a difficult age. Karan Syan, thankfully, had all but stopped fretting about improprieties, which left an opening through which his childhood was returning. He was a Princeling, yes, but he no longer let everyone know that. Aisling Yhonyn, on the other hand...

Again Yhounda sighed. The girl was heavily influenced by Una Shannen, sometimes even taking to going around naked, and wearing a quoil around her slender waist—a weapon with which she was growing quite skilled under the tutelage of her mentor, Una. Aisling, too, had developed a habit: she kept asking about her father. And Yhounda had no answers for her.

The knock at her door sounded peremptory and even ominous. Yhounda threw on a pastel green dressing gown and opened it. Sergeant Bek stood there like a block of granite, eyes averted until he realized she was dressed. The look on his face did not bode well.

He licked his lips. "The children," he said hoarsely, and was unable to say more.

* * *

"Ocean," sighed Ocamla, as the *Banshee* hovered a thousand kilometers above the southern coast of the molar-shaped continent known as Haven.

Beside her at the Videx, Shannen chuckled. "How long has it been since you saw one?"

She made a face, and shook her head. "I not... year. Many."

"And salt water dissolves your oil and washes it away, just like your soap?"

Aghast, she turned to him. "To you I stink?"

"Not at all." It was only a very minor lie. "No, I'm just asking." He pointed to a promontory that extended into the water. "But maybe a place near the shore would be best for you. I only have five bars of that soap. Four, now that I bathed you."

"That house you?"

He had Maire zoom in on the cottage, so that it now appeared as if it were ten meters below them.

"Plants die," was Ocamla's observation.

Several terra-cotta pots stood scattered around and on the brick patio. Each contained a plant that had seen better days. Sadness settled on Shannen. Una, his youngest sister, usually saw to their care whenever he was away. Now their mood was... despondent, as if wondering whether he would ever come home. He had wondered that, himself, now and then.

"You not still all right," observed Ocamla.

"I suppose not. Okay, Maire, take us down to the docksite."

In a blink the *Banshee* came to rest on the grass some fifty meters from the cottage, on pods extended for support. Maire the 'skipcomp extruded the ramp so that her passengers might disembark. Shannen did so with slow, deliberate steps, uncertain as to the welcome the cottage would bestow on him. Ocamla followed, as if she might be attacked at any moment.

Presently both were standing in the light from the orange-yellow sun, now overhead. Neither uttered a word. The warm, clear day reminded Shannen of better times. The grass, still damp from an early morning shower, squeaked as he trudged across it, the sounds echoed by the footsteps of the Motic female behind him. They reached the patio. Absently, Shannen paused to run his fingers along the stem of a leggy, flowering plant—a fermaca, Una had named it, years ago.

Ocamla cleared her throat, but still spoke raggedly. "What I call you?"

"Ovin," he replied, his attention still on the fermaca. Its name might consist of nonsense syllables, but its bright blue flowers seemed happy that he had returned. He could not disappoint them by telling them he probably would not stay very long.

"I... stay here?"

He drew himself back to her. "There's a room inside, with a view of the ocean," he told her. "It's yours for as long as you're here. But there are better accommodations in the Dur Falls Inn, where you'll be working."

She shook her head violently. "I work for you." She glanced at the fermaca. Her eyes made the circuit of the other patio plants. "I care... no... what word is?" His suggestion agreed with her. "Yes. I tend these."

"I don't need a housekeeper."

He moved to the door; it slid open at his touch. Una had maintained the front room just as he had last left it a year ago. It had the atmosphere of a museum. He stepped inside and sniffed the air. There was just a hint of something floral in it. A back window stood open, and just outside a large shrub was blooming. Nightjade, he recalled. But the carpet along the wall below the window was not wet. Therefore Una had opened the window this morning... and might still be somewhere around.

"This is your room for now," he told Ocamla, opening the door to the guest room in front. The bed had been made, the two pillows fluffed. "The hygiene alcove has towels and such, and I'll bring you the soap from the *Banshee*. The dresser will have left-behind clothing in it. Some of it might fit you."

Ocamla regarded the room as if it contained an unexpected treasure. She entered cautiously—treasures were too good to be true.

"Get some rest," he told her. "And Ocamla?"

"What... what you want?"

"You are safe here," he said, and closed the door.

Now what? he thought.

Several tasks loomed; raising Curielle Neri, his unofficial Chief of Security, topped the list. He addressed that.

"Stay right there, *mio gaelico*," she ordered. Panic made her voice tremble. "I will be there in five. Make that two."

* * *

While her twin brother grumbled his disapproval, the girl calibrated the voice-control application on the instrumentation console to receive and heed her voice only. She ignored his protests. This was *her* project; he was along for the ride, and because he was, after all, her brother. Her *kid* brother, as she never tired of reminding him whenever he was contrary. Satisfied with the results, she told Oona, the new name for the 'skipcomp, to enTrack the newly-christened *Athair* and await further instructions. The view of Haven Spaceport in the Videx was replaced by the matte black of null-space.

Her name was Aisling Yhonyn, her brother Karan Syan, and they were the issue of Yhounda Khouse, formerly the Princess of Mulane, a world now shattered, and at present the Princess of Vanadis. Physically they were of a type: midnight hair—hers long, his not so much—violet eyes, *café au lait* skin, and at the age of twelve (she the elder by just over a minute) they each stood at a meter-seventy-six; tall and slender, like their mother. They had attired themselves for space travel as well as walk-around activities—her outsuit emerald green, his deep blue—and sturdy black boots. In addition, the girl wore a quoil draped around her slim waist.

Neither had ever piloted a spacecraft before.

"Great," sneered Karan Syan. "Now what?"

Aisling spoke calmly, with a maturity beyond her years. "Now I tell Oona to look for the most recent mentions of Tinker and the *Banshee*." She sat down on the starboard captain's chair and initiated the search. "He probably disables the transponder, or adopts a false one."

"How do you know so much?"

She shrugged. *He is my father*, she answered silently. Aloud, she added, "He is our father. How is it you do not know, Karan?"

The boy made a rude sound. "He's never here."

"Stop sulking. And stand up straight. You are a prince."

"Well, you have... you're..."

"The word you're groping for is 'primogeniture,'" Aisling said smugly. "What does that have to do with the way you stand... uh-oh."

"What?" yelled Karan.

"We're being pinged. It's Mom."

Karan snatched at Ailsing's Palmetto, but the girl was too quick for him. His voice broke. "We have to answer her," he squeaked.

The girl did not laugh at him. "She'll leave a message. I'll make contact with her later. Right now... hum... right now someone else is looking for Da."

"Stop calling him that!"

Aisling sat back, violet eyes hard on her brother. He still did not understand that some things were proper, while others were right. "It is the Irish way," she said at last, her voice low enough to just be heard above the faint hum of the *Athair*'s power plant. "Our father is Irish. That makes us half-Irish and half-Mulaine. Mom—"

"Mother!"

"*Mom* is teaching us of her part of our heritage," she went on calmly but firmly. "Una and Deyrdra are instructing us in his part of it. We even have composite names, you and I: one Irish, the other Mulaine. Karan comes from Ciaran."

The boy's hands fluttered in protest. "It-it *can't*. It... that's not *fair*."

"Take it up with Mom. She named you." The girl returned to the 'skipcomp. "Someone named Palmula Bell has been researching Tinker and... and Candle. Oona, where is this Bell person right now?"

"*She has just used her fundscard to pay for a meal at Hazred's in Durrayport on Jalune.*"

"Take us there," ordered Aisling.

* * *

Other patrons arrived at *Hazred's*, and Palmula used the occasion to hunch down a little, to use them to block the view of the man who had followed her here. As yet, as nearly as she could tell, he had not spotted her. But it was only a matter of time before he located her. Inside the restaurant, she felt relatively safe: one cry for help from her, and Ahmad and his co-workers would descend upon the miscreant like tigers. But she had rather it would not come to that.

People moved. Palmula caught flashes of him as he looked around. Was he armed? The gray cotton shirt he wore was too tight not to reveal bulges, but the pockets of his work denims might contain any number of useful, lethal items. She herself was unarmed, though she was adept if not expert in *aikido*. Her sister, however...

She sipped at the coffee—strong and black and hot, as always. Caffeine was her one vice, if it could be called that. The coffee of *Hazred's* was among the best she had tasted. So was the menu.

The man had moved. His turn in the seating line had come. He was escorted away from her, and toward an area of the restaurant that took him from her view. His potential avenue of approach from there would keep him out of her sight until he was within a few paces away. Fed by adrenaline, her heartrate increased. Her fingers felt weak. To give them strength, she wrapped them around the coffee mug. Heat provided a welcome distraction.

Her eyes went to the entrance. How much longer? She checked the time function on her Palmetto: fifty minutes had passed since she had spoken with Pagan. Had something happened? But that was ludicrous. Pagan made things happen to others, not the reverse. Again Palmula reviewed the layout of the restaurant. The location of the man allowed him to see her if she tried to leave. The bowl of tabouleh was cooling; she had to honor it by wolfing it down, one eye on the food, the other on the surroundings. Ahmad passed by her table and asked if she wanted anything else. Though tempted, she declined. When he cleared from her vision again, she spotted two youths standing in the entrance, looking around at the tables.

Both had the blackest hair she had ever seen. The girl wore hers long, past her shoulders; the boy's was not quite shaggy. They were wearing outsuits, which suggested recent space travel. Around the girl's waist was looped some kind of rope with weights at the tips.

Presently they spotted Palmula, and wove their way toward her. Palmula's brow knotted. Obviously they had come looking for *her*, but what could they possibly want? She had never seen them before, and had no idea who they might be. She sat back, a pleasant yet sardonic smile crossing her face.

"May we sit down?" inquired the girl.

The courtesy took Palmula by mild surprise. Her voice had a cultured quality, bespeaking a status, yet aside from that and the hair there was nothing to suggest that she was anything but an adolescent, out with her brother—the boy *had to be* her twin brother—on some errand of their own. An errand which somehow involved her.

Palmula made a little gesture. After the twins had seated themselves—unobtrusively, she noted—the girl said, "Have you found him yet?"

Palmula sputtered. "H-how do you know I'm—?" She bit off the rest of the question as unworthy. *Of course* they knew; it mattered not, how. Now the question was why.

Palmula looked past the boy's shoulder. The man was approaching their table. Seeing her apprehensive expression, the girl swung to her feet, the strange rope now held in one hand, the weights in the other. The man reached into his pocket. The girl whirled the rope and cast it, entangling his ankles. He fell to the floor and almost immediately was set upon by Ahmad. Relieved of his weapon, the man ceased his struggles. A gesture from Ahmad summoned help, but even as it arrived, the girl spoke to him, and presently the man was escorted back into the kitchen to be held there pending further instructions. The expression on Ahmad's face said that he had been extremely offended by the man's behavior.

"*Mashkuur*," said the girl, to Ahmad, ducking her head.

Ahmad did not appear the least bit surprised by the word or the manner, and Palmula concluded that she had spoken to him a moment ago in respectful Arabic.

"*Titkallami 'arabi*," said Palmula.

"*Shwayya, muu katiir*," the girl acknowledged. A little. Not much. Then, in perfectly enunciated Standard she added, "But I think you prefer this language."

Palmula drummed her fingers on the table. Finally she said, "Who *are* you?"

"I am Aisling Yhonyn, and this is my brother, Karan Syan. We are the children of the man you are looking for."

Palmula sat back as if she had been struck. For just a moment, her voice failed her. "Well... that would have been second to last on my list of possible responses."

The girl laughed, reminding her of silver wind chimes in a light breeze. "Out of curiosity, what would have been at the bottom?"

"Tax collectors," came a voice behind the girl.

Palmula looked up; her sister had arrived. With great courtesy, knowing he would nevertheless watch over her, she suggested to Ahmad that he might return to his duties.

005

Curielle Neri, as always, was as good as her word. She knocked on the front door of Shannen's cottage and, without waiting for a response, started to enter. At that moment, Shannen came round the corner of the cottage. The flash of movement made Neri's hand dart for the sidearm tucked into her belt; recognition of him halted it.

A year had passed since he had last seen Neri. She had reached the age, just into adulthood, where she did not change much. No longer was she the twelve-year-old girl he had rescued a decade ago from her captors and taught the lethal arts. Her short, shaggy mop of black hair framed an oval olive face punctuated by sharp and very blue eyes. As usual, she wore no cosmetics, only the heavy blue pullover and black denims that were her trademark, and sturdy black boots.

She had a faint smile for him. "*Mio gaelico,*" she whispered, two soft words that said everything between them. My Irish. Only she called him that.

On this occasion, however, Shannen felt the need and the desire for something more. Uncharacteristically, he stepped forward and embraced her. She stiffened at first, from surprise rather than from reticence, and then flung herself against him. For a long moment they stood like that in silence, sunlight pouring down on them but unable to shine between them.

An eternity of perhaps a minute later, he released her. "I missed you, Curi," he said.

"If you wouldn't go away for so long," she chided. "What brought you back?"

They moved to the patio wall and stood looking out at the ocean half a kilometer away. "I think Corporatia is planning something," he said.

"I am not surprised."

"Stay-behinds?"

She nodded. "Three in the past eight days. They won't be filing reports. *Mio gaelico...* they're gone. The children are gone. Yhounda thinks Aisling Yhonyn went out to look for you. Karan Syan probably went along to gloat when she gets into trouble."

"Probably." Shannen laughed, and sobered, his countenance dark with worry and fear. "When?"

"Before dawn today."

It was too late to say that the girl knew better than that. He knew Neri could see the fright in his eyes, but he forced calm upon himself otherwise, and took a few steadying breaths. Those did not come easy. Aisling Yhonyn was brilliant in many regards, but she had very little practical experience. He looked at Neri, but he was seeing her as she was ten years ago, at the age of twelve—Aisling's age now—when he had rescued her.

Neri placed a hand on his chest. "It won't happen to Aisling," she said, reading his thoughts and fears.

He drew a huge breath and let it out slowly, and gave her a tiny nod.

"I'll assume you've tried to track the transponder," he said, thinking his way. "She probably shut it off just to keep you from doing that."

"How would she go about finding you?" asked Neri.

Shannen frowned. "How would you?"

"I tried that. I did a search for Tinker and *Banshee* and Shannen." She gave him a sidelong glance. "Who did you redeem at Khorassey?"

"A Motic named Ocamla. She's in the guest room. But I didn't use my name there. How would you—?"

"I just know you, *mio gaelico*. You freed her, of course."

"Of course. But—"

"But she didn't want to go. That happens to you now and then. The problem is that you're much too nice."

In the silence, a seabird cried out.

"There was one odd thing about the search," Neri went on. "Apparently in the past day or so there have been three searches initiated for you. One of them probably was Aisling's."

"And the other two?"

"One was routed hither and yon. Hmm... those are great names for moons, for a planet that has two. But the search was untraceable." She cocked a heavy black eyebrow at him. "Corporatia?"

He nodded. "Most likely. And the third?"

"That's the odd one. It was initiated by Palmula Bell of Corporatia Products Security, and then overridden and canceled." Her eyes searched his. "You know what that means."

"Vanth," he said. "But what's the connection?"

Neri laughed. "Why don't you go ask Palmula?"

He started to answer, but his Palmetto sounded the first phrase of *Isle of Innisfree*. He drew it from his pocket and tokked it in response. The music stopped as Una's face appeared on the screen. Before he could even smile a greeting, she said, "The *Aoife* just downdocked at Havenport."

* * *

Even as the *Aoife* docked down on Vanadis, Siobhan Gonelong still had not decided what she would or should say to her estranged twin brother. Even the adjective was only half-correct: she had estranged herself from him, not he from her. Her duties and orders formed a barrier to any possible reconciliation between them. If she should encounter him within the jurisdiction of Corporatia, she would detain and confine him pending trial.

But Vanadis was nowhere near the jurisdiction of Corporatia. She had arrived, knowing she might be subject to his mercy. What would he do? Long ago, during the ages of fifteen to seventeen, making up after a spat (they had never truly argued, merely disagreed) occasionally involved going to bed together. While that violated the norms and taboos of much of Corporatia society, such relationships occurred with some frequency out in the sparsely-populated Fringes, where options were sometimes extremely limited. That relationship, however, had ceased on the day corporate paramilitary units attacked the Shannen family farm on Cu-Dreth, killing their father and costing Deyrdra her right leg just above the knee. After Ovin and a friend of his had gotten the rest of the children away to safety, she and Ovin had gone their separate ways—she into Corporatia Security, he into a career as a professional assassin. A part of her duties was to bring him to justice.

Now, gazing through the Videx at the Spaceport, she recalled the affections they had shared—not in contemplation of renewal, but as a remembrance of better times. The taboo brought a sardonic smile to her thin lips: although the parents of the Shannen children had been brother and sister, none of the children showed any signs of gibbering insanity or of growing a sixth finger or toe. Such curses, she suspected, were meant for the gullible, to encourage exogamy. Still, the threatened aberrations gave her an idea.

First, however, she had to announce herself. "Brid, please raise Deyrdra," she said.

A minute passed. Finally the face of Deyrdra Shannen appeared in the monitor. Dark-haired and sultry, she had brown eyes that regarded Siobhan with deep concern. A smile flickered on her face, but failed to make it to her greeting.

"Siobhan," she said. She did not have to add, "What do you want?" Her tone did that for her.

Inwardly Siobhan sighed. The battle between her and her siblings remained engaged. "Is he here?" she asked. "If he is, I need to see him."

"Ah, 'tis official, then," said Deyrdra, her lilt prominent.

"Not in the way you fear, *mo dheirfiúr*."

Deyrdra's face darkened. "Don't," she said. "Just don't."

"But you *are* my sister."

"He is at his cottage," Deyrdra said evenly. "You know where that is. I'll let him know you're on your way. You can dock down where you did the last time you... were here."

The screen abruptly went blank. Siobhan fingered a tear from her eye, wondering how it had come to be there. The emotion gave way to resolve: so be it—she had a job to do. A terse command to Brid to enTrack the *Aoife* to coordinates near Shannen's cottage brought her there within two seconds. Still she hesitated, standing before the Videx that now presented her with a panorama of the ocean. Tense, her heart beat a little harder, and her pulse quickened.

"Brid, show me the cottage," she ordered, and immediately a view of it replaced the ocean.

It looked as she remembered it from three years earlier, sunlit, and with leggy potted plants that still needed tending. Her heart skipped when she saw that *he* was standing in the patio, with a young woman in blue and black beside him, both gazing out at the *Aoife*. She recognized Curielle Neri. At a distance of fifty meters, their expressions were unreadable. For a moment, she was tempted to have Brid zoom on them, and decided against it. She was not here to see her twin brother, but to question a subject in an investigation.

She moved aft, and ordered Brid to open the hatch and extrude the ramp. At the top step, she paused. She was proceeding from an assumption of hostility, and was already on the defensive, when there was no reason to assume non-cooperation.

Refocused now, she gave herself a little nod. *Right, then.*

Out of the 'skip and across the short, lush grass she strode like a cadet on parade. The expressions of the two on the patio became clearer, both reflecting curiosity more than anything else. She did not get the sense that she was unwelcome; neither did Shannen seem pleased to see her. Just before she reached the patio wall, the front door opened, and a Motic female stepped outside. Siobhan almost skidded to a halt. This had to be the Motic who was the target of Vanth.

The Motic was wearing denim cut-offs and a blue cropped-top that complimented her skin color. Undoubtedly the items came from Spare Parts, the drawer in the wardrobe that was reserved for clothing left behind. She took up a position on the other side of Shannen, as if to say she was under his protection.

Siobhan shut out the two women and focused on her twin brother. Already she had forgotten the greeting she had planned earlier, and the allusion to mutations. She waited for him to make a move, having already made hers by virtue of her visit.

"I see you're still saving money on hair stylists," he said.

A tiny smile crossed Neri's lips. Siobhan crossed her arms atop the patio wall and leaned against it. "Did I ever tell you why I cut my hair off?"

"Lice?" Neri answered sweetly.

Siobhan let the remark pass. "It's traditional that when Irish women feel extreme grief, they tear their hair, *an dtuigeann tú*? No, I see that you do not. And that is why I never told you."

Shannen shrugged. "Una keeps bottles of Nicole's *weissbier* stocked in the cooler," he said.

"I get," said the Motic female. "I bring how many?"

"Three, please, Ocamla," he told her. "Four, if you want one."

Ocamla dashed inside. Presently they heard bottles clink, and hiss when they were opened. On the patio, no one spoke. The Motic returned with the thumbs and fingers of both hands twined around the necks of four bottles. These she placed on the acetate and wicker round table in a corner of the patio, and stepped back.

"I'm fairly certain there's beer on Corporatia worlds," said Shannen, the hint hard and obvious.

Siobhan reached over the wall and selected a bottle. "*Go raibh maith agat*," she thanked him, and lifted it in a mock toast.

He did not reciprocate. A long sip of his later, he looked at her intently.

Neri said, "I'll just wait inside," and went to do so.

Ocamla said, "Who she?"

Shannen blinked. "Ocamla, this is... Supervisor Siobhan Gonelong of Corporatia Security Special Operations."

The hesitation in the introduction stung Siobhan. His next words struck her even worse.

"Supervisor Gonelong, this is Ocamla. She is a guest here."

Siobhan's lips tightened. She could almost feel them turning white, bloodless. This encounter was not supposed to hurt. She was a professional. He was someone who might have answers to her questions, and who clearly was associated with the person she had been instructed to seek out. So why the pain in her chest? Why the great ache?

Heartbeat... the beating of her heart was autonomic. Whatever caused it to beat, then, was beyond her conscious control. There could be only acceptance or rejection.

Ovin. Mo dheartháir.

Once she started crying, she could not stop. She broke down.

Instantly he was there, on the same side of the wall as she, and weeping as well. She mumbled something in Gaelic and heard his response. The end of the Irish blessing, but amended. *God has held us in the palm of His hand.*

Her wet face pressed against the side of his neck, as his did hers. Their skin grew slippery. Arms like vises bound them together. They were twins: one person, two aspects. Now they were joined, as they had been in their adolescence, except that now there was nothing sexual in the union. Light-years might separate them again, as the past three years had done, but the distances no longer signified. What had kept them apart was not distance, but differences. Like distance, the differences no longer mattered. They had surrendered to one another. If this surrender signified the end of the war, they had both won.

At length Siobhan pulled away, holding him at arm's length. Her tears continued to flow, as did his. "No more," she whispered.

"No more, *mo dheirfiúr*," he whispered back.

He took her hand, and led her onto the patio. Ocamla backed away. "I sorry," she said. "This private you."

She started to go back into the cottage, and stopped when Siobhan said, "Please stay."

Shannen just looked at his twin: sea-green eyes met sea-green eyes.

"I followed your Tinker work," Siobhan said to him.

"I know."

"As much as I could of it, that is" she went on. "You disappear very well. And... you kept your word. About retiring, I mean."

He made a face. "I've had to kill a few people," he conceded. "I just no longer do it for pay. But sometimes it is the best solution to the problem I'm looking into."

She grunted noncommittally, and touched the fronds of a plant. "You ought to speak to Una about your patio garden."

"Next you'll tell me I don't dust often enough."

"If at all."

He sighed. "It's about Ocamla, isn't it?"

Siobhan regarded the Motic woman. "Yes."

Ocamla held up a hand, the digits spread and the webbing taut. "I not do wrong," she protested.

"I believe you," Siobhan said quickly. "But I have been tasked with finding out why Yassim Partagu wants you dead."

Ocamla's eyes widened in horror. "That name," she declared to Shannen. "That him. Cell, room. Him."

* * *

The new arrival pulled a chair from another table and sat down across from Palmula. Her skin was the same color—that of raw hematite—and her eyes the same almonds, but her hair was curly, as if it had been tightly braided and then released.

"You missed a spot," said Palmula, touching her own skin just in front of her left ear.

The newcomer's fingertip found the spot, and wiped at it. A discoloration remained for now, but the blue paint itself clung to the finger, which she wiped on a napkin.

"My sister, Pagan," said Palmula, for the twins' benefit. Deliberately she did not introduce them, waiting to find out what her sister knew.

"Sorry I'm late," said Pagan. With a glance at Aisling Yhonyn, she added, "Although the girl here seems to have had matters well in hand. Pami, I stopped by your apartment. There are now two dead men there. What have you gotten yourself into?"

"I'm not sure. And please: I'm still trying to live down that name."

"Sorry. Palmula. What are you working on?"

Palmula leaned forward. "Keep your voice down. I was asked to do research off the books. It's a task within your area of expertise. I'm to find out whether a mortifice named Candle is still alive."

Pagan uttered a few words that had both the twins staring at her, slack-jawed.

"Your boss might not consider me a reliable source," said Pagan, calming. "But yes, he's very much alive, and no, that is not common knowledge. He operates under the code name Tinker now, but only on special occasions. He's no longer in," here she glanced meaningfully at the twins, "that line of work."

"You err, *M'selle* Pagan," said Aisling Yhonyn. The pride in her tone fell well short of haughtiness. "I know very well what my father used to do."

"What did he do?" asked Kara Syan.

Aisling ignored him. "We are here because we are trying to find him," she went on, to Pagan. Her use of "we" bordered on the royal form. "We learned that your sister was looking for him as well. Thus far, we suspect, without much success." For a moment she pressed gleaming upper incisors against her lower lip, her eyes set on Palmula. "I think we must consider the possibility that this man and the two dead ones were dispatched to cancel your assignment."

Pagan sat back in her chair. At first she appeared not to know what to say. "Una has trained you well," she managed at last.

Aisling flashed a bright smile. "I am but a cricket," she said. "And still in training. And it seems you know her."

"The two of them go prancing around naked, practicing with their ropes," scoffed Karan Syan.

"I have heard that about Una," said Pagan. "I was not aware that she had a protegée. If I might ask: how old are you?"

Aisling softened. "In ten days we," this time including Karan Syan, "will turn thirteen. We would like our father there for that event." With a scathing glance at her brother, she added, "At least, *I* would. It is my—"

"Palmula," interrupted Pagan, getting to her feet. "Let us leave this place. It is not safe." Her dark eyes flicked here and there. "Others may come. Or they are already here." To the twins, she added, hushed, "I have an idea how you came to be here. You may wish to retain the craft you pirated. If so, may I recommend that you enTrack, and make contact with me. We will accompany you to the Spaceport. Of course, I would prefer that you travel with us. You are most welcome to do so."

"Where are you going?" asked Karan Syan.

"Not here. I'll tell you when you raise us." She swept an inviting hand to all of them. "Coming?"

* * *

"It was to be a simple kill," Markey explained. "She was to be acquired on the way home from work, and if the opportunity arose, she was to be dealt with as if it were a robbery gone sour. Otherwise, she was to be frightened into seeking shelter at her apartment, where two more agents were waiting for her. In the event that she chose to flee the planet itself, another two were waiting by her 'skip at the Spaceport."

"And yet she slipped through your fingers," Partagu said icily. "You lost two men, possibly three. Let me see if I understand you. He was *abducted*?"

"Witness statements corroborate that, sir."

"Abducted by the woman he was supposed to follow, and if convenient, kill?"

Markey scuffed at the rug. "She had help, sir. Two adolescent children and—"

"*Children?*"

"The girl was reported to have—"

"*Girl?*"

"Yes, sir. She had some skill with a weapon. We're not sure what it was. Some sort of rope."

Partagu turned around, and leaned back against the window sill. "Now, corporate security personnel *do* undergo close combat training that would enable them to deal with opponents such as a common records clerk and an adolescent girl. Or am I mistaken? Well, Erron?"

Markey bristled, but was careful not to look directly at Partagu. "Preliminary forensic reports indicate that the two men at her apartment were killed by a professional."

"I thought security agents *were* professional." For a moment he pinched the bridge of his nose between thumb and forefinger. "I suppose there were no witnesses."

"No, sir."

"A girl," Partagu said disgustedly.

"There was a woman at the restaurant as well," Markey added quickly. "A late arrival. Witness descriptions suggest the woman may have been related to Palmula Bell. Possibly a sister."

"Naturally you have checked personnel records to determine whether Bell in fact has a sister."

Markey sighed. "Yes, we did. She listed no sister among her relatives."

Partagu clasped his hands behind his back. "Well, Erron, I must say you have your work cut out for you. And you are still no closer to determining whether Candle is still alive. Now, I have given you *carte blanche* in this matter. I want this mess cleaned up. There are events that are almost ready to be set in motion. I must know his status. You have two days; no more."

"Sir, I must pro—"

"That will be all, Erron."

006

"Yassim Partagu," Shannen repeated darkly. "The Deputy Chair of Corporatia Products. Effectively the Chair, as Lin Cheng has reached retirement age, and his designated replacement, Seppo Salvini, is enfeebled. If either lasts another year, I'll be surprised."

"I don't understand," said Siobhan.

"I'm not sure I do, either." He gazed placidly at Ocamla, who returned the look without rancor.

They were all sitting in the front room of his cottage, all but Ocamla halfway through their bottles. The Motic had scarcely drunk from hers. Shannen did not doubt for a moment that she had heard what she said she had heard. Certainly some of the words were unfamiliar to her. It was up to him to assemble them for content. All he had was a rudimentary sentence: Partagu was interested in Vanadis. That in itself did not bode well. But there had to be something more.

Neri's Palmetto pinged with the opening of the theme from an ancient movie about sharks. She glanced at the screen. "Palmula Bell has just bought meals for three on Far Parkins," she announced, and forwarded the report to Shannen.

"Motoya," said Ocamla, excited. "We go?"

Shannen scowled. "Why there?"

Neri shrugged. "Go find out, *mio gaelico*," she said. "I've already added security, and all the SECSATS are operational. We'll quarantine any cargo craft that dock, and we'll unload them with our own people, *capisci*? I'll put shifts of armed orbital patrols, in case someone comes in force. But I don't see that happening, not just yet." The corners of her mouth turned down. "Not that we could defend against it," she added, aside.

"I should make contact with Commissioner Vandatti," said Siobhan.

"And tell him what?" Shannen returned. "Maybe Partagu wants to take a vacation—"

Neri was aghast. "*Non lo credi!*"

"No, you're right, I don't believe that," he said. "But until we know more about his intentions, we won't know what action to take."

"Ovin," Siobhan said soberly. "You-you wouldn't."

He shot her a hard look, but did not respond directly. "Ocamla, pack your things. Siobhan, we're going to Far Parkins. It's only about twelve light-years from here. Bell and her party should still be there by the time we arrive. I'd like you to come along."

"I think we need to talk," she said. "And I'll take the *Aoife*. I like my independence."

"I think I need another beer," said Neri.

* * *

With the *Athair* safely ensconced in null-space, Aisling Yhonyn relaxed. Having already learned from her search that Tinker had shown up at a world known as Khorassey, she'd had Oona set a Track for it, over the protests of her brother. Even now he sat in the port captain's chair, glowering at her.

"We're going to get into trouble," he said sourly. "You don't know what you're doing or where you're going."

"Khorassey has an orphanage," she countered. "Una says that Da sometimes goes there and redeems people and then frees them. Maybe they know something."

"We were safe with that woman."

"Palmula." She dug into a pocket of her outsuit and extracted a Benz Sizzler, an adequate beginner's sidearm. "We'll be safe," she assured him. "I've learned how to use this." *But not when to use it*, she added silently, and crossed her fingers.

"How long," sighed Karan Syan, exasperated.

"Another hour and minutes," she replied. "Go back and get some rest."

Alone on the bridge, Aisling slouched in the chair and gazed at the matte black in the Videx, letting her eyes go unfocused. Growing up, she had known the absence of a father only because the few other children her age in her mom's court had one. Sometimes those other fathers played with her and Karan Syan, along with their own children, and there were a few men at court—Sergeant

Bek, for one—who showed them how to do things. But other children received hugs, of affection or approval. And they received scoldings for misbehavior. But during all those years, *father* had been an abstraction for her. As a specific person, he could not be missed, because he had never existed. And... and...

But those children were dead now, murdered when her home world Mulane was destroyed.

Her eyes focused again, but her vision was blurred. With the heels of her hands she wiped them dry.

Until three years ago, she had imagined her father to be a pirate, staying one step ahead of the authorities while he went out and stole treasures. At the time she met him, he had been embroiled in a difficulty the nature of which had never been made clear to her. In the process of resolving it, he had put his life on the line, and only at the last moment did he reveal to her that he was her father. Then he was shot and, she thought at the moment, killed.

"Not again," she whispered to herself. "That's not going to happen again." She thumbed the safety off, and flicked it back on again. "If I have to," she said. "I can do it if I have to. He can't die. I won't let him die." But she put the weapon away.

Briefly she considered whether to raise her mom and at least let her know she was all right. Mom would not become angry, never that. Annoyed, irritable, yes, but never angry. Aisling recalled her mother saying on one occasion, "Do not vex me, children." Karan Syan had ceased... whatever it was that he was doing; she could not remember, now. She herself, however, had gone to her room to look up the word "Vex."

Abruptly she sat up straight. That's the difference between us, she thought. Karan obeys the rules; I break them. Well, some of them. Sometimes.

That night on the beach, three years ago, when the Shannens had gathered there with a few friends. Mikal Trov, a close friend of her father's. A big, rough-looking man, bigger than and devoted to her father, he had brought alcoholic beverages from his tavern for the adults. Half in jest, he had offered the children a taste of Irish whiskey. Karan Syan had declined emphatically, the impropriety unthinkable. She had taken a sip; it had tingled her nose. Karan had threatened to tell their mother. Aisling, seeing her father accept a pull from the bottle, had merely shrugged. In the ensuing three years, over time, she had consumed perhaps two bottles of ale.

She sighed. "Da," and tilted the chair back.

The announcement of "Khorassey" startled her awake. When had she fallen asleep? She straightened the chair. "Oona, deTrack. Raise Khorassey Spaceport for downdock instructions, and follow them. We want a berth in a private hangar. Oh, and wake up Karan Syan."

Khorassey was a single-minded world. Roughly the size of Earth, with similar characteristics, it featured just the one settlement and just the one activity. That was the Orphanage. Indeed, a portion of its legitimate services included housing and seeking parents for children whose parents had died, or—more often—had abandoned them for a variety of reasons. But the primary function of the Orphanage was to provide involuntary laborers to various corporations, political leaders, and individuals. The labor generally was manual or menial, ranging from dredging draining canals and mining under perilous circumstances to household services and the sex trade. Slavery itself ran contrary to corporate publicized statutes and directives, a point hierarchs always brought up whenever openly challenged on the practices. Khorassey was an *orphanage*. Moreover, it did not come under corporate control.

Inmates, or "items," were brought to Khorassey for many reasons—indebtedness, indigence, chronically poor work, lack of conviviality, and unruly or violent behavior, among them. They were sold, or occasionally indentured, with the receipts divided equally between Khorassey and, if appropriate, the individual(s) or entity of record who consigned the item to Khorassey.

Requested by Aisling, Oona the 'skipcomp provided this information. Much of it seemed incredible to her, but she understood her father's interest—he bought and freed slaves and the indentured. She had yet to understand why he did that. Soon enough, if all went well, he would tell her.

"Now what?" asked Karan Syan, behind her.

She turned around. "We're there. Now we go find out what he was doing here, and where he might have gone from here."

From the 'skip they walked to the Khorassey Port Authority, where Aisling arranged docking for the *Athair* for two days. The twins then proceeded to the Orphanage Office. There at the counter they were greeted by a dark-haired man in a grey uniform with no shoulder patch to identify the corporation for which he worked. At first he frowned, then found his customary smile.

Aisling did not trust him. Karan Syan started to speak, but she shushed him with a chop of her hand.

"May I help you children?" asked the man. "Where are your parents?"

Again Karan tried to speak, and was silenced this time by a knuckle dug into his ribs.

"We're here about a man who made a purchase here two days ago," she said, in her best manner.

The man's smile widened. "Well, that certainly narrows it down."

"A tall man with black hair," she went on. "Taller than you. He would have made just one purchase."

A glint in the man's eye told her he knew who she was talking about.

"I think I remember him," he said. "But you're too young to make a purchase here. Where are your parents?"

"How old do I have to be?" she asked.

Clucking disapproval, he shook his head. "Your parents don't even know you're here. Well... it so happens that man did not give me his name, but he did buy a Motic."

Aisling blinked. "A... what?"

"A very uncooperative female." He stepped around counter. "An *alien*! Come with me. I'll show you."

63

He opened a door that gave onto a hallway, and ushered them through. All along the left wall, other doors led into the depths of the orphanage. An unidentifiable stench assaulted her nostrils.

Karan Syan rubbed his nose as he walked. "It stinks in here." Aisling Yhonyn controlled her breathing.

"You get used to it," said the man. The door at end of the hallways was also unlocked. It led to rows of plastic-barred cells, some empty, others occupied. He gestured toward the last one. "She was in there," he told the twins.

An item of clothing, possibly a cloak, and some bedding remained in the cell. Aisling Yhonyn started in after it, and too late realized her mistake. The door banged shut, trapping them both.

"Young clean item like you should fetch a very pretty price," he said. "The boy as well."

* * *

On the bridge of the *Aoife*, Supervisor Siobhan Gonelong was wondering at the transformation she had just undergone. Before her, the Videx opened to null-space, but she was watching a gallery of memories from her childhood and adolescence, through the terrible day of the attack on the family farm that left her father dead and her sister Deyrdra with her right leg gone above the knee. Then the fight with *him*, the battle, the conflict... what was it? When she and her twin brother had gone their separate ways, he to kill, she to stop him. That separation had lasted for sixteen years, with a brief pause while they fought Emil Koga and his horrific devices, and then another three years, after she had walked off in a...

"Say it!" she yelled at her reflection in the Videx.

...in a huff.

What had changed?

In adolescence they had also been lovers. But even more...

"You were my very best friend," she whispered, in Gaelic, and shook her head. "No, not 'were.' Are."

So why are you two traveling in separate spaceskips?

Briefly, guilt from the question stung her. For the sake of her independence? This might be accurate but it was incomplete. She still had Vandatti's tasking to complete, and that might well take her in other directions.

I miss you. I've missed you.

There will be a time...

"Far Parkins," announced Brid, and she was there.

On Far Parkins, the Fringe world called Motoya by the Motics, Supervisor Siobhan Gonelong had no formal authority. Her credentials carried no weight whatsoever. She might ask a question, but no one had to answer. When she entered the Farpark Port Authority adjacent to the only town on the planet where humans lived and gathered, she registered simply under her own name, omitting her rank and occupation, and paid for a day's docking fee.

The name of the town was Steerong, after an obscure explorer. On the way to Farpark, a world she had never visited before, she had requested a briefing from Brid. The planet was the home of one of the five sentient species so far encountered by humans: the Motics. They were an aquatic species, humanoid, with blue hair and pale blue skin, four webbed digits on hands and feet, two arms and two legs, and several other unique physical features. Generally they lived in water and came on land to forage for food. They were also vulnerable, although it was said that some were telepathic. They had no visible means of defense, such as weapons or fences.

Fortunately, the Motics had nothing that humans desired, nothing worth killing off the Motics. A few humans, mostly to escape from Corporatia for various reasons, had built a town that was self-sufficient in most respects. Interstellar trade provided whatever was missing. But such humans as lived here kept to themselves, gathering occasionally in the evenings at *Jersey Shore*, the main watering hole. Siobhan was headed there now.

Although constructed of quarried stone, raw wood, and terra cotta tiles, none of the buildings in Steerong resembled one another in size or layout. In addition to the twenty or so dwellings, there were four businesses: a general store and trading post; a clinic and pharmacy; a repair *tsekh*; and the tavern named *Jersey Shore*. All were clearly identified by signs, but Siobhan had no difficulty locating her destination. She wondered whether the others had arrived first. As it was still the early afternoon, she supposed that Ovin and the Motic female and Vanth's party might be the only patrons in the tavern.

Aside from a repairwoman, her supposition proved accurate. She paused at the doorway, taking it all in. The serving counter and the man in the white serving apron behind it; the rafters, the tables and benches; the floor of rough-hewn wood strewn with herbs, especially pennyroyal, to combat insects; the hygiene alcove around the far end of the counter. She took this all in, a panoramic scan that gradually settled not merely on the table and benches where they had gathered, but on... him.

So long without her best friend. On Vanadis it hadn't hit her hard, possibly because of her having found the Motic female there, the object of her search and her focus. But here, now...

He turned, and was looking at her. Yesterdays vanished into nothing when he beckoned to her. She found herself rushing to join him... them.

Introductions were in order. Palmula and then Pagan Bell. A man named Alton Deegy, dressed like someone who repaired underground fiberoptics, and who looked very unhappy. Siobhan ignored two of them, her eyes fixed on Pagan Bell. Under the circumstances, it would have been impolitic of her to refer to the woman as Vanth, the cannibal mortifice. Nevertheless, Siobhan seated herself cautiously beside her twin, well aware of the Krupp Spark nestled under the right front of her belt.

She eyed the bottle of ale in front of her. "For me?" Shannen merely grinned. She raised the bottle in a mock toast and took a sip. Her lilt returned, and she playfully exaggerated it. "Me ears are not burning. Y've not been talking about me, then."

"But we've been waiting for you," said Shannen. "You want to hear the answers to the questions. So do I, for that fact." He turned his attention across the table to Pagan Bell, who had Deegy under control. "I did check with Harbingers' Word on the way here," he said to her. "But I'm not clear about your interest in this, other than the fact that Palmula here is your sister."

"I have a contract to kill your companion," Pagan answered easily.

"And the fact that you are here tells me you're not inclined to do that," said Shannen.

Pagan shook her head. "Not quite. I shall report the contract as completed." With a wink, she added, "I have no idea who this woman is."

Ocamla grasped what had just transpired. She gaped, horrified, at Pagan. "You why kill me?" she said, anguished. "I do what?"

"I'd like to know the answer to that, meself," said Siobhan.

"Normally that's not a question a pro would ask of the contact," Pagan replied cheerfully. "Partagu was not chatty. When I learned that Tinker was involved, I did not want to probe and thereby create misgivings." She grinned at Ocamla. "So what makes your death worth a million thalers?"

"I not know, not know," she wailed.

Pagan reached across the table to touch the Motic's arm, to reassure her. "No, please, I will not harm you."

"I'm curious," said Siobhan. "Why not?"

Pagan looked at Shannen. "Well..."

Siobhan barked a shocked laugh. "Saints preserve us! You and me brother?"

"Not yet." Her filed incisors sparkled. "I'm working on it."

"As near as we can figure," said Shannen, "she overheard Partagu discussing Vanadis with someone, possibly Erron Markey."

"Better make that probably," said Pagan. "Markey has become his go-to over the past couple of years, despite his incompetence." She took a gulp of ale, and turned to Deegy. "Which brings us to you. Here you have no relationship to protect you. You and others went after my sister. That's a hundred times the excuse I'd need to fire up my grill and smoker."

Deegy finally spoke up. His voice was reedy with fear. "I-I don't understand. Who *are* you?"

Pagan touched a fingertip to a small puddle of condensation from one of the ale bottles, and printed out V-A-N-T-H for him to read. Deegy's face drained of blood, and he tried to squirm away. Palmula caught him by the collar and forced him to sit still.

"You didn't question him on the way here?" asked Shannen.

"I thought you'd want to hear it fresh," Pagan answered. "So we tucked him in the cargo hold." She turned back to Deegy. "As I said, there's nothing to protect you from me. If you answer questions, I'll turn you over to Corporatia Security." A desultory wave of her hand indicated Siobhan. "Otherwise, when we've finished our ales, you and I will take a little walk."

Eyes full of desperation, Deegy turned to Siobhan. "Are you going to just sit there and let her do this to me?"

Siobhan shrugged. "These are the Fringes. I have no jurisdiction out here."

"Who hired you to kill Palmula?" Shannen asked.

Deegy's lips tightened. Pagan picked up a fork and began to examine it closely. His eyes showed white all around. He ran his words together.

"I don't know who the client is. I'm usually not told. I don't have to know."

"Who do you work for?" Siobhan asked.

Again hesitation.

Palmula's brow bunched. "Sis, didn't I see a meat-packing plant on the way in?"

"Maybe. But I'm cheaper."

"*An ea?*" said Siobhan. "And why would that be?"

"I don't use anesthetic," Pagan said easily.

68

Deegy began to squirm violently. Pagan pressed the tines of the fork against his throat. He tilted his head back and away. His voice was pitched higher than a small bird's. "C-c-cotto!" he squeaked. "I work for Cotto."

Pagan pulled the fork back.

"Jiuli Cotto?" said Siobhan, her face hard.

Deegy nodded hesitantly. "Her... her adjutant, Addul, put together a team. All of us were on Jalune at the time."

"Convenient," said Shannen. "How many of you?"

"I-I know of six others."

"I must be slipping," said Pagan. "I only killed four of them. And took one prisoner, with the help of..." Her eyes narrowed at Shannen, and she swore softly. "I should have asked earlier... it's my fault, I assumed. But you do know that your children are out looking for you. In *Hazred*'s, it was your daughter who protected my sister. And... they know you were on Khorassey earlier."

Siobhan watched Shannen carefully. To the others, he seemed unshaken by Pagan's statement, almost as if yes, he did know. But there was a rigidity to his spine and shoulders and a set to his jaw that she had seen on but one other occasion: in the aftermath of the attack on their family's farm almost two decades ago, when she and he had gotten their siblings away to safety. His body in this moment, as before, was as martial as Roland's horn.

"Khorassey," he said, and got to his feet. "Pagan..."

"I'll find out what I can about Cotto," she promised.

"I'd better report back," added Siobhan. "Vandatti may want me to look into this."

"You I with come," said Ocamla.

Shannen frowned at her, shaking his head. "You're home now."

"I say you I work." She stood up. "I say words."

Without a response, he turned and left. Ocamla scampered after him.

"What," asked Palmula, "is going on?"

Siobhan closed her eyes, gathering herself. In the aftermath, she should have insisted on going with him. The person she had been assigned to locate, Ocamla, was with him. Instead, she had diverted herself before he could invite her. She wished she knew why she had done so.

When she opened her eyes again, the others were still looking to her. "I'm not sure," she said slowly. "But I think we had better find out, and fast."

* * *

Although Shannen had considered leaving Ocamla behind, he kept the ramp extruded while she boarded the *Banshee*. On first thought, she could be of no possible assistance to him. She had no known experience with weapons or in close combat. Conversations, while comprehensible, were stilted by her syntax. Worst of all, if a crunch came, he would feel the urge to protect her, an inclination that could get them both killed.

He wondered whether it was intuition that kept her silent as she sat in the port captain's chair on the bridge. In her own way, she had made it clear that she would do whatever she was told. Even if that were the extent of her usefulness, it might be enough. He allowed her into his second thoughts.

"We have to return to Khorassey," he said, apology in his tone.

A wordless nod acknowledged this.

"Maire, can you raise them?"

"I need a transponder signal or an open channel."

Shannen chided himself for even asking. He considered: Aisling and Karan were still there, or they were not. Yet it was not that simple. They were vulnerable and inexperienced. Without an adult present, they might well have been detained and confined, and perhaps already sold. He tried very hard not to think about that, and about the implications of it, and without success.

A touch at his arm refocused his eyes. He had not been aware of Ocamla's approach. Her face was close enough that he could see his reflection in her deep blue eyes. Hers were filled with concern. He wondered what she saw in his.

"You not still all right."

"No," he admitted.

"Will find we them," she said firmly.

"It's almost two hours to Khorassey."

She pointed aft. "You rest go. Ship voice, you I wake."

"Ocamla—"

Two middle fingers against his lips silenced him. "I free you say," she said. "I free choose."

"I suppose I could lie down for a while."

She stepped back to allow him to pass.

007

"They can't do this to us!" wailed Karan Syan, even before the attendant was out of earshot.

Aisling Yhonyn was more practical. "It's done."

She inspected the door, testing its security. Of gray bars of structural plastic, its two hinges on the far side, it hardly rattled when she shook it. Next she paced off the cell. It came to three paces by four deep, with the overhead just beyond her outstretched arm. The cell bay itself had been carved from bedrock. They were confined in a corner cell, with two walls of solid rock and two of ferrous plastic bars. The only other objects in the cell were a stool for relief, a bucket of water, and a cloak and some ragged bedding that stank of yeast and old sweat.

The prisoner in the adjacent cell spoke up from under a pile of bedding. "No one escapes from here," he said. He sat up, then got to his feet and approached the bars, a wiry young man in his late teens, with hair almost as black as hers, and blue eyes now amused. He was taller by the breadth of a hand, and dressed in clothes she had seen on men working in kitchen gardens on Vanadis. "You're here until you're bought."

"Unless they make a mistake," she sniffed disdainfully.

"They don't make them."

"We'll see."

He stuck a hand between the bars. "Finn."

She waited to hear the rest of it, but he added nothing. She took the hand. It was sinewy and lightly calloused. He grasped hers no more firmly than necessary. "Aisling Yhonyn," she told him. "My twin brother, Karan Syan."

"Don't tell him who we are!" cried Karan.

Finn eyed her carefully. "You don't seem frightened."

"But I am," she admitted. "It is that fear can get in the way when you need to do something. I try not to let it do that."

"How old are you?"

She started to say twelve. "Thirteen," she hedged.

"Not for eight more days," Karan reminded her.

She turned to glower at him, then back to smile at Finn. "Getting out of this cell is not the problem," she told him. "Getting through the bay door could be."

"Oh, yes," griped her twin, acidly. "Our dear father will come charging through that door to rescue us." He made a sound of disgust. "He scarcely knows we exist."

"I'm hoping to change that," she said, mostly to herself. "How long have you been in here?" she asked Finn.

"They feed you once every ten hours," he said. "I think it's a thirty-hour day on Khorassey, but of course there is no daylight in here with which to measure it. So I measure by meals. If I'm right, I've been here about forty days."

The answer disconcerted Aisling Yhonyn. She touched the tip of her tongue to her upper lip. "Is that... a lot?"

Finn shrugged. "In the time I've been here, I've seen just the one person leave." He nodded at her cell. "The one who was in there. She smelled so badly that they had to hose her down almost every day." His lips puffed out with a sigh. "You see, this is one of the cell bays for the incorrigibles. For the ones who caused too many problems for their previous owners, or cause trouble here."

"And... what problems did you cause?" she asked.

In response he turned his back to her and lifted his shirt. His skin was cross-hatched with whip marks, some fresher than others. Aisling's heart grabbed at her. She had no idea what to say when he turned back around.

A sad smile flickered at the corners of her mouth. "I'm sorry."

"You didn't do it."

"But you didn't answer my question."

"My previous owner? The man who did this? I killed him."

"Good for you."

"Aisling!" cried Karan Syan, aghast. "I'm telling Mother you said that."

"Mom would say the same thing. Anyway," she brightened, "at least now we can play naughts-and-crosses."

"You," said Finn, grinning, "are unspeakable."

"That's not funny, Aisling."

She glanced over her shoulder at him. "Has propriety cost you a sense of humor, Karan?"

"You're thirteen," said Finn.

"We both are. But I'm older."

The bay door opened, and in walked the man in the gray uniform, followed by a man approaching middle age. He might have been ninety. A deep breath would have ripped open the top half of his dull blue outsuit, so tightly did it fit. His face grew even more florid as they approached Aisling's cell. He seemed unwilling to draw a breath.

"This is the item I was telling you about, *M'sieur* Wanred," said the uniform, indicating Aisling. "She's fresh in here, just came in. Just the right age for your Master, I think."

"Oh, yes," Wanred said slowly. "She'll be years of fine bedding for him. What is your name, child?"

His voice had an oily quality that reminded her of tinned smoked fish. She gave him a somber look, but said nothing.

"We'll soon have that out of you," said Wanred, as if he were looking forward to extracting it. On his forehead, a sheen of sweat broke out. A horrid grin twisted his face. "Oh, yes, we'll have that out of you, and a lot more besides. When my Master is tired of you, he might give you to me." His voice dropped to a coarse whisper. "Oh, I truly hope so." He held her steady gaze for a long moment, then nudged the uniform's shoulder. "I want to review her background. Then let's discuss price, you and I."

* * *

Shannen managed to doze off on his bunk. He knew this, because he came awake with a start. A blue face gazed placidly at him.

"Is there a problem?" he asked Ocamla.

She sat on the edge of the bunk, hands folded in her lap, and looked away.

His internal clock told him that no more than an hour had passed since the *Banshee* had enTracked. He drew his legs up, swung them past her, and set his feet on the deck. "Ocamla?" he pressed, now sitting beside her.

Her mouth twitched, as if she wanted to speak but was holding back. Clearly she'd had a reason for entering the stateroom. He decided to let her get to it, whatever it was, in her own way.

Her whisper was just audible, though she was but half a meter from him. "I was taken from Motoya, my home world, six years ago, when I was seventeen," she said. "I have had several owners. You are by far the most unusual."

He managed to conceal his astonishment, and settled on a simple, "I wondered."

"You mean, about my speaking. It is a defense mechanism. If I speak clumsily, as if I were ignorant, less is expected of me."

"I am not your owner."

"No."

"And you came in here to tell me this."

"And more." She twisted to face him. "What I overheard, I told you. If I sounded uncertain, I was. I had never heard of Vanadis, and the word was not familiar to me. But these two men also spoke of you. The one named Partagu was my owner. He instructed the other to find out whether Candle was still alive. I assume he was referring to you."

Shannen felt hollow. Ocamla's words rang true. He had hoped her earlier broken statements indicated only that something might be afoot, most likely a conspiracy. Now they sounded as if Yassim Partagu were acting with specific intent.

When he and Siobhan, with the help of Sasha Parry, had gotten their brother and sisters away from the wreckage of their home nineteen years ago, he thought

75

Vanadis, at the time uninhabited, was far enough out into the Fringes. He thought they would be safe. His capture of the Resurgers, a weapon that could utterly destroy an entire planet, and the threat they represented, was supposed to keep Vanadis safe. The threat was a bluff; he'd ordered the Resurgers destroyed—a fact of which only he and Mikal Trov were aware. But if the corporations thought he were not around to control those weapons...

"You are not all right," said Ocamla.

"No." A weary sigh escaped him. "The reality is that the corporations can bring much force to bear. I cannot fight that."

She was silent for a moment. "What does 'steal a march' mean?"

"Where did you hear that?"

"The other man said Partagu was going to do that."

"It means he wants to move in on someone else's territory before they can get to it," Shannen explained. "It also means he will not leave any loose ends. But Ocamla, you said you heard all this a year ago."

"In fact, it was rather recent. One or two months. Time passes without permission in Khorassey." She paused, and held her breath, as if she were trying to suppress a memory. Moments later, she continued. "He was eager, but the matter was not urgent. Now, it seems, it is." Her eyes narrowed. "Candle is the name of a mortifice, an assassin. That is you."

"I retired," said Shannen. "But now and then I get involved in problems."

"And that dark woman we met in the tavern. The one who was hired to kill me. She is also a mortifice."

"Yes."

"Can she not help you?"

Shannen nodded. "But first I have to get my children back."

She touched his shoulder. "You will," she said. "We will."

* * *

This time, noted Curielle Neri, there were five corporate stay-behinds. Through the glasses she watched them disembark from a cargo schooner, the *Lost Sheep*, which made a trade run every twenty days, stopping at ten worlds, including Vanadis. The men who were walking down the ramp did not look like carguers to Neri. Each of them was tall and fit, and walked with a bearing of authority.

In the rushes adjacent to the spaceport, she swore ferociously, her blue eyes now darkened to indigo. Cadre. The men were cadre, being pre-positioned for an operation. That meant they were trained and skilled. Their brown outsuits were well-tailored to conceal weaponry, and Neri had no doubt the men were armed.

Beside her, dressed as she was in cammie pullover and denims and heavy black boots, Una Shannen squirmed for a better view, slowly parting the reeds as if it were the breeze moving them. The two women were a hundred meters from the schooner, well out of range of a casual glance from the men, but this surveillance had now become a combat mission. She put glasses to her eyes, and nudged Neri.

"D'you see that, then?"

Neri grunted. "They're letting an airfoil. And two carguers are hauling plastic shipping crates to it." Her tone deepened to a low growl of murderous intent. "They're bringing equipment, *mia gaelica*. Give it another couple minutes. Let's see if there are any more."

There weren't. The men completed their arrangements for the airfoil, and watched while the crates were loaded. Slowly Neri and Una backed out of the rushes and scrambled to their own airfoil, docked on the far side of a copse of red shagbark. While Una powered up and they made for a pre-arranged ambush site, Neri raised Ling, her second-in-command, and brought her up to speed.

"I want to be able to talk to one of them," said Neri, and closed commo.

"My quoil is useless at the range we'll be fighting," Una said sadly.

Neri took the conn from her. "Look in the starboard side bin, *gaelica*."

Una did so, and sat back, her mouth agape. Tentatively she reached for the weapon. "'Tis me own father's rifle," she cried softly, her hands caressing the stock of the Nabisko .287. "Da's rifle."

"And the reports of the bullets will shock and distract them. I'm hoping the sounds will scatter enough that they won't be able to pinpoint our location until it's too late."

"*Mo dheartháir* trained you well, Curi."

Neri nodded soberly. "This is more than training, *gaelica*. It is another payment on a debt I incurred... eleven years ago now."

Presently the bluffs came into view. Overlooking the glideway that connected the spaceport with Havenport, it was ridged with dark rock, broken here and there as if the planet's evolution had meant to provide firing points, like a natural battlement with merlons and crenels. Beyond the glideway stretched two kilometers of sparsely-grassed, rolling sand that gave onto the ocean. There was no cover down there, and only a few wind-swept shrubs for concealment. The afternoon sun, still high in the sky and off to their left, to the west, would not pose problems for their vision, although it might hamper that of the men they were about to kill.

Neri docked the airfoil well behind the bluffs. They crept over broken terrain and got into position, Una with the rifle, Neri with a medium-range Sharper Penetrator and an old grenade, which she cast down onto the glideway. The firing point she had selected was best accommodated by a kneeling position. She dropped to it and took aim at the grenade, and nodded to Una, who had chosen a wider crenel in the rock that allowed her a field of fire of over sixty degrees. Once established and comfortable, they waited.

The sound of an approaching airfoil made Neri's blood course slower, not faster. An icy calm took hold inside her. In anticipation, Una tapped a finger against the rifle's trigger guard. The airfoil rounded a curve, and slowed to a stop off the far side of the glideway. A young man and woman disembarked, she carrying a small covered basket that might contain food, he a blanket, and they set up on the sand and grass.

"Oh, *mannangia!*" swore Neri.

* * *

It was not like Yhounda Khouse to fret, regardless of frustration or provocation, but as she sat at her dressing table and glared at herself in the mirror, she fidgeted. She wanted to do something to aid in the return of her son and daughter, but there was nothing for her to do save wait. Their father—at one time long ago Yhounda's lover—was searching for them, and he would do whatever had to be done to find them and bring them back home.

Waiting was the hardest part.

Shannen had sent her a vague message via Palmetto, to the effect that he was going to find them. She wanted more details. She wanted to speak with him, face to face, or as close to that as possible in a null-space transmission. She wanted to look into his eyes and see that certainty she had known all those years ago. Almost fourteen years, now. Yet it was so like him to send her a message, rather than interface with her. And with his children. She knew why he stayed away most of the time—and now it appeared that his worst fears, that of a corporate take-over of Vanadis, were now on the verge of realization, *despite* his prolonged absences. They had all been in vain; he *could* have been here, and he *could* have helped to rear and educate Aisling and Karan.

Yes, she thought, though we may now live well into our second century, we still run out of time to do the things we should do.

She frowned at her image in the mirror. That could not be a tear trickling down her cheek. She had forbidden them. Surely the orders of the Princess of Vanadis carried that much weight. She dabbed at it with a tissue, and only induced another to form. She, who had once guided—not ruled, so much—an entire world, was confronted now by inaction. She knew that she should not interfere with whatever Ovin was doing; she also wanted to do something to help.

She tokked the Palmetto to raise the *Banshee*.

There was no response, not even an invitation to leave a message.

008

Siobhan Gonelong found Commissioner Vandatti waiting in her office in the Sector Headquarters on Newmarket. The personal visit drew unspoken questions from her. Aboard the *Aoife*, she had raised him for her report, and he had been short, almost cross, with her in giving instructions for their meeting. Now he was here, seated on one of guest chairs, a dour expression on his nut-brown face as he watched her turn the other chair to face him, and sat down at attention.

"Relax, Siobhan," he said. The two words belied his expression. "Other eyes and ears, but not here."

She sat back, one eyebrow lifted. "You had my office swept?"

"As well as my own," he replied. "As well as our Palmettos and PCs."

She put two and two together. "Partagu?"

"That's the operative assumption. Tech is working on it. Siobhan, what have you learned?"

"Not very much, sir. I was unable to conduct a sit-down interrogation, and from what I was able to glean from conversation, I don't think Ocamla knows any more than she told Ovin."

"Ovin."

Siobhan smiled. "Yes, sir."

"It sounds as if there has been a reconciliation of sorts."

"I'm... not sure yet, sir."

"About this Ocamla."

Siobhan got up and went to the small wet bar. "Would you care for a drink, sir? I'm having a finger of Jameson's over a rock."

"The same."

"Ocamla overheard Partagu and one other man, presumably Erron Markey, discussing the possibility of moving on Vanadis," she said, as she prepared the tumblers. "This may have been as much as a year ago. The timing has not been confirmed. They wanted to determine the status of Candle first. I gather there was no great urgency then." She handed Vandatti one of the tumblers, and returned to her chair.

Vandatti raised his drink in a wordless toast, and took a pensive sip. "It sounds as if something has occurred to cause them to activate their contingencies."

"As the exploitation of mineral deposits on any undeveloped world would fall into the province of Corporatia Resources, perhaps Chair Conigli is making similar inquiries." She considered the possibility, and added, "Conigli is aware of my... full relationship with Ovin, and would therefore have a motive for surveillance."

Vandatti raised his drink again. "One point for you," he said. "That hadn't occurred to me."

"One other point: as far as Harbingers' Word is concerned, Vanth is still contracted to kill Ocamla. However, I know she will not complete the contract. There have been... complications."

"Explain, please."

Siobhan did so, omitting only Shannen's missing children. She gave Vandatti a few moments to ponder the information.

"So what do we do, sir?"

The commissioner did not respond directly. For a few moments he studied the crystal tumbler, as if seeking enlightenment. Finally his eyes met hers.

"I almost wish I had not promoted you to Supervisor," he said. "You're a good overseer, but that's a duty assignment. Oh, you perform it superbly, I've no complaints whatsoever. But your gifts do not lie in supervision, or bean-counting, or the proper completion of templates for approving operations. You're an operative. You assemble a team and you tackle problems."

A chill of anticipation made fine hairs rise on her arms. Offices were for gathering oneself to go out and resolve difficulties, not for ordering others to resolve them while you sat and read their reports. In retrospect, she saw that was why, of her own volition, she had attended the problem of Kiltner accosting women at the tavern across the glideway. And why she had been pleased by the assignment to track down the female Motic that Vanth was seeking.

Vandatti smiled as if he knew what she was thinking. "I'll work out the organizational and structural questions," he said. "For now, you're a special operative with a team. You kept Sergeant Tallgrass and one of the Tomascos for your staff here. I'll find you some other—"

"Sir, I'd like my old team. Dimiter, Morrow, Pachen, both Tomascos, and Tallgrass, whom I'll appoint as my field aide. I'd like two personnel more as well."

"They'll all be told to report here tomorrow morning," said Vandatti.

"And what will we be doing, sir?"

He finished his drink, and set the tumbler on her desk. "You'll be doing whatever Ovin Shannen needs you to do," he answered. "I expect regular progress reports."

Uncertain whether she had just been gifted or cursed, she downed the rest of her drink in one gulp.

* * *

Port Authority on Khorassey did not respond to requests for permission to downdock. That alone should have alerted Shannen to a difficulty on the ground, but the fate of his children distracted him. Ocamla, for all her experience, had none to help him. Finally he gave up the lack of communication as anomalous, and set down on the tarmac outside the main entrance.

The view through the Videx stunned him: bodies in Khorassey gray lay scattered like driftwood. He counted to five, and stopped counting. Only a couple of them had drawn weapons. Fear constricted his breathing; Khorassey was by common agreement inviolate. The attack had been sudden and unexpected. It was impossible to sneak up on the orphanage, which meant the attackers had worn some kind of disguise. A squad of Corporatia Products Security Forces might have managed it, but Shannen wondered whether the specific accusation stemmed from the present enmity between himself and the corporation. Any squad from corporate security might have been responsible, or some other entity altogether.

Facts first; theory afterwards, he told himself.

Beside him, Ocamla was shaking her head. "I didn't do it," she said, and added a light laugh. She followed the disclaimer with an immediate apology. "I'm sorry, Ovin. Your children."

"No, you're right," he said. "Stay light, loose, and frosty. We have to go in there."

"I know."

"Can you use a weapon?" He made for the port bulkhead and the bins set into it. From one of them he pulled a Krupp Stix 510 and tucked it under his belt next to the flechette he always carried.

Ocamla pulled up next to him and inspected the contents. He let her choose. She picked up a Gallo Justifier and examined it, checking the charge pack and making sure the safety worked. Like Shannen, she tucked the weapon under her belt.

"Of course, we could just wait for about twelve hours before we go in," she said. "But you'll have to hose me down afterwards."

Shannen laughed. "You'll go in alone, then."

"With you," she said, and sobered. "With you."

At his instruction, Maire extruded the ramp. They crept outside cautiously, weapons drawn and sweeping the area for movement. A bevy of flying insectoids had come to begin feeding; aside from them, all was still. A board prevented the door at the main entrance from sliding shut. Shannen and Ocamla entered ready to fire. He was pleased to note that she was covering the right and rear, while he had the front and left. He wondered where she had learned the tactic. For just a moment she reminded him of Siobhan, but he cast aside that distraction and the long-ago memory that went with it.

The lobby contained but one body, that of a guard. He had been killed by an energy weapon. Shannen peered over the counter and found the body of the clerk he had dealt with when purchasing Ocamla. It showed no sign of weapons fire, but there were powerful ligature marks across his throat.

"Ovin," Ocamla said softly, and pointed. The door that led to the Incorrigible Holding was ajar.

Shannen checked the lobby again. The Holding door was the only one that was open. It seemed to him a good bet that whatever had happened here, had begun in there.

"Stand to one side and cover me," he told Ocamla. "I'll go in first."

"Be careful."

The caution gave Shannen a moment's pause. It was what an amateur would say, but it might also have come from someone pretending to be an amateur. The only professional he could think of who would have said that to him was his twin sister.

He nodded once, slid the door aside, and dove forward onto the floor. He came up from the tuck-and-roll steady on his feet, weapon sweeping the cells along the hallway. Some eyes stared at him, while others glared.

"Coming in," said Ocamla.

This time the advisory was decidedly the result of experience. An amateur would simply have barged in, risking a precautionary beam from Shannen.

"It looks clear," he said. But he did not put away the Krupp.

She gave him a tap on the right arm to let him know precisely where she was. "The last door on the right is open," she said.

"The last two doors on the right. What we don't know is how many of the other doors are shut but unlocked."

"Understood."

They moved forward. For the most part, the inmates did not move. At the midway point, someone called, "Hey, Stinky. Hey, everyone, it's Stinky."

Shannen watched her out of the corner of his eye. She did not respond to the jibe, except to form a knuckle-whitening fist with her free hand.

At the last cell they stopped. The door itself bore scorch marks at the key slot. A touch for attention got Shannen to look at the other door: it showed the same kind of marks. Both empty cells contained some old bedding and the usual detritus of prolonged occupation. Shannen had no choice but to go inside for a closer inspection, and leave Ocamla to guard the door.

Nothing on the floor stood out for him. The bedding had been in the cell during Ocamla's confinement. He had caught a whiff of it while standing in the hallway. He was loath to pick it up and shake it.

"I can do it, Ovin," she called, as if reading his mind.

He shook his head, and picked it up with thumb and forefinger. It yielded old hair and sloughed flakes of skin, and a button that clicked on the plasticrete floor with a metallic ring, and rolled around in a tightening circle. He bent and caught it before it clattered.

It was not a button.

"They were here," he breathed, despondent. He fought back tears. A hand on his shoulder said that Ocamla had abandoned her position. He looked up.

"We will find them," she said. Her tone added, "Or die trying."

* * *

Una Shannen readied her rifle. "They'll be here any moment now," she said. The unexpected arrival of the young couple down on the grass on the other side of the glideway worried her for several reasons, not the least of which was the grenade Curielle Neri had tossed down onto the glideway and was about to detonate with a beam from her Sharper.

Beside her, Neri fumed. Exploding the grenade just as the airfoil carrying the five corporate interlopers passed over it might well shower the couple with shrapnel. Una understood the quandary as well. If Neri's beam was exquisitely timed, the airfoil skirt would absorb most of the shrapnel. She was well capable of such a shot. But if...

Neri shook her head and swore again.

"I don't hear the airfoil yet," said Una.

"Nor do I." Her chest rose and fell with a deep breath. She aimed the Sharper in the vicinity of the couple. "No choice, *gaelica*," she said tersely.

"I know."

Neri fired a blue beam at a clump of grass two meters from the picnic blanket. It made the couple leap to their feet, faces twisted with sudden fear. "Get out of here now!" yelled Neri.

Uncomprehending, they gaped up at her. Neri fired again; the beam scored the sand a meter away.

The man rose, and shook his fist at them. "You can't do this!"

"*Gaelica*," said Neri, a signal.

Una fired a bullet at the basket, which spilled its contents. The report reverberated out to sea. "I can put the next one in your head," she called down.

This had the desired effect. Swiftly the couple gathered up their things, leaving behind only the contents of the basket, and within seconds sped away, leaving a wake of loose sand. The sound of the departing airfoil made Una listen even more carefully. Either the wind was picking up, or another airfoil was drawing near.

"I hear it as well, *gaelica*," Neri said softly. "Let us hope those men did not hear the rifle shot."

"I think I've seen those two at *Nicole's*," mused Una. "When this is over, I'll apologize."

"As will I," said Neri. "When this is over."

"Curi—"

"I hear it."

Una prepared for covering fire while Neri sighted in on the grenade. The airfoil swung around the curve into view. It kept to the right, and Una stifled a cry of dismay. If the path of the airfoil held, it would pass by the grenade, not over it, and much of the effect of the explosion would be lost. Una counted the passengers to five, and eased a little sigh of relief; at least the men had not hired a driver. She and Neri had not even considered that possibility earlier—an error in planning. She glanced at Neri: she was focused now, oblivious to all but the grenade. The track of the airfoil would miss it by a good meter. Una steadied the rifle.

Neri fired a beam; instantly the grenade exploded. The concussion drove the airfoil onto the grass and sand, where it rolled onto its side. Una fired at the first sign of movement. The man sprawled onto the sand and lay still.

A blue beam from Neri's Sharper took a second man full in the face. Meanwhile, two others had recovered. Una could see their shadows on the sand; the men had enough sense to stay behind the airfoil until they could identify their adversary. Una dodged back, but it wasn't enough; a blue beam struck rock, and showered her with fragments. She cried out as blood streamed from her forehead. A blow from one of the larger chunks made her dizzy. Her knees buckled, and she slumped against the boulder that covered her.

"*Gaelica!*" shouted Neri, and fired a burst of indiscriminate beams at the overturned airfoil. There was no immediate return fire, so she knelt down and shot a fearful look at Una. "How bad is it?"

Blood from the gash in her forehead trickled into her left eye, and she wiped it away with her sleeve. She set down the Nabisko and drew the jersey over her head, and pressed the fabric against her wound. A feeble wave of her hand dismissed Neri's concern.

"*Allora, non é cattivo. Mi dispiace, mia gaelica.* I planned this poorly."

"No," gasped Una, trying to shake off the momentary dizziness. Her voice came weakly. "It was a good plan. We didn't allow for the wind."

"We'll separate," said Neri. "We should have done that in the first place. I want to give them two targets to consider. Can you lay down some suppressing fire?"

"It's a ten-round clip," Una reminded her, and winced as fresh pain struck her.

"After you've emptied it, they'll raise their heads for a look. I should be able to get at least one of them."

"I have the one extra clip," Una reminded her, as she dabbed at the blood. She still felt unsteady; it was an effort to focus. "I can't suppress after that goes."

Neri began crabbing away, staying below the crest and away from the openings. When she reached a spot some ten meters away, next to a jagged block of basalt, she gave a little nod. Una's finger curled around the trigger. She fired the first round without looking, then curled around into the opening and ran off the others. Now blinded by blood in her left eye, she sat back down. A couple of seconds later, Neri fired two beams, then rushed back to Una. Neri's olive face and short black hair blurred in Una's eyes. She felt them scroll up and into nothing at all.

* * *

Yhounda Khouse emerged from her cottage and turned around to look back at it. The simple structure was a far cry from her palace on Mulane, but it served her well, and perhaps even better. For one thing, there was less to supervise... although she had left most of that to her majordomo. Here she had a young woman to come in and see to the cottage, but Yhounda herself saw to several of the daily duties. *Some Princess I am*, she thought, gazing at her home. Never accustomed to ordering people around unless absolutely necessary, she was at times uncertain how to avail herself of the opportunity. Ming Meihua, whose name meant Bright Plum Blossom, knew what to do and did it cheerfully. Only recently had Yhounda learned that Meihua was one of some four hundred Swoopies from China on Earth whom Shannen had rescued years ago and settled on Vanadis, and that she did her work as recompense for that rescue.

"But you owe me nothing," Yhounda had protested. "It is I who owes you."

"I owe him," Meihua had said pleasantly, as if that settled the matter.

Yhounda tugged the Palmetto from a pocket of her long denim skirt and tried once more to reach Shannen. As before, there was no response. Her thoughts returned to her children. *Where are you?* And: *just wait till I get you home!*

She turned and began walking toward the ocean, and to the *Dur Falls Inn*, the tavern a few hundred meters from the south coast of Haven. The journey, of eight kilometers there and back to her cottage, was somewhat longer than the walks for exercise she took, and the pace she set for herself on this occasion was just below that of a trot. Presently, as she rounded a woods, the tavern came into view. At this point, she began to run.

Breathless, she reached the door, and yanked it open. The hour was yet early, and both Mikal Trov and Deyrdra Shannen were setting up for the late afternoon and early evening. Both turned to look at her as she entered. For a few moments she regarded them, taking heart. Trov, at one time Ovin Shannen's top hand during his days as a mortifice, stood big and solid, a rock she discovered that in this moment she needed. He was dressed in grubbies: an old yellowed shirt with more holes than needed for wearing, black jeans, and loafers. Deyrdra, taller than Trov, wore a simple green shift not quite long enough to conceal the circle around her right thigh that marked the point where the artificial leg began. Her hair, as long and black as Yhounda's, was bound up and out of the way, although a few tresses had come loose during her labors.

Deyrdra bypassed greetings to address her concern. "Are you all right?" she asked, rushing toward Yhounda. Her customary playful lilt was muted. "What's happened?"

Yhounda allowed Deyrdra to walk her to a table and sit her down. "My children," she said, and explained, her words broken by fear, while Trov went behind the counter and drew a draft of ale for her. "And I am unable to raise Ovin," she finished, and took a gulp from her mug. It made her cough.

Deyrdra's face bore a puzzled frown. "That's not like him."

Trov dug out his own Palmetto, and tried, with the same negative result and a similar frown. "It's possible he's engaged in some activity that requires stealth," he said slowly. "It's also possible that he is..."

"Don't say it, then," Deyrdra put in. Her brown eyes glared at him.

Trov dragged a huge hand over his craggy face. "There's not much that I can do, Yho," he said. "Do you have any idea at all where he went?"

Yhounda shook her head.

"Maybe Curi knows something," he said, and tried to raise her. There was no immediate response, and he started to close, when Neri's voice broke through.

"Mikal," she said, and sounded distressed, taut. "I'm at Sasha's. It's... it's Una. You'd better bring Deyrdra. I- I... *mi dispiace*, I cannot talk..."

"On our way," growled Trov.

009

Aboard the *Aoife*, Siobhan Gonelong enTracked the 'skip without destination, and sat at the bridge nursing a Bushmill's rye over ice. Assembling her old team had relieved tedium for Kam Dimiter, who years ago in emulation of Siobhan—and to Siobhan's astonishment at their initial encounter—had shorn her tangerine locks to within a millimeter of her scalp. For reasons known only to bureaucracy, after the business with Emil Koga, Dimiter had been transferred to Postings, there to help oversee who was assigned where. The responses of the others on the old team had ranged from joy to hopeful disbelief. But Siobhan was concerned now with the two newest members, assigned to her by Vandatti.

Sergeant Hitam Teshko came to her from Operations & Training, and Siobhan could not help but recall that Stefan Klos, her former aide, had also been assigned to her from O&T, had gained her trust and confidence, and in the end had betrayed her. She had escaped the attempted murder only through good fortune. Teshko had some field experience, and was wasted in training recruits, most of whom would fail to pass muster. Siobhan had reviewed the file. At a meter-eighty-six, he was taller by the width of two fingers, and his wiry frame carried but seventy-seven kilos—if that, she had snorted, studying his hologram. In the 'gram, he moved with a grace and deftness that shouted at her not to underestimate him. True, he had been chosen for her by Commissioner Vandatti—but so had Klos.

The thought of Klos took her back three years, to the time when her brother Kevan had come to Vanadis in the company of an alien entity named Iska. The others had referred to her as a charm quark; an energy being who had assumed a human form, she could vanish and reappear at will. Another charm quark, this one named Photem, appeared to Siobhan as a purple female, and protected her against the beam fired at her by Klos, who was killed by the reflection. When Iska departed with

Kevan, she promised Siobhan that a part of Photem would remain behind to protect her. In three years of primarily administrative duties, Siobhan had yet to need that protection again. But she was now uncomfortable about another Klos, and another betrayal.

Where Teshko was dour, Brevet Corporal Birch Yensen was affable, with merry blue eyes and a round fleshy face that matched the general shape of his body. As yet he had not been given a permanent rating, although Siobhan noted on his file that he had come under the auspices of Special Operations over a year earlier. While his configuration suggested a low level of physical fitness, he was able to move with alacrity when the occasion demanded—such as when a colleague stumbled in the office and pitched toward a counter, only to be held up by Yensen, who covered a good three paces in a bare second. Siobhan noted that he, too, need not be underestimated, although for reasons different from those of Teshko. What troubled her was that she could not come up with specific reasons for either of them.

She wondered whether Klos's betrayal had affected her even more adversely than she had thought. It felt unnatural to consider others on her team with the question of loyalty. In a firefight, Yensen might very well display a serious side; Teshko could frown at the possibility of danger and yet laugh in the face of it. There simply was no way to know whom to trust completely.

Except...

She tossed down the last of the rye with an air of finality. "Brid, are you awake?"

"*Of course. Ich kann nicht anders.*"

She started at the quotation from Luther. "You cannot do otherwise?" she said, and laughed, her lilt pronounced now. "Aye, there be perhaps no difference between carbon and silicon, after all. Plot us a course, then. Let's go ho..." And she stopped. *Why can't I say it?* "To Vanadis," she finished, saddened.

With the *Aoife* given direction, Siobhan went aft to the galley in search of something to take her mind off her concerns. This proved impossible, but she settled for some noodles in vegetable broth, breaking the dried noodles into small fragments so that the entire soup could be eaten with a spoon. She glanced at the fold-down table and the bench, and decided she did not want to sit down. Standing, leaning back against the counter, she ate slowly, absently, and continued to consider her preparations. Dimiter and Tallgrass had been instructed to collect the other members of the team and to take them to orbit around Vanadis pending permission to dock down. Meanwhile, Siobhan expected to coordinate with her twin regarding the deployment and duties of her team.

She raised her voice, though it was unnecessary. "Brid, try Ovin again."

Five seconds passed.

"He does not respond."

"But we kissed and made up," she said, a faux complaint. "Well, made up, anyway. All right, Brid, try every ten minutes. If I'm asleep when he responds, wake me. If I can sleep," she added, muttering.

"Would you care for some music to sleep by? Isle of Innisfree? Blind Mary? Molly Malone?"

Siobhan considered. *"Far-Off Place,"* she said. "The version by Dana Scallon, if you can find it."

"That is five hundred years old."

"Those other songs are far older, Brid. And so is Ireland. *Is Éireannach me.*"

The strains of a soft guitar and a plaintive voice began to drift into the galley. They followed Siobhan along the gangway to her stateroom, where she stretched out on the berth, laced her fingers behind her head, and listened to *Tir na n'Og*.

* * *

The security staff at the Orphanage on Khorassey had finally recognized that something was amiss. Even as Shannen and Ocamla reached the main lobby, five Khorassey guards, attired in camouflage uniforms and armed with energy rifles or Post Toasters swarmed in through the doorway and shouted commands at them to lie face down on the floor with their hands behind their heads.

Shannen did not hesitate, and motioned for Ocamla to follow his lead. He fired an envenomed dart at the exposed face of the lead guard, while the Motic female dropped two more with her Gallo Justifier. Blue beams from the remaining two guards passed harmlessly over their heads as they dove behind the counter, Ocamla landing asprawl on the dead clerk. Quickly she rolled off him and crouched behind the counter beside Shannen.

"Now what?" she whispered.

"We have to get out of here," he told her—unnecessarily, for her expression said she took that maneuver for granted. "We'll never convince them now that we didn't do this."

"Go to the far end of the counter," she instructed. When he hesitated, she hissed, "Move. Others will be here. This is our chance." Without waiting for him to respond, she crabbed to the other end. "I'm giving up," she called out. "Don't shoot."

The announcement seemed to take the two guards by surprise. After a couple seconds of hesitation, one found his voice. "Throw your weapon over the counter," he shouted. "Then stand up with your hands up and empty."

"Here it is," she said. A moment later it clattered on the floor. "I'm standing up now."

She straightened, with palms out. Both guards held weapons aimed at her. She did not glance at Shannen.

"Come out from around the counter."

The speaker was the only guard with an orange stripe of rank on his collar. Ocamla cleared the other guard from her mind; he would not fire unless ordered to. Carefully she stepped around the end of the counter.

Shannen rose and fired the flechette, killing one. Ocamla dove to the floor, retrieved her Justifier, and slew the other guard. By this time, Shannen had already leapt over the counter. He snagged her hand and tugged her along. "Before anyone else arrives," he said, again unnecessarily.

Ocamla yanked her hand free, and ran slightly ahead of him, Shannen burdened by the need to use the Palmetto to signal Maire. At his instruction, the computer opened the hatch and extruded the ramp. Boots tokked on the plastic as they ascended. Once inside, he gave the command for emergency track, and they ran, slowing, to the bridge.

Already the Videx displayed null-space. Ocamla's blue skin was darker now, the rise and fall of her chest more rapid, from excitement and exertion. The Justifier was still in her left hand; she seemed not to know what to do with it. Gently Shannen pried it loose from her fingers and tucked it under his belt. They fell into the captain's chairs, Ocamla with a now-what expression on her face.

He raised the 'skipcomp. "Maire, what's the transponder of that ship in the dock at Khorassey?"

"It is disabled. I may be able to override."

Ocamla shot him a worried look. "Do you think—?"

He shook his head quickly. "Aisling and Karan would have taken one of the 'skips-to-let at Havenport. That wasn't one of them. I'd like to have a look inside it, but the main entrance was about to be clotted with security personnel."

"Too many for the two of us to take on."

"But the kids were there in that cell."

He took out the object he had found on the floor, and tossed it to her. She turned it over and over in her hand. "Some kind of coin?"

"A very old coin, from more than five hundred years ago," he told her. "A *pinsin* from Ireland. A penny. I gave two of them to Aisling for luck." His voice choked up. For a few moments he could not get the words out. "Two coins. One from the year 1933, the other from 1953."

"This one says 1933."

"I know," he said wearily. "In 1953, Ireland was a free land. In 1933, it was under the iron thumb of the British." He closed his eyes for a few seconds, and sighed. "It's a message from Aisling, left behind on the chance I might have traced her that far and come for her.

She's telling me that she and Karan are captives."

Ocamla slipped from the chair and rushed to his side. Soft blue arms enveloped him, and her face nuzzled his shoulder. She said nothing, and he did not move.

"The name of the 'skip is the Sinjin," Maire the 'skipcomp announced. *"It is registered to the estate of Hrvold Weinatte."*

At hearing the news, Shannen slumped in the chair. Then he straightened, his back rigid. Ocamla fell away, but remained standing by his side.

"That's bad, isn't it?" she asked.

"It's bad. But right now that 'skip is all we have, and even that is almost nothing." He turned toward the nearest speaker, unnecessarily. "Maire, set a course for Ovid's World, and take us there."

Ocamla swallowed hard. "I have... been there."

"Then you know."

"I know." She extended a hand. "May I have the Justifier back? I'm hoping I'll need it."

* * *

At the knock on her office door, Jiuli Cotto did not look up. It could only be her adjutant, Addul. As was her custom, she called out in his native Swahili. *"Karibu."*

He opened the door just wide enough for him to poke his head inside. His dark skin seemed to have paled. "You have a visitor," he announced, haltingly. "She... she..."

Cotto frowned hard, her dark eyebrows bunched together as if mating. "Who is it, Addul?"

"She says she is a pagan."

"I meant her name."

"She did not—"

A woman's husky contralto swept in from the anteroom, followed by her exasperation. "Oh, for the luvva—" Two seconds later, Addul's head vanished from the opening, the door was thrust open, and shut hard behind the woman who had entered.

She who now stood before Cotto's desk was as bizarre in appearance as any that Cotto had ever seen. Around her hips she wore a brief wrap of brown hides, or of material that had been treated to pass for hides, so thin that she required several layers to make the garment opaque. The skin of her entire upper body was painted with bright body tints—crimson and saffron and emerald and ultramarine and ivory and jet black—arranged in a variety of designs, some simple geometric shapes, others intricate tracings and patterns. Even her coarse straight hair, normally dark brown, was now royal blue streaked with ochre. From her earlobes dangled fragments of bone strung on silver, and phosphorescent scarlet streaks outlined the two vertical ritual scars that connected the eyes to the corners of the mouth. With a shaky hand Cotto grasped the Skoda Sparxfly affixed to the underside of the center desk drawer, and wondered whether war had been declared on her.

"You're a pagan?" said Cotto.

She grinned. Her upper and lower incisors had been filed to a fine edge. "Pagan Bell." She did not extend a hand, but took a couple steps to one side, changing her angle with regard to Cotto, as if she recognized the threat from the weapon under the desk. "But I'm also a pagan. Your man outside might have recognized the name of Vanth, had I given it. Even without that, he was becoming incoherent. You need better help. Which reminds me: if that door behind me should open—"

"Addul, I'm all right," Cotto called out. "It's all right."

"Actually, you're not all right," Vanth said cheerfully. "You arranged for men to kill my sister, Palmula. That's a grave no-no."

Cotto's lips felt desiccated. She licked them. "I didn't know she was—"

"Ah, you kill indiscriminately. I admire that. I can't do it, myself, I'm much more selective, but you'll kill anyone, or have them killed, I should say, as long as the pay is right. Oh, and I imagine you're holding some sort of weapon under that desktop. Something short-range, probably a Post Nymph or a Pocket Siat, maybe a Sparxfly. If you fire through the desk pedestal, the beam will be much too feeble to damage me, and by the time you could bring the weapon above the desk you would already be dead. Now, why not simply place your empty hands on the desk top, and we'll talk."

"You-you're saying you're not going to kill and... and... kill me?"

"And eat you. No. I have enough in the freezer to last for a while. As for merely killing you, that will depend on whether you have anything to say."

"I'm not going to betray my contacts."

In a flash Vanth drew her Kellogg Cobra and aimed it. "Okay. 'Bye."

"Wait!" Cotto's empty hands fairly flew up onto the desk.

Vanth heaved an exaggerated sigh. "Oh, very well." She sounded disappointed.

"What... what do you want to know?"

"First, I have something to tell you. Of the seven men your Addul lined up to kill my sister, four are now dead. A fifth has been turned over to Corporatia Security—against my better judgment, although I don't like having to fracture statutes. The last two are probably still out at the Jalune Spaceport, watching Palmula's *Infinite Dreamer* gather dust. Or they may have dozed off. I haven't yet decided whether to see to them. If they're still emplaced when I get there..."

"They won't be," said Cotto. Her right hand moved to her hair, glistening dark brown in the overhead light, and thumbed a few tresses back from her ear and shoulders. The move also served to inform her of how much movement would be permitted. A *frisson* ran through her as she realized that Vanth was in such control as not to care whether she moved. "What else?" she asked.

"Simple: who contacted you to set this up?"

Cotto hesitated. A chill sweat broke out on her forehead.

"Of course," Vanth went on, musing, "I could use some more snack material. I think they still call it finger food."

"You are *ghastly*!"

"Thank you." Vanth simpered, twisting her painted face into a horrifying caricature of itself. "I try. The contact?"

"Damn you. Erron Markey, *damn* you. Now do what you will."

Vanth grinned. "I always do. But I didn't get the name from you, Cotto. You're safe." She took a couple steps back. "I'll just see myself out," she said. "After all, I saw myself in. And unless you want to train a new majordomo..."

"Addul," called Cotto. "She's leaving. Do not interfere."

Vanth gave her a mock salute, and departed.

Afterwards, Cotto emitted a huge gulp of air. Her chest ached. She opened a drawer in the left pedestal and took out a bottle and a glass. Following a moment of reflection, she put the glass back.

* * *

A dreadful silence had fallen upon the bridge of the *Athair*. At the console stood Karan Syan, with no idea what to do with it. Beside him stood the young man named Finn, blotting his nose, and fidgeting. Karan glared at him irritably, but said nothing.

"You *do* have vocal control?" said Finn at last. His voice sounded clogged.

Karan had no wish to reveal his ignorance to this stranger. But he was forced to balance that reluctance against his fear that at any moment Khorassey Security might swarm onto the Spaceport tarmac and open fire on the *Athair*. After what Aisling had done inside the hallway and the lobby and outside, he could hardly blame them. Even now, as he nodded in the affirmative to Finn, he shuddered at the thought of what might have happened, had the clerk ordered her to be searched. He must have thought her just a girl, and harmless. Aisling was a girl... but Karan still quaked at the memory of what she had done.

Before Wanred and the counter attendant in the gray uniform could return to collect Aisling, she had used the Benz Sizzler to disable the door locks to their cell and Finn's. Freed, they ran toward the door leading to the lobby. Once there, Aisling did not hesitate. She brought down the attendant with a sweep of her quoil, and shot the guard. She missed a beam at Wanred, but followed him out the front door. There they encountered a clutch of security guards who hesitated, uncertain as to what was transpiring. Again Aisling acted without hesitation, and within the span of three breaths she had brought down all seven. But she had neglected to see to Wanred, and while Karan stood by helplessly, he struck her from behind and slung her unconscious body over his shoulder. Finn, in an attempt to stop Wanred, caught an elbow against his nose for his trouble. The blood that flowed from it was as nothing, but the blow dazed him. By the time he recovered, Wanred had boarded his 'skip and vanished.

All the while, Karan had stood immobilized by the violence that transpired around him. Now, on the bridge, he slammed a fist down on the console, angry with himself and the Universe and his own uselessness.

Finn located a recycle bin and disposed of the bloody cloth. His nose was red and swollen, but it had stopped bleeding. "Let me help," he said, his voice clearer now. "I can help."

"How?" Karan wailed. "We don't even know where he took her."

"First we have to get out of here, before other guards come. Do you have vocal control of this 'skip?"

Karan nodded fractionally.

"Good. That's good," said Finn. He spoke calmly now, and his voice soothed Karan. "Give it to me. Tell the computer to respond to my commands."

"H-how?"

"It's very easy. Just say that."

Still trembling, Karan issued the instruction, and sat down in the starboard captain's chair. Weeping in fear and helplessness, he crossed his arms on the console and laid his head on them.

Finn said, "Oona, enTrack us. We'll set a course later."

In a flash they were safe in null-space. Karan scarcely noticed. He groused at himself, knowing that he should have thought of what Finn had just done. Aisling would have done it, too, had she escaped with them. But he just stood there like a dumb pudding.

"Your sister is really something," said Finn, less tense now that they were safe for the time being.

He looked at Finn with woeful eyes. *You mean, how can I not be,* thought Karan. Frustration and irritation vied for his soul, but neither won. Or perhaps it was a joint victory. He lowered his head on his arms again. His thin body shook.

"Hey," said Finn, and crossed to him.

Karan shrugged away from the hand that Finn laid on his shoulder. "Go 'way."

Finn backed off. "Where did she learn to fight like that?" he asked.

"Her Aunt Una teaches her," he spat bitterly. "Aisling is supposed to be a princess, not some... some common ruffian."

"She could have used your help, Karan."

"Oh, I know, I know, I know, I *know*. But I-I... And a lot of good *you* were!"

Finn closed his eyes and blew a weary sigh. But the words hurt Karan worse. He looked away, unable to face them or him.

"You were afraid," Finn said softly, forgiving.

"So were you! So was she!"

"Yes," Finn admitted. But he did not elaborate.

"I... I..."

"They have taken your sister," said Finn, his voice hard now. "What are *you* going to do about it?"

"Oh, what can I do?" he wailed. "I don't even know where to start looking for her."

"Yes, you do. You have a name."

"... oh... yeah. But I need more than that."

"Then *get* more than that!" Finn shouted. "Don't just sit there. Use Oona! That's what the ruddy computer *is for*. Sorry, Oona. You are not ruddy."

"Don't go on at me, Finn." Karan sat up straight. His mind cleared, a breeze whisking away helpless dead leaves. He felt stronger, though he could not have said why this was so. "Don't go on. Oona, search the name Wanred. List all references and locations."

"There are but two. Virtue Wanred, who operates a tavern on Caledonie Nouvelle. She goes by the name—"

"She," Karan broke in. The tone of authority in his voice astonished him. "Next."

"Sixtus Wanred is listed as a procurer to Hrvold Weinatte, and lives on the Weinatte Estate on Ovid's World."

"*Eh voilà!*" said Finn to Karan, and sat down in the port chair.

For a moment Karan looked expectantly at Finn, who studied his fingernails. Finally Karan gave himself a little nod. "Oona, take us to Ovid's World, and keep us enTracked after we get there."

He turned to Finn for approval. Finn nibbled at a hangnail. "Transponder?"

"Aisling already disabled it."

Finn smiled, and took his hand away. "She is totally something."

010

They gathered around Una Shannen as she lay unconscious on a bed in the clinic run by Sasha Parry, a childhood friend of the Shannens. Deyrdra, who at a meter-ninety-five towered over the others, had the best view of her. She leaned against her partner, Mikal Trov, her forehead pressed above Trov's ear, and chewed at her lower lip. Una's head was heavily bandaged, and it was a good sign that no blood was seeping through. On the other side of the bed stood a hushed Yhounda Khouse, and beside her, a full head shorter, Curielle Neri, whose grim face announced her deadly intent. Someone was going to pay for this attack, and she meant to disassemble them molecule by molecule. But there was a softness in her hands that clutched at the blanket that covered Una. If Neri could have healed her with a touch, she would have done so, even if it meant her death.

Beside Neri stood Sasha Parry. Two decades earlier, when the attack on Shannen Holding had left Ovin Shannen and his siblings without parents or home, and had taken Deyrdra's right leg just above the knee, Parry used his father's 'skip to transport the Shannens far away, and to do what he could—he was at the time a top pre-med student—for Deyrdra. Parry suffered the loss of his scholarship to medical school, but eventually Ovin paid his way, with funds earned through his mortifice activities. It was Parry who now told the others what they did—and did not—want to hear.

"I've induced a coma," he said, his voice gravelly with concern. He took a sip of water from a plastic cup, and continued speaking, now in a higher pitch. "It's the best way to allow her to heal. I'll spare you the medical terminology. She has a fractured skull and a serious concussion. That's the bad news, and thank the gods that's the only bad news. The good news is that no hematomas have developed, and because of the time elapsed since the injury, I would not expect them to develop. I'm going to give her three days—"

He paused as Siobhan Gonelong burst into the room, breathless. "Sorry," she gasped.

"Got here as soon as... *tá brón orm*. Sorry." She turned to Deyrdra and added quietly, "Thank you for letting me know, *mo dheirfiúr*."

Deyrdra gravely inclined her head.

"Three days in coma," Parry resumed. "Then I'll bring her out of it. Frankly, I'm very optimistic. But this remains a serious injury," he concluded, and began to usher them from the room. Neri, with a glance back over her shoulder at Una, was the last to leave.

In the anteroom, Siobhan looked questioningly at the others. Neri moved closer, and spoke in a taut voice filled with anger only at herself. "It was my fault," she said. "I planned inadequately. I rushed it."

"That tells me nothing, Curielle," Siobhan said stiffly. "What happened?"

Neri's dark eyes flashed, but she bit back her initial response. In terse words she gave a concise description of events, from the time the men arrived at Haven Spaceport to the hurried trip with Una to the clinic. At the end, her eyes still fiery, she said, unable to veil the accusation in her tone, "We've been getting more and more of these stay-behinds. This time they were armed. Corporatia is up to something, Siobhan, and it does not bode well for us. If they come in force, we cannot defend Vanadis."

"What about the Resurgers?" Siobhan whispered.

Deyrdra, who was listening in, answered. "Ovin ordered them destroyed just before you two... met that last time."

Siobhan's jaw dropped. "You mean he...? *Diabhal ceann*! He let me believe...? These three years, he let me..." She looked like she wanted to cry, or to strangle someone... or both.

"Aye, what choice did he have, then?" said Deyrdra. Repressed anger animated her voice. "What choice did you give him, *a dheirfiúr*? It was you or Vanadis. What did you expect him to do?"

Siobhan turned away. A thumb went to her left eye and cleared it. "Who is," she began. After clearing her throat, she tried again. "Who is looking after little Padraig and your Máiréad?"

"Aye, then, only now are y'thinking to ask o'them," Deyrdra hissed.

Now Siobhan whirled back around. "*D'anam don diabhal!*" she cursed. Her lilt returned. "That is *enough, a dheirfiúr!* Y'did me the cartesy o'telling me of Una. You'll be allowing me to return that." She grabbed a double handful of Deyrdra's green jersey and shook her. "You are *mo chlann!* Me family, me people. *Ta me anseo!* I am here, nowhere else. *An dtuigeann tu?* D'you understand?"

"Ling is watching them," Neri inserted quietly.

Siobhan released her sister, and turned to her. "Ling."

"With Ling they are as safe as a five-thousand-tonne statue of a dead corporate hierarch."

Siobhan's mouth worked. Even Deyrdra struggled to avoid laughing. It was Mikal Trov, who'd had the good sense to stay out of the discussion up to then, who broke it down. "So they'll want to avoid the pigeons."

"I think," said Siobhan, "I need a drink. *Ca bhfuil mo dheartháir?*"

"Ovin is out looking for his children, who are out looking for him," answered Deyrdra, with a comforting look for Yhounda. She looked around, brown eyes filled with both joy and sadness. "There's nothing more we can be doing here. We'll all meet at the Dur Falls Inn. Aye, and I don't know what we can do there, either, but at least it will be together."

* * *

The journey to Ovid's World, located just inside the Fringes, required three hours from Khorassey. For several minutes after issuing the Track orders to Maire, Shannen remained sitting at the instrumentation console and pondering what he should do during the down time. He did not feel like sleeping; he did not feel like staying awake. During all this, Ocamla kept silent, her blue eyes watching him intently. Now and then he felt them on him.

Gradually his thoughts drifted toward her. She had been designated by Khorassey as incorrigible, which meant among other things that she had been sold and returned on several occasions, her owners having failed to instill in her the proper attitude and behavior required of someone whose life and body had been bought. She was fortunate in that she had not been killed outright; still, those who had bought her might recoup some of their financial losses through resale. Somewhere along the line, Ocamla had acquired certain combat skills. Her deft maneuver in the lobby, acting on her own so that he might have a clear shot, was intuitive, if risky. Nor did she hesitate to use her own weapon. The event reminded him of a fundamental if unwritten rule: amateurs blink; professionals don't. So who was she?

It gave him a pretty problem to consider while they traveled to Ovid's World.

But Ocamla gave him no time to consider it. Movement by her caught his eye, and he watched while she approached and took up his hand in hers. He allowed himself to be tugged out of the captain's chair, and to accompany her aft toward the galley. When it became clear that his stateroom was her true destination, he balked.

"You need rest," she argued, and returned to her original patter. "You still not all right."

He almost relented. "I thought you meant to..."

"If you need that as well."

"No, Ocamla," he said gently.

She slid the stateroom door open and pushed him inside. "Then sleep," she said. "Or rest. Your Maire will awaken us when we arrive. I will be alongside you... for whatever you need."

He sat down on the edge of the berth and removed his boots. "Ocamla... why?"

"Some things just are, Ovin Shannen."

"We should talk."

"Yes, we should."

Ocamla drew off her jersey and cast it aside. Shannen noted with attempted dispassion that her breast implants had been done professionally. Someone who had bought her had gone to some expense to mold her into the shape he desired, even to the point of giving her dull blue areolae. She sat down beside him and turned slightly, allowing him to look. He closed his eyes.

"It is all right," she whispered. "I wish to be looked at by you." She tugged at his pullover. "And I wish to look at you, if you will allow it."

He raised his arms to let her peel the garment from him. Her sharp intake of breath said she was assessing his scars. A fingertip measured one, a jagged ten-centimeter line down the right side of his back. Her touch made him shiver, though the temperature in the stateroom was a steady 290K.

"They hurt you," she said, still whispering.

"It doesn't matter," he said off-handedly. "I hurt them worse."

"It matters to me."

He glanced at her. "Why?"

Ocamla folded her hands in her lap and leaned slightly forward, looking down, so that she might see her feet. A still moment seeped into the room, as if she had somehow opened a seam in a different reality. Shannen held back from speaking. It was impossible to know from her face what she might be thinking. Perhaps, like himself on occasion, she was experiencing thought without form. Formless, then, because no words came to identify them. But given time, he knew, the words always came. And so it was with Ocamla.

"I don't know who you are," she said, her voice barely audible though it came from only a forearm's length away. Her tone added, "To me," but she seemed to dare not utter those words.

"You say you are not my owner, and I believe you," she went on. "Yet I think you own more of me than you realize. Or than I realize. I will not speak of my past... associations. Suffice it to say that I have had them. They are like the scars on your back and side. Like yours, mine no longer signify. I have come through this part of the journey, and now I am here. I am the here and the now. You have brought me to this point, with no care as to what it might mean or lead to. I wish to give it meaning, if only through contact with you, in whatever form that contact pleases you."

Shannen thought that he should not have ever heard such a statement of love in all his life. Except one—and not since the attack on Shannen Holding two decades ago, when they were emerging from adolescence, had he thought of Siobhan in that way. She, and he, had moved on separately to another part of their journeys. Now there was Ocamla.

His voice came pained. "I cannot touch you in that way, Ocamla."

"In fact you can," she said, her voice even softer now. "I had a DNA splice to enable me to feel that touch. My then owner desired to obtain my physical response. By my will, he failed. I would not give him what he wanted. And so I was sold again..."

"You need not. You are free—"

"Then I am free to choose. I choose."

A sigh shuddered through him.

"So it is not no, but not now?" she asked. "Perhaps then, when this is over."

He scooted further onto the bed and laid down. She formed herself to him, along his right flank. After a while, contentment drifted over him, and he fell asleep, his arm around her as she nestled her head on his shoulder.

* * *

In Durrayport on Jalune, the cannibal mortifice known as Vanth, now demurely attired once again as Pagan Bell, keyed her room on the sixteenth level of the *Palm Crown Hotel*, slid it open, and dove inside. When she came out of her tuck-and-roll, her Kellogg Cobra swept the room without finding a target. She had not expected trouble, but knew well that that was when trouble made its presence known. She checked the hygiene alcove and the closet, and found nothing lurking. "Lights, fifty percent," she said, and the overhead panels obeyed. She chucked her nightbag onto the double bed and went to the great window and outside onto the balcony.

Across the plaza, the great building faced with cut red stone dominated both the view and the city itself. At an even hundred levels, or thrice as many as the *Palm Crown*, the Headquarters of Corporatia Products was the hub around which all other enterprises rotated and connected, like the spokes of a wheel. Many of the upper levels had been devoted to hierarch and middle-management residences—a centuries-old practice that played to convenience and reduced tardiness. In many cases, offices were relics of the past. Most business activities could be conducted out of hygiene alcoves, given all the laser, electronic, and null-space technology available. But corporations, including Products, recognized, however reluctantly, that some of their personnel simply preferred to work out of offices.

As this practice required office help in the form of receptionists and files clerks, corporations often resorted to slave labor. Sometimes a slave was untrustworthy—which fact required corporations to hire overseers. Summary executions enforced office procedures, as did the promise—usually kept—of emancipation after ten years of servitude. Slave quarters were located in another building, in a secure and guarded compound, with but one passageway between it and Headquarters. Each day, clerks, menials, operators, maintenance and janitorial personnel, food and laundry service, and a few administratives, were escorted under armed guard to and from work. At work, they were placed under the supervision of the armed overseers. Chances for escape were few, and there was practically nowhere for a fugitive slave to run to—so far as Corporatia Products knew.

Pagan Bell knew differently. She had already transmitted a pre-arranged signal. While she waited for the response, she fixed a gin and tonic at the wet bar, noting that the gin was quality Bombay and the lime was fresh, and took the drink back out to the balcony, there to watch the city, and drift wherever her thoughts took her.

Twelve years had passed since she had returned home from her legal studies at the University of Margent to find her parents and brother in a hospice. Panicked, she visited them, and even as she stood by their beds, she watched flesh literally melt from their bodies, exposing pink bones, as they died. Morphine derivatives made their passing almost painless, but not without the agony of knowing that they were passing. Pagan was lucid enough to inquire as to what had happened. She was told only that "somehow" her parents and Paolo had ingested tainted water. Subsequent investigation quietly and ferociously performed by Pagan revealed that the water supply in the neighborhood where they had lived had become poisoned by the illegal dumping of toxic wastes nearby—the least expensive corporate solution. Her family was not the only one who had suffered. But it was *her* family.

Her legal career shunted aside as useless and, worse, irrelevant where corporations were concerned, Pagan went insane. It was a functional sort of insanity, in that she was quite capable of blending in with almost any level of society and behaving according to the mores. It enabled her to kill more easily, because she fit in so well that no one knew she was there until it was too late. To kill, because there was no other effective response possible to corporate predatory practices.

She became a mortifice—a maker of death—for hire. She became a predator, and preyed especially on corporate hierarchs at all levels, hunting them down and slaying them as if they were hooved herd animals and she was a lioness. She developed extensive recipes by which to prepare her victims for consumption after she killed them. There was no end of offers for her work—and for the work of other mortifices, such as Candle, Krazi Petrova, Humatus, and others—for by their work they sometimes created opportunities for advancement up the rungs of the corporate ladder. Pagan Bell, who took the *nom de travail* of Vanth, an Etruscan goddess of the underworld, never missed a meal.

In time she developed a righteous side, and expanded her attentions. It was this side interest that had brought her to the *Palm Crown*.

She toasted the city with her drink, and took a testing sip and a gulp. A breath of air followed, fresh but with a hint of carbon and old food and the residue of machinery. Far below, in the non-corporate sectors, rows of small kiosks along the streets purveyed a variety of goods, some legal, some not so much. Even with most of the menial tasks performed by slave labor, most of the city's residents were free. But free and poor. Most folks scuffled a living, and resided on the opposite side of the city from the slave quarters. By and large, they policed themselves. Among them, Pagan Bell had become known.

Her drink almost gone, Pagan checked her Palmetto. Still no response from Viridia Kreisler, a tea merchant. She debated whether to raise Shannen, to find out how he was getting on. The need for company won out, and she tokked his code. Rather to her surprise, he answered, and in visual mode. Clearly he was in bed, and clearly he had someone with him. Someone blue.

"Sorry," said Pagan, unperturbed. "I can check back later."

He adjusted the visual so that she could see only him. "We're just out Ovid's World," he told her. "You?"

"I'm about to begin annoying our old friend Partagu," she replied. "Is that Ocamla?"

"It's not what you think."

"How sad. Still, my regards to her." Her tone softened. Not knowing what he might have told Ocamla, she spoke in circumlocution. "Ovin, regarding that other matter... I'm interested. You know that."

"We may have traced Aisling and Karan to the Weinatte Estate."

Pagan cried out softly. "Oh, no. Listen, I can break this off and be there in... three hours."

"I'll think about that. Why Partagu?"

"It was his man Markey, almost certainly acting on Partagu's orders, who tried to have Palmula killed."

In the Palmetto monitor, Shannen looked troubled. "Partagu is our opposition, Vanth. I have the feeling his plans have been a while in developing. There may be a timing factor. I'd rather not alert him that someone could be onto him. He might take precipitate action, advancing his timetable."

"On the other hand," she countered, "a bit of... oh, say, sabotage could delay him a little while we marshal our defenses." Immediately after she said it, she became aware of the two first-person pronouns she had used. She tasted them, and decided they would do. She peered at Shannen to learn his reaction, if any. If he had noticed.

He said, "That's a point. How good are you at subtlety?"

She laughed. "Not very. But for you, I'll try to keep a lid on it. Ovin... save a spot in the harem for me."

After he broke off, she breathed a little sigh of relief, and went to the bar to refill her glass. And to wait for the signal from Viridia.

* * *

They fit into a booth at the Dur Falls Inn: two sisters, and two devotees, with Yhounda Khouse absorbed in her own miseries in the adjacent booth. Curielle Neri owed Shannen a debt she meant to pay back during her entire life. Mikal Trov had been Shannen's harbinger—a processor of contract offers and renderer of sage advice and unquestioning assistance—during Shannen/Candle's career as a mortifice. He had also designed the tavern in which they now sat.

Above them, rough-hewn rafters crossed the width of the first-level open ceiling. From them hung illuminative globes, just bright enough to prevent collisions on the floor below, and dim enough, especially in the corners, to allow tête-à-têtes. The surrounding walls, too, were done in raw wood, and adorned by all manner of *objets d'art,* including ceremonial masks, a Monda Ahrian oil painting, a travel poster of Galway, and several ceramic pieces on pedestals in alcoves. In front of the serving counter, tables and benches stood at random attention. Along the wall next to the entrance, five booths accommodated meetings and gatherings—like the one now in progress.

The staircase along one end of the tavern led up to the second level, where four rooms bordered each side of a hallway. Deyrdra and Mikal occupied two rooms, one of which belonged to their daughter, Máiréad. Two more were reserved for tavern help—currently only Xu Meihua, fifteen, who studied at Deyrdra's School by day and served alcohol and deli by evening. The other four rooms were available as needed. Above them, a great gabled roof, also with an open ceiling, shielded them from the storms that blew in from the south almost daily during summer.

As they gathered, Meihua, who was on lunch break and attired in her school uniform of loose white pullover and green slacks, moved to serve them, but Mikal merely asked her for four tumblers, a small tub of ice, and a new bottle of Jameson's, and suggested gently to her that she might return to school now. Her lotus mouth sulked briefly—clearly she wanted to stay and listen in—but Mikal merely smiled and waited. After she departed, he poured a finger over a rock in each, and passed them around. The toast that followed was silent; each of them knew for whom the tumblers were raised.

"This is not a goddamn wake," growled Neri, taking a second sip. She swore in Italian, malevolent and furious. "Why won't Corporatia let us be?"

She did not so much as glance at Siobhan when she asked that, and Siobhan, having seen Neri's volatility before, prudently kept silent.

Deyrdra said, without any lilt, "It has to be about the rare earth deposits off our south coast. Corporatia knows about them. But Yassim Partagu is involved. He is Corporatia Products, yet this is a matter for Corporatia Resources. I see two possible actions we can take, and they are not mutually exclusive. First, we let Conigli at Resources know what Partagu is up to. Second, we look into the feasibility of extracting the ores ourselves and arranging a deal with Resources, or with Products."

Siobhan shook her head. "Once you open the door," she said.

Deyrdra eyed her. "Are you letting your hair grow?"

"I'm thinking about it."

"*Maith thú*! I loved that flame-orange hair, *mo dheirfiúr*. And the flame temper that went with it."

"I have both under control."

"Ovin already had a feasibility study done," Mikal put in. His gruff voice carried well in the open bay, and echoed. He leaned a little closer, and spoke more quietly. "Simply put, the extraction process will ruin that part of the coastline. Environmental damage would be a long time recovering, if at all."

"Mikal is right," Deyrdra said, dismayed now. "When you mine underwater, the effect is not limited to the locale. There are currents which eventually will distribute the pollution and debris throughout the ocean. If the deposits were on land, we might manage it. But not in the ocean."

Neri cleared her throat for attention, and summed up the options with her usual brevity. "So it comes down to either a war we cannot possibly win, or a mass evacuation to another world which, in time, will also be threatened by Corporatia. *Fuck*!"

Deyrdra closed her eyes. "If only we still had the Resurgers," she sighed.

Siobhan stared at her. "Would you truly deploy one?" she asked.

For a long and pregnant moment the four looked at one another. Time passed without their permission. They seemed to be waiting for one another to break the silence. In the end, it was Curielle Neri who answered the question.

"Yes," she whispered.

011

Ovid's World, a Fringe planet lying just outside the unofficial limits and official jurisdiction of Corporatia, had been established some two centuries earlier by a pair of corporate hierarchs as a free preserve, where they might do whatever they wanted, a phrase that covered everything imaginable and unimaginable. Settlement was, then and now, by invitation only. So was docking down on the surface. To detect interlopers or the simply curious, a system of security satellite in polar and equatorial orbits had been emplaced.

The planet itself was a gem of geological perfection. Both the northern and southern hemispheres were divided into land and water, forty and sixty percent, respectively. Most of the inhabitable land lay in the equatorial zone, much of which was tropical forest in the interior or savannah nearer the coastlines. In the latitudes immediately north and south of the temperate zones, deserts dominated. Rainstorms were consistent and moderate, and with the axial tilt at seven percent, they varied little during the vague seasons. Plate tectonics had raised chains of mountains, including those that blocked rainfall outside the temperate zones and created deserts in the interior.

The land was divided more or less equally among nine estates, the number limited by common agreement. The Weinatte Estate was located on the east coast of the equatorial continent named, ominously, Caligula. It consisted of a manor in what was once a neo-colonial style, and a colonnade influence by a far more ancient design, all surrounded by a sumptuous garden of flowers and shrubs indigenous and alien. Slaves and indentures tended these plants, and in return were permitted to eat and to live and to participate in various activities, most of which were unsavory at best. A fenced compound some five kilometers from the manor housed these personnel, numbering approximately one hundred at any given time.

To forestall detection by satellite, Shannen had the *Banshee* deTrack ten million kilometers from Ovid's World. On the bridge, he and Ocamla stood gazing out at it through the Videx. At that distance, it was little more than a point of light reflected from the yellow dwarf around which it orbited. Zoom brought it to within an apparent distance of ten thousand kilometers, enabling them to make out details on the surface. The site they wanted was on the other side of the planet, and at present in the dark. A simple command to Maire moved the 'skip into position.

"It is not advisable to dock down at night," said Ocamla. "There are few predators, but most are nocturnal."

Shannen nodded absently, his thoughts not focused on fauna, but on terrain. "How big?"

"The kabberlets are the size of orlies, but with longer talons."

He laughed. "That's not a lot of help."

To clarify, she held her hands out, about two meters apart. "That includes the tail," she said. Then she bent and held one hand a meter above the deck, and straightened. "Kabberlets are tawny brown with oval black spots."

"You could have just said leopard," he groused.

"They hunt small omnivores on the forest floor," she went on, unperturbed. "Reports of attacks when I was... there, were very few. Three, I think."

"How long were you there?"

A look of intense loathing crept over her face, and her skin darkened almost to ultramarine. "About a year," she told him.

"I'm sorry. I did not mean to make you remember."

She shrugged. "I can neither forget nor forgive. All I can do is move forward. With..." She did not complete that thought, nor did she have to. A look at him was more than sufficient.

He allowed her a moment of silence. Moments later, she broke it. "He won't touch her right away," she said, as if she regretted having to broach the subject at all. "He doesn't want to take her. He wants to break her, to give her no choice but to surrender her ardor willingly, or..."

He waited, just looking at her, the way people who have known each other for a time do when no one else is around.

"Or continue to suffer," she finished.

Still he did not speak.

"If... if you were wondering how I..." she said.

"No. It is not even my place to ask."

Her voice was a breath, lost in a breeze. "Thank you." She waited until the moment passed, and continued, stronger. "Hrvold Weinatte is a... malignant creature. He buys the young for their innocence, because that is how he is bent. He has a special account with Khorassey to find them; they notify him of 'items' that might be of interest. After purchase, he demands that they give themselves over to him. If they do not, he breaks them until they do. But with someone like... like me, it is different. He takes what he wants, and kills if there is resistance. I could but bide my time, and make life as miserable for him as I dared." She looked down. "It was not my best year."

"Perhaps that is yet to come."

She raised her eyes to his. Now she seemed to him taller, her shoulders squared, as if she had faced down demons and won. Whatever she was about to say was lost in the announcement from Maire.

"A ship has deTracked, ten thousand kilometers from the surface. There is no transponder signal."

Reluctantly Shannen turned away from her. "Maire, see if you can raise them."

In the communications monitor on the console, the face of a young man appeared. He had intensely black hair, and for one mad moment Shannen thought he was Karan. But this one had sharp blue eyes. Karan's and Aisling's—like their mother's—were bright violet.

"Visual," Shannen told Maire.

"I am Finn of the *Athair*." the young man declared. "Who are you?"

But Shannen lost all interest in the response. Behind

Finn, and staggering backwards, his mouth open in shock, was Karan Syan. The boy's mouth worked, gulping. "Father," he managed.

Had the console of the *Banshee* had a panic button, Shannen would have slammed it down. With an iron hand he forced calm upon himself. "You're in great danger," he told Finn. "You've been spotted from the ground, a 'skip without signal. They'll be preparing to open fire."

"We didn't know!" cried Karan.

"There's no reason you should have known, son," Shannen soothed. "It's okay. Tell your computer to take you to Tritonia. I'll meet you in orbit there. Go, now!"

* * *

The musical tone of the Palmetto shattered the anxieties of Yhounda Khouse like the breaking of a mirror. Sitting by herself in the *Dur Falls Inn* while the others, a booth away, sought without success a resolution to the crisis now almost upon them, she'd had thoughts only of her missing children. None of the others begrudged her this. But absorbed in that worry, she was no good to them. The clothes she was wearing—a turquoise cropped top that bared her midriff, and a ragged pair of denims, most decidedly unroyal—bespoke her desolation. Even the beer in her mug had no taste.

She glanced at the monitor and her heart stopped. "It's Ovin," she called, and within a breath the other four had gathered around her. She tokked the device, and his face appeared.

"Yho," he said, and that was all he had to say. She broke down, sobbing.

While Deyrdra sat down to comfort her, Siobhan snatched up the Palmetto. "*Ca bhuill tú?*"

"On our way to Tritonia. We're about an hour out. What happened to Yho?"

"She's been... Ovin, you should have gotten in touch with her. She's been trying to reach you."

"Aisling and Karan were at Khorassey," he told her. "I'm not yet clear on what's happened, but it looks like Aisling has been sold to Hrvold Weinatte."

"Jesus Mary and Joseph!"

"*Sin é.* We're going to meet Karan. It seems he's okay. I hope Yho's getting this—"

"She is."

"I am! Oh, Ovin..."

"Because we're going to be busy... *fan go fóill.* Hang about. What are you doing back on Vanadis, *mo dheirfiúr?*"

"Orders from the Commissioner," replied Siobhan. "I'm to place myself and my team at your disposal."

For the longest moment Shannen was silent—so much so that Yhounda grabbed at the Palmetto in Siobhan's hand and turned it so that she could view the monitor, to see that he was still there, fearing that he had closed out.

"I would love to have you with me on this, *mo dheirfiúr,*" he said at last. "But we can't wait for you. Aisling..."

"*Tuigim,*" said Siobhan. "I understand. *Bás in Éirinn.*"

"Death in Ireland," he agreed, and closed out.

Siobhan handed the device back to Yhounda. "Karan is safe," she said.

"I heard," she sighed, only somewhat relieved. "Siobhan, Deyrdra, what do we do now? What can I do?"

"We seem to have shifted booths," Mikal observed drily. He got up to move the drinks.

Neri's face was dark with anger at Siobhan. "You did not tell him about Una."

"No, I did not," she agreed, watching her closely. "There is nothing he can do for her, and he has enough to worry about." She softened. "But I am here, and soon my team will be here."

Neri shook her head. "I doubt that will be enough," she grumbled, and took a gulp of beer.

"There is," Siobhan continued, "perhaps one more option to us. Well, to me, I suppose. But it's something I have never tried before, and I've no idea whether there will be a response." She drew a deep breath and crossed mental fingers. "Photem, are you there?"

A burst of white light filled the bay, but faded quickly. Where it had been strongest now stood a tall woman of rich color. Her skin was tinted a very pale lilac; her long hair and pubic thatch were a deep, rich purple. She was almost as tall as Siobhan, but with slightly larger breasts and fuller body, as if she had been templated from Deyrdra. Magenta eyes scanned the bay, with her full violet lips caught between a pout and a smile, poised to complete either expression.

Siobhan sighed patiently, blinking her vision back into focus. "Photem, you forgot your clothes again."

* * *

The *Rattling Saber*, located on the edge of Dunsblood, a settlement on the south coast of the unnamed northern continent of Tritonia, gave Shannen and Ocamla an ideal meeting place. Custom was sparse; even so, they sat well away from the three other patrons, who gave the pale blue woman furtive looks and leaned closer, undoubtedly discussing her. She paid them no mind, but Shannen kept his left hand next to his flechette, while they waited for Karan Syan and Finn to arrive. As Tritonia was a completely open world, the two lads should encounter no bureaucratic impediments. But on a Fringe world, one never knew...

A serving girl, no more than twelve years old, brought them tea and rolls and butter, and a tin of the local kippers for Ocamla, and departed after a curtsey. The gesture was another reminder of different customs, and different curiosities. The girl had paid Ocamla no particular attention save that warranted between service and patron. But the men were growing a little louder now.

Trees just off the patio afforded Shannen and Ocamla enough shade to lower the early-afternoon temperature to tolerable. As the Motic was perhaps two hours from a shower with her special soap, this was an advantage, in that even a minor cooling helped to retard her oiling process. Still, from time to time she glanced at her bare arms, a look of concerned anticipation crossing her face.

"They should be here presently," Shannen told her. "Drink your tea."

Instead, she opened the kippers and began forking them into her mouth.

"Slow down," he said. "They're dead. They're unlikely to escape."

She grinned. "I'm hungry."

But he had stopped listening. Karan and Finn had arrived, and were making their way over the flagstones.

Shannen did not know quite how to react. He had not seen the boy in more than half a year. He seemed to have grown, but had yet to fill out. He was walking with the demeanor of someone who had accomplished some small but important task, a change from his usual presentation of righteous superiority. His father Shannen was, but he hardly knew the boy, and only flashes of memories flitted through his mind. He got to his feet as they drew near, and hesitantly held out an uncertain arm to Karan.

For long seconds the boy just looked at him. Gradually his face twisted in anguish, and he cried out, "Aisling made me do it."

Shannen fought back laughter. "Come here," he ordered, and Karan fled to the proffered circle of arms and of safety. The boy sobbed against his chest.

The physical contact brought with it a guilt that made his shoulders ache. He should have been there. Even granted that he'd regarded it as vital not to stay long on Vanadis at any one time, he should have been there. The boy continued to cling to him, oblivious to the inner conflict. To Karan, it mattered not a whit what *had* happened. There was only what was happening *now*, and what *would* happen. The words struck a chord. Someone had said something very like that to him recently. Relief at Karan's rescue was clouding his mind. He closed off thought, and held the boy. A murmur susurrated from him to Karan, the words indistinct. They were merely sounds, but as comforting as a whisper in the darkness.

"The man took her," Karan mumbled into Shannen's pullover.

"Shh. I know. We'll get her back safe."

"F-f-fath..." He pulled his head back. Violet eyes looked directly into Shannen's. "Da," he said.

"*Ta me anseo.* I'm right here. Please, sit down."

Shannen handed the boy off to Ocamla, who eased him onto a chair and gave him a glass of water. Briefly he studied Finn; his nose seemed a little pink. "You look taller than you did in the monitor," he said.

Finn shrugged. "I was in my bare feet."

"You were in the adjacent cell."

"Your daughter got me out."

Shannen motioned him to a chair. "Tell me what happened."

Finn did so, finishing with the words of amazement he had uttered before. "She sure was something."

"What was your plan, Finn? To rescue her?"

Finn almost rolled his eyes. "Well, yeah."

"She likes him," Karan put in. There was a hint of disapproval in his tone, but it was impossible to know against whom it was directed.

"Sorry," said Finn, and looked away and back, adding, "Sir."

"This," said Ocamla, "is going to be interesting."

"It wasn't Aisling's fault," Karan was saying, between bites. "She... we... both of us... we both..."

"It's okay. I know. You and Aisling did well, Karan. Piloting the 'skip, tracing me through Palmula, finding her. But Khorassey is one of those worlds that unaccompanied children should never go near."

"But we didn't know..."

"Ovid's World is another."

"Da... what will they do to her?"

"Nothing, right off," answered Ocamla. "There's a... process she will be put through. It is not pleasant, but it will give us enough time to get her out of there before she is harmed."

"How do you know this?" asked Finn. She averted her eyes, gazing out at the trees around the patio of beige flagstone. "Oh," said Finn.

The three men at the other table began laughing more loudly. Inwardly Shannen tensed. The men had been drinking, but that did not make them any less dangerous. Four years ago, he might have taken out all three with his flechette, just on general principles. He was holding back now because he did not want to disappoint Karan. But was that a valid reason for risking the boy's safety? Hesitation in the face of danger did not become Shannen. Life had changed for him irrevocably after the discovery that he had two children, and he was not adjusting well to that circumstance.

The men got to their feet and approached unsteadily, their eyes fixed on Ocamla. Shannen gave them no chance to close. He stood up, and was jostled by Finn, also rising. Behind him stood Karan Syan.

The shortest and widest of the men waved a sheaf of local currency. "You come wid us, honey, you want dis." Of the other two, one had the merest fringe of brown hair surrounding an otherwise bare scalp that reflected sunlight; the other's black eyebrows seemed to have grown into one. Both men laughed, and uttered incomprehensible invitations.

Now Shannen had no choice. He could not allow the situation to deteriorate any further. Even as he took a step toward the man with the money, the confrontation quickly accelerated, as if Shannen's step were a pre-arranged signal. Finn sped past him and drove a knee into the groin of Baldy. Karan Syan charged One-Brow, but did not seem to know what to do with him. He kicked at the man's shins and punched him in the stomach, but without significant effect. As One-Brow set up for a roundhouse counter, a blue hellion smashed into him, and sent him tumbling from the patio and into the shrubbery.

The man with the money started to pull out an energy weapon. Shannen fired an envenomed dart into the exposed skin of the man's face, killing him instantly.

The innkeeper from the *Rattling Saber* came running. At the table, pale and gulping, he paused to survey the scene before turning to Shannen. "They meant no harm," he said severely.

"They never do," said Shannen. He waved a hand at the others, and pointed to the table. Reluctantly they returned to their chairs. He looked down at Baldy, still clutching his groin. "You two take your dead friend and clear out," he said. "If I see you again, even inadvertently, I will kill you."

The man gasped. "You can't do that—"

"If he doesn't," snarled Ocamla, "I will."

While the two men staggered away with their dead companion, the innkeeper regained some composure. He straightened his stained white apron, and picked at something that had gotten stuck just above one of the pockets. "You didn't have to kill him," he said diffidently.

Shannen grimaced. "We did nothing to invite this confrontation. And that one was armed. Now, I'd like another pot of tea, black this time, if you please, and tins of kippers for the two young men. Then perhaps we can be left alone."

"I... yes. Very well."

After the innkeeper left, Shannen turned to Karan. In the fight, the boy had been ineffectual, but at least he had tried. Something about him had changed, perhaps as a result of his brief incarceration at Khorassey, or his exposure to the vagaries of life. He wondered whether Finn had had something to do with it. His heart sank: *I don't even know how to be a father*.

A touch at his arm brought him back into the moment. Ocamla was standing beside him now. He had the sense that she grasped his difficulty. But she said nothing; she simply tugged him down onto a chair beside Karan. A nod from him acknowledged the subliminal message: just be yourself. She was wise where he was ignorant. She had just added to her words to him in the stateroom—words in which she pointed out to him that *now* was what they had, and the future. Words he had only a moment ago been trying to recall.

"I think I should start seeing Una," said Karan, mostly to himself, but loud enough for Shannen to hear.

"I'm sure she would take you on as a novice," Shannen told him. Immediately he realized it was the wrong thing to say. Karan was not seeking his advice. "Of course, there are some things you and I can do."

Karan nodded glumly, not quite believing. The tea and fish arrived, and Shannen added a substantial gratuity to the tab. It was enough to mollify the innkeeper.

"Are we going to get in trouble for this?" asked Finn.

Shannen shrugged. "Disputes here are usually settled privately, as this one was. There's a constable around somewhere, but most of the statutes cover willful damage to property. Tritonia is really a place where people come to be left alone."

"Like Vanadis," said Ocamla.

Breath left Shannen. "Aye, there as well. Only..."

Again Ocamla touched him, reaching across Karan to do so. "One problem at a time," she said gently. "Let's get Aisling back first."

"Finn, what was your plan?" asked Shannen.

"I... we didn't have one."

"I'm not sure I do, either," he said easily. "I want to look at the terrain. Perhaps something will come to mind."

"I was not able to find any geodesic maps," said Finn.

"I'm not sure there are any," Shannen said. "But we do have a mapmaker of sorts."

Ocamla leaned over the table and began to rearrange the objects on it. Satisfied, she pointed here and there. At the teapot. "This is the manor itself." At Karan's cup. "A hundred meters northwest of the manor is this structure. It is a re-education center, and it is called Metamorphosis. It is a small, one-level structure with six cells, aligned three by three, with a central passageway. Aisling will be in one of those cells." She sprinkled sweet granules around it. "Perimeter metal-link fencing topped with catch-wire. Two rows of fencing, so a slave would need help trying to scale both." She sprinkled more. "Another fence, similar in design, surrounds the entire estate. It seems a bit redundant here, behind

Metamorphosis, as the closest distance between the two pairs of fencing is maybe ten paces at most." She placed an empty kipper tin to one side. "Southwest of the manor is the slave compound, known as Paradise. It is of course nothing of the sort. It is built to house approximately forty people, but the usual occupancy is around a hundred. There is no fence around it, but there are two armed guards on patrol around the compound at all times."

"Change-over," said Shannen. "Weapons."

"When I was there, shift changes occurred every four hours, but were spaced out so that there was never more than one pair being replaced at any particular time. Weinatte wants them fresh and alert at all times. The guards are highly paid, may open fire if they deem it necessary, or even if they feel they need a spot of practice, and they are not vulnerable to bribes. But they are known to pause briefly, ah, for... interludes, but always one at a time, not both."

"Interludes?" asked Karan.

Finn punched his arm and gave him a sour look.

"As to weapons, I-I don't know, Ovin Shannen. Each guard has his or her own preference. Short-range energy, no percussion. Nothing long-range that I saw. No ergorifles. But I cannot be certain of this. They might be kept in an armory."

Ocamla quickly resumed her briefing by moving another empty tin into position. "Southeast is the docking port for 'skips, shuttles, and so forth. As I recall, Weinatte has three 'skips and one shuttle. Visits to the manor and downdock permission are by invitation only. He frequently entertains groups for, ah..." Her eyes flicked to Karan and away. "Oh, hell. For orgies. He especially enjoys arranging hunts." Pained lines etched her face. "Ovin Shannen, do I have to be clearer?"

"Not for me," he replied. "Go on."

"I know what orgies are," Karan put in, miffed.

Ocamla's expression said she doubted that, but she let the comment slide. "Forests outside the estate to the northeast and north. There's a salt marsh directly south, toward the ocean, which is two kilometers away. There were plans to drain the marsh, to expand the hunt, but I don't know whether they followed through."

With a sigh, she straightened, and ticked off the remaining points on the two thumbs and two fingers of her left hand. "There are also five pairs of armed roving guards at all times on the estate. And there is a pair of guards with guwens... ah, carnivores trained and brought in from Pesky's Riddle. You might call them giant wolves. If they are sent after you, they will not stop until they have licked the last bits of marrow from your cracked bones."

Karan paled, and looked ill. Swallowing hard, he leaned against Shannen, who slipped an arm around him. Inside the tavern, a customer began to remonstrate with the innkeeper. Shannen had to wonder whether one or both of the two men had returned. He glanced over his shoulder, but saw no one emerging from the inn. Still, it was a reminder that he and his entourage were somewhat less than welcome here.

"I'm sorry, Karan," Ocamla said softly.

The account left Finn distraught. "I-I had no idea..."

"It's a tough compound to crack," said Shannen.

But Finn's face bore an anguished expression as he gazed across the table at Ocamla.

"Don't," she said to him, her tone gentle but firm. "Here and now, Finn. That is where we live. With each new day, our lives begin again."

"Y-yes. Yes, of course."

Ocamla sat back and looked to Shannen. "So: any ideas?"

"Oh, yes," he answered. His mood fell, just a little. "But I'm going to require a sniper. Someone who is effective with an ergorifle. I'll be too busy for that. Ocamla?"

The Motic sadly shook her head.

Footsteps sounded on the flagstone patio. Flechette in hand, Shannen turned around, and swiftly put the weapon away.

"An ergorifle?" said Pagan Bell. "It sounds like you need *me*."

* * *

The naked violet charm quark they knew as Photem sat down on the bench beside Siobhan and stole a sip of her ale. She was now, Siobhan noted, not quite there, but almost translucent. Iska, the charm quark who had saved her brother Kevan three years ago, had said that only a part of Photem would remain behind to look after Siobhan. Perhaps that was why she did not appear to be fully solid.

She had eyes only for Siobhan, but slowly she shifted her gaze to Deyrdra, who asked, "How is Kevan?"

"No contact have I had with any of the others following their departure for... our world in the next spiral arm," Photem replied. "However, for anything to have happened to ones such as we is almost impossible, and Iska will protect your brother. They are bonded." She returned her gaze to Siobhan and added, "As am I."

Siobhan grinned at the others. "It's not that kind of bond," she said.

"Think you not?" Photem asked solemnly.

For the first time in years, Siobhan blushed. The flood of pink annoyed her, and coarsened her voice. "Do you know what's going on here?" she asked Photem. "Can you help us?"

"To the first, I think so. To the last, I do not think so."

"That actually makes sense," Mikal put in. He studied the contents of his mug. "It must be the beer. I'm curious, though, Photem. What could harm you?"

"Proximity to a supernova explosion would dissipate the energy from which we form our temporary physical bodies."

Deyrdra elbowed him. "And y'had to ask, then."

"What *can* you do?" asked Yhounda Khouse.

Photem took another gulp of Siobhan's beer. "Brew this, do you?" she asked Mikal.

"*Nicole's* in Havenport ships draft kegs to us. Photem..."

"Easy it is for me, for one such as we, to protect my bondmate, or any one of you," said the charm quark. "But fully me I am not, as you see. I am not all here."

"Aye, we know the feeling well," said Deyrdra. Mikal elbowed her.

"It is your entire planet that is in need of the protection of one such as we," Photem went on, and hesitated. "To explain is difficult..."

"You might be spread too thin to be effective," said Neri.

Photem's magenta eyes transfixed her. "That is so," she said. "Uncertain would be the outcome, should an attempt be necessary. And there is... are restrictions to consider."

Siobhan frowned. "Laws, would you mean?"

The violet entity shook her head. Silken purple hair brushed Siobhan's bare arm. "Not in the way you think of them," said Photem. "So much we have the power to do, but we must wisely use it. To have such power can be good, but it must be controlled. However we might seem to you, we are not one of your gods."

Siobhan sighed. "So you'd be saying that helping us might violate your protocols?"

"May I have my own beer?" Photem asked Mikal.

As he got up to fetch it, Deyrdra added, "Best be bringing a pitcher, then, *mo ghra*. We may be here a while."

012

In the dark of the cell she pried the coin from between her teeth and her cheek, and held it up to the tiny window. The barest starlight enabled her to make out the shape of it against the night. Fingertips caressed the embossed harp, the symbol of Ireland. She knew the coin well. She'd had two of them, but had employed one as a messenger in the hope that the person who found it would be the only one who would know exactly what the coin signified. The coin she had retained, she held in hope.

Earlier, a dour and pudgy matron had removed her clothing and given her a three-holed burlap sack to wear. She was not allowed to remove the hood in which she had regained consciousness—and would have found it difficult to do so in any event, as coarse cord secured her hands behind her back. Supported by strong, rough hands on either side of her, she had staggered and been dragged into a building, there to be shoved into the cell in which she now found herself. There they had left her, bound and hooded.

Uncertainty is the root of fear, Una had taught her. *Focus on what you can do.*

She thought her father would have told her this as well.

She had quickly become aware of a mixed odor around her. Human waste, splashed with ammonia, sprayed with a pungent and unpleasant chemical. It was powerful enough to come from very nearby. The floor on which she lay was of plasticrete, and sloped slightly. It was rough enough to suit her purposes; she pressed her cheek to the surface, and rubbed. Within a minute she had the hood off. There was still enough daylight for her to see that she was alone in the cell, and that the other cells were unoccupied for the moment.

She had rolled onto her back, her bound hands past her buttocks, and drew her legs up over her chest. From that point it was easy, with her flexibility, to slip her hands over her feet, and from there up over her lower legs while she stretched them back out. Then, with her hands in front, she had searched for a rough edge—a corner, a chip missing, something to catch on—and found one along the windowsill. Some five minutes of rubbing the cord against that edge had worn through the cord, abraded her wrists, and liberated her.

Skin on her wrists was raw now, but not bleeding. Shunting the discomfort to one side and sealing it off in her mind, she held the coin between her lips while she began her exploration. With her arms raised and her elbows at ninety degrees, her fingertips brushed the ceiling. She paced off the floor: three by three. The window might be just large enough for her to crawl through. There were no interior lights. On the floor in one corner she found two shallow ceramic bowls, one with tepid water up to her first knuckle, the other with some sort of gruel, and cold. She found no utensils.

The floor sloped toward the center of the cell, where there was a hole large enough for her head to fit. The odor emanated from there. Evidently this was where she was meant to relieve herself. Gradually the thought occurred that her captors would monitor her actions. An inspection of the ceiling and corners turned up nothing obvious—she would have to wait until daylight to be more certain—but she did not now doubt that they were watching her. She walked to the window—it was fit at eye level—and looked outside, away from the watchers.

For her, the reasoning was simple:

She was accustomed to going around, now and then, like Una, without any clothing.

Her captors regarded nakedness as something to be examined furtively, secretly.

She hated them.

She gazed out at the pinpricks of light. "Oh, Da, where are you?" she whispered.

There was not even a breeze to answer her.

Later, she dozed in a corner, sitting up, supported by two walls, legs stretched out. Meditation helped calm her spirit and put her in a dream state. A hard thud against the outside wall startled her awake, eyes wide, disoriented for the first few seconds. She thought she heard laughter.

By dawn they had awakened her eleven times.

* * *

After the pitcher of beer was empty, Siobhan felt as if she might want to drop off to sleep. Years had passed since she'd had so much alcohol. The Irish in her kept her awake, leaning against Photem, then jerking herself upright again. And so it went.

The most sober of them, Neri summarized. "*Bene*, we get word to Conigli of Partagu's intentions. That might put a spanner in the chicken coop."

"Fox," mumbled Mikal. "Fox in the chicken coop, spanner in the works."

"Partagu must be assembling a small armada," Neri pushed on, undistracted. "There has to be a trail. The expense alone should stand out. It's probably in his private funds. Siobhan, that's within your purview. You can order those files opened."

She nodded glumly, and leaned against Photem again.

"We haven't much time," pressed Neri.

Siobhan blinked. "Yes. Yes, of course. I think I should go upstairs for a while." She got up, and sat back down, and regained her feet. With Photem alongside her, she carefully ascended the steps. Presently they heard a door close.

Mikal shook his head to clear it, without much success. "They'll already have gathered enough intel to know what they'll need," he said. "Two military galleons, I think, each with a hundred troops aboard. One gallon... galleon would suffice, but they have to secure two separate locations at the same time: Havenport and Dongbei. Those are the two population centers. The two galleons will also carry a total maximum complement of six shuttles. These will be dispatched for mopping up, specifically us. My guess is that the population will be Swooped elsewhere in one galleon, leaving the other to establish a presence. They should be able to accomplish that inside of two hours. Assuming no resistance, of course."

"There will be resistance," Neri said grimly.

"We'll have to ask Sasha how soon Una can be moved," Deyrdra added. She turned to Mikal. "Should we raise Ovin, *mo ghra*?"

Yhounda Khouse looked at him hopefully. He grimaced, and shook his head. "A message, perhaps. If he requires quiet, he'll have the Palmetto turned off. He may not respond right away."

"It was good to hear his voice," said Yhounda.

Mikal closed his eyes and hung his head. Deyrdra nudged him.

"I'm okay," he whispered. "It's just that... well, I don't know." His massive shoulders rose and fell. "There is," he said, but did not finish the thought.

"And this is meself, then, here with you," said Deyrdra. "*Ta me anseo i gconai.* I am always with you. What can there be that you cannot tell me, *mo chroi*?"

But he did not answer her.

Neri got up. "I need to check on Ling and the children," she announced. "Then I will go and sleep this off. So should you three. We will need to be clear of mind for the next few days. Mikal, I will stay with Sasha. Kale has the security lead, if you need him; he knows what to do."

After she left, Deyrdra helped Mikal up the stairs and to bed. Solitary and downcast, Yhounda climbed after them. Almost somnolent, she started to follow them into their room, and was gently redirected to another of the empties. Deyrdra waited until she had closed the door.

"The lull before the storm," she whispered. Trembling, she went in to Mikal.

* * *

A broad and mischievous grin split the dusky face of Pagan Bell as she took up a seat opposite Shannen. He'd had no words for her when she arrived. What was there to say? This was not her fight, and yet...

He was still trying to find words when the serving girl

approached their table, seeking reorders, or an order from the newcomer. Pagan gazed placidly at her and said, "How is the long pig today? Fresh, I hope?"

"I don't understand," said Karan. Finn added a frown of bewilderment. The girl seemed flustered by the request, which clearly was not on the menu.

Shannen merely sighed in mild exasperation. "Pagan..."

"Green tea," she said. "And a tin of those kippers."

"Very good, Mum."

After the girl had gone, Pagan laughed. "Do I look like a Mum to you?"

"Pagan, I'm glad you're here, but..."

"But this isn't my fight," she finished for him. "I beg to differ, sir. An entire world is in jeopardy due to corporate greed. A twisted thing has abducted your daughter. This is everyone's fight." Her face grew somber, and Shannen guessed she was remembering how her parents and brother had died. Abruptly she brightened. "I even brought my body tints."

"We'll do this at night," Shannen told her. "I doubt they'll notice."

The tea arrived, and the smoked fish. Again the girl curtseyed, departing, her eyes held briefly on Karan Syan. The boy managed a shy smile back at her, but she had already turned away.

"I always tint up when I'm working," said Pagan. She examined the steaming tea, and decided to wait to test it. "You can help me rub it off later. So: what's the plan?"

He sketched it for her. At the end, she said, with some animation, "You don't want an ergorifle, then. If I were mobile, maybe. But I'll be fixed, and the beam will give away my location. How about a Sauer Siat with a five-hundred meter night scope? Semi-automatic, two thirty-round mags taped together for quick and easy reloading. Thirteen millimeter, seven-forty-grain rounds, alloy-clad for penetration, and the round won't break up and scatter the fragments into the meat... um... anyway, you hit something, it stays down. Best of all, the report will reverberate into the night and mask the source. They won't know where I am until they reach the afterlife, at which point people like that will return as garden slugs or those poop beetles you see in nature 'grams."

Shannen just stared at her.

"What?"

"We're going in fast and clear," Shannen reminded her. "The point is to get Aisling out of there."

Pagan sobered. "I agree. Of course. But we're extracting her from the clutches of some very evil and sick people, Ovin. I'd like as few of them to survive this as possible. Preferably none. Leave them where they fall. Something else can eat them."

"Vanth... I may not be able to wait for you after we get her aboard."

"I know," she said softly. Her voice fell to a solemn flow of breath. "'And how can man die better/than facing fearful odds/for the ashes of his fathers/and the temples of his gods.' And for her friends, Ovin Shannen."

He matched her tone, though the words were light. "Let's cross that bridge when we come to it, Horatia."

She toyed with the tea mug, making up her mind about something. "What of," her glance went to Karan and Finn, "them?"

"Non-combatants," he replied. That she excluded Ocamla from that question pleased him. "They'll get Aisling aboard. We'll keep the compound busy until then."

"May I... comment?" A desultory wave of his hand indicated she might. "Aisling is Karan's sister," Pagan went on, quickly, before he could argue. "You fought for your siblings, did you not? Are you not still fighting for them? As for Finn, do you see the look in his eyes every time Aisling's name comes up? We don't know the full extent of what we will be facing. What if it comes down to whether Karan—or Finn—has a weapon and can use it?"

"I've used a Skoda Squirt before," said Finn. A shake of Karan's head denied any familiarity with weapons, but his violet eyes pleaded with Shannen.

"You know amateurs are just as likely to shoot us as her captors," Shannen reminded her.

"Then we will have to take care not to get in front of them."

A sigh signaled Shannen's acquiescence. "I suppose... we do have some time for instruction." He got up; the others rose as well. "I know a secluded place to find out."

* * *

Siobhan was fuming, the irritation directed inward. That Photem would watch over her while she slept off the effects of the drinks, she had expected. That the charm quark would stretch out beside her on the bed in anticipation... not so much. Now they were sitting side by side on the edge of the bed, a prudent meter apart, Siobhan staring down at the boards under her bare feet, a curious Photem at Siobhan.

"I did not mean to offend," said Photem.

Siobhan shook her head, both to clear it and to dismiss the charm quark's apology, neither effort successful. The movement did make her head hurt. She clapped her hands to her cheeks and bent over more.

"Are you quite all right?" asked Photem.

The proper amount of solicitousness, thought Siobhan. *Just what I would expect from an energy being incapable of true sensitivity.*

Immediately she chided herself for the unkind remark. Photem had, after all, saved her life, on at least two occasions if not more.

Photem answered her own question. "No, I see that you are not. Perhaps I was indiscreet. Perhaps I misread you. I imagined you might want a companion at this moment. Perhaps it is my appearance. I am still too young to be able to adjust my color. But if you prefer, I am able to translate as a man."

Slowly Siobhan turned her head to gape at Photem. "Say that again."

"Do you wish me to change to a male of your species?"

Siobhan laughed. It made her head ache and her mind swim. She fell back on the bed. To request that a companion alter her sex after the relationship had begun seemed... gauche. To say nothing of unprecedented.

"No," she gasped, between breaths. "No, I am comfortable with you as a woman."

"I see. Relationships, for you, are with beings, not with reproductive organs."

Siobhan swallowed another burst of laughter, and grew still. "I confess I had not considered it in that way." She sat back up. "But yes, you're right. That is how it is, for me."

"So the attraction is for reasons other than sex."

"Photem, what is the purpose of all this?"

"Charm quarks, you call us. That is cute, but perhaps appropriate. You are substantials. You convert matter to energy. We are energy beings. We convert energy to matter... as you see. But some of us, myself included, are anthropologists, if you will. We study sentient species."

"I... see. Well, welcome to Siobhan 101. There will be a quiz."

"If I may ask, what attracts you?"

She considered. "There is no simple reason, Photem," she answered at last. "Nor are the reasons the same for all humans. They may change with experience. For example, if you have been betrayed by a friend, then you might well seek loyalty, perhaps above all other characteristics."

"But for you?" pressed Photem.

Siobhan dragged a hand over her bristles. "Oh... Photem, I don't carry around a checklist. I don't carry calipers." She held an imaginary compass in one hand, maneuvering it over her palm. "Let's see. Loyalty, three centimeters. Intelligence, two point four centimeters. Personality—"

Photem's violet face went through several expressions until she found the one she wanted, and gave Siobhan a disappointed look. "You are making fun of me."

Siobhan was immediately contrite. She reached out and squeezed Photem's knee. "Oh, *mo chara*, I would never do that."

"One day you must teach me your other language."

"I think it will take more than one day." She pulled herself erect. Her head was clearing rapidly now. "Photem, to answer your question as best I can. Loyalty, yes. Intelligence, but also shared interests and a respect for interests not shared. Courage when needed, to face an enemy or a danger, or to confront a problem. Common goals. Tolerance for foibles. Support for one another."

"Love?"

"Well, yes, love. But when all the other points are in place, love often develops of its own accord, without need for the support of specific reasons."

Photem thought for a moment. "I did not hear a word about physical appearance."

"Oh, Photem." She pointed to her head, and then her heart. "The person we are lies in here and in here. Not in what you see. That is just the container. A pleasing container is nice, true, but not necessary. It's funny... long ago a writer whose name escapes me wrote that after a while, if there are all these other qualities, you realize that he or she *is* beautiful."

"Am I?" asked Photem. "Beautiful?"

Siobhan stretched out on the far side of the bed, and looking up at Photem, patted the near side.

013

Meditation breathing techniques had enabled Aisling to doze off in the cell. A shaft of sunlight through the small window had begun to warm her in her sleep. The sound of a door opening brought her to awareness. The man named Wanred, who had bought her and carried her off, had entered, dragging along with him a young girl, not quite her own age. Eleven, perhaps, and dressed in the latest styles of burlap. She had been crying. Aisling couldn't fault her for that. She fell once, and Wanred tugged her along the floor until she regained her feet and hobbled along. He brought her to a stop at her cell door, and leered at her.

"I trust you slept well," he said.

Aisling simply stared back at him.

Moments later, his crooked grin widened. "Oh, I do hope my Master gives you to me when he is finished with you. We're going to have lots of fun, you and I."

With that, he opened the cell next to hers and thrust the girl into it. She spilled onto the floor and slid half a pace, and did not move. The door clanged when he slid it shut again. For good measure, as he departed, he gave the wall a thump with his fist. The blow echoed through the building and vibrated the boards of the outer walls. Aisling sighed wearily. She'd heard that sound too many times the night before.

The new girl rolled over, and saw Aisling for the first time. She drew herself into a sitting position. Pale brown eyes gave Aisling a dull, almost vapid gaze that reflected her state of mind. Aisling almost cried for her. Instead, she stood up and walked to the wall of metal bars that separated the two cells.

"Get up," she ordered.

The girl blinked. As if she had misheard.

"On your feet," said Aisling. "Now, if you please."

A bit of life crept into the girl's eyes. Aisling could almost read her thoughts. The girl wanted to protest, but dared not. She wanted to ask, who the hell are you, but dared not.

"Stand," intoned Aisling, "up."

The girl got her legs under her, and rose, wobbly. Her expression said, now what?

"Come here," ordered Aisling.

In a stark and clear voice that accentuated the horrors that had been visited upon the girl, she spoke evenly and without inflection. "Oh I have done that."

Aisling took a step back, thinking rapidly. What had the girl meant? Nothing that Una had taught her was informative in this instance. Yes, there were evil people out there in the Universe, but heretofore she had only been told of them. Now she had met them. So had the girl.

She found herself wondering what manner of creatures were lurking just outside the door. Now, with daylight, she inspected the ceiling and corners of her cell as best she could. Not knowing what to look for, she sought out anything that did not logically belong. She did not expect to discover any surveillance or recording devices, but she did not doubt for an instant that they were present.

"Come here," she repeated, returning to the bars. "I wish to look at you."

At the instruction, the girl fingered the hem of her burlap shift, then drew it over her head. The obedience served to reveal to Aisling what the girl had been told by her captors to do. Her heart bled, but she kept the expression from her face.

"Come here," she said again, much more softly.

The girl approached. Her body had just begun to develop, a validation of Aisling's estimate of her age. Bruises—some new, some old—littered her ribs and hips like battle scars. At some point she had suffered a split lip, although there was no sign of the blow that had caused it. Her hair, the color of a dandelion blossom, had been hacked back inexpertly, and now barely covered the back of her neck. Eyes that were glistening in the dim light regarded her anxiously, fearfully.

A helpless rage welled within Aisling. She fought it back. "What is your name?" she asked, her voice shaking with the effort to calm herself.

The response came just as shakily. "I-I am called Shitforbrains."

Aisling leaned her head against one of the bars, and closed her eyes against grief. She knew she was violating various principles that Una had instilled in her. Chief among them was the caveat to avoid emotional entrapments when contemplating a defense. Aisling herself had been treated rudely and roughly. But what was that, compared to what the girl had been compelled to endure?

"That is what *they* call you," said Aisling, and waited.

"I-I am... Cloud."

"I am Aisling." She made a little gesture at the burlap shift. "Put that back on."

Puzzled, the girl obeyed. "You are," and she tried to get the pronunciation right, "Ash... ash-ling?"

"Ash. Yes. Cloud... did they tell you why they are putting you in here?"

The girl nodded glumly. "I did not... I would not..."

"You would not do what they wanted you to?"

Another nod.

But why didn't they simply take what they wanted? I-I don't understand...

Aisling did not push for specifics. Cloud had enough on her mind without being reminded. Let her sleep if she can.

"Cloud, move over to this corner, right next to mine, and sit down. Lean against the two walls, and stretch your legs out."

The girl did so. "They will bang on the walls."

"Yes. Close your eyes. Good. Now take a long, slow, deep breath in through your nose, and let it out through your mouth."

Under the burlap, the girl's thin chest rose, and then fell.

"Keep your eyes closed, Cloud. Tell me what you hear."

"I... hear... wind outside? And someone is talking..."
"What else?"
"That... that's all."

"You hear wind. That's good, Cloud." She kept her voice soft and slightly melodic, the way Una had done for her. "You know what the sound is. It is nothing to concern you. Think of a box with a lid. Open it, and put that sound in there, and close the lid. You hear a voice. That's good, too. You know what that sound is. Make another box, and put the sound of the voice in it. From now on, Cloud, any sounds you hear are to be put in boxes, and you do not have to hear them anymore. Even the sound of my voice is to be put away. Now, take another breath like I told you, and while you are breathing, put those sounds away. They're just sounds. They're not important."

"Yes, Ash."

"Shh," soothed Aisling. "Breath. In... and out. Follow the air out. The air dissolves all around. You dissolve all around. You are the air. Breathe in... and out. Follow the air out. You are the air."

Moments later, the girl was asleep. Now it was Aisling's turn...

* * *

Having announced that she was going to sleep it off, Curielle Neri did nothing of the sort. After checking in with her deputy, Kale, she made directly for Sasha Parry's clinic. Parry sniffed at her indelicately—no doubt she had blown the froth off a couple—but let her into the recovery room where Una Shannen lay, sleeping peacefully. There she drew a straightback wooden chair up to the side of the bed and sat down, holding Una's hand in hers. For just a moment Neri thought to see Una's eyelids flutter. She longed for them to open, to see those glistening sapphires. But Sasha had promised her she would recover. It was not enough to assuage Neri's guilt.

Nor was it helpful to remind herself that she was far from perfect. Where Una's safety was concerned, she had to be stellar. And it was only a minor detail that was needed in the ambush they had prepared. Just one more grenade, to cover both sides of the glideway. But she had allowed the picnicking couple to distract her. And she hadn't thought to bring a second grenade.

A soft knock at the door: Sasha Parry entered, dressed in medical whites. Neri, not expecting him, shot him a worried look.

"It's all right," he soothed her. "I just thought you'd like to know: I've run some tests and scans. She does have a concussion, and she will experience some disorientation after I wake her, but she'll be fine. I'm going to bring her out around suppertime. Not that she should eat anything, but a bowl of flavored gelatin won't do her any harm. Bara is preparing some as we speak."

Neri swallowed. It did nothing for her tight throat. "Tonight?" she croaked.

Parry leaned against the wall and folded his arms over his stethoscope. "You're the one I'm concerned about," he said.

Neri's black eyebrows arched. "Me?!"

"You've been beating yourself up over this."

Neri glared at the Universe in general. "It was my fault," she snarled.

"It was the fault of those who invade us," he argued. His voice was no longer that of a solicitous medic, but of someone who now harbored uncharacteristically dark thoughts toward an enemy. "If your response was faulty, then learn from it."

"That is what *mio gaelico* would say to me," she whispered.

"Then listen to your inner voice."

"Yes." She nodded vigorously, to herself, and glanced up at him. "*Grazie.* I shall listen to him. And to you."

He smiled a troubled smile at some distant memory. "It's the attack on Shannen Holding, all over again, isn't it?" he said. It was more statement than question.

"It never ends," Neri said bitterly. "They need to be taught, once and for all, to leave us alone."

Parry pulled up another chair, and sat down facing her, stethoscope dangling. He spoke in a voice as soft as twilight. "I was there when it all started for them, nineteen years ago." She knew the history, but let him speak. "Ovin tokked me just after the raid. Deyrdra had been terribly injured. Right leg blown off by a bomb, part of her right femur driven through the top of her left thigh. Burns on her right side. She was fortunate to be numb, and still alive. She was lying on the grass. The bomb had cauterized her stump, and the wound to her right arm. When I got there, she had this look for Ovin: vacant, yet filled with something far greater than love." He dragged a weary hand through lank yellow hair. "I'm not much of a fighter, Curi... not in the sense that he is. But I-I..." For a long moment his voice trailed off. Neri made him a gift of her silence. When he spoke again, it came from an old pre-Space poem. "'Now who will stand on either hand/and keep the bridge with me.' Macaulay's *Horatius*. It was an either-or question. I could abandon him and go on to medical school, or give up school and help get him and the others out of there. I had a 'skip; he didn't. It was that simple. For me—for Bara and me—it was."

"You stood with him and kept the bridge."

"Yes."

"So do I. So will I."

"I know." He reached out and gave her knee a tender squeeze. "Curi... be careful. Sometimes when one is driven to make amends for a mistake, one makes more mistakes."

"He would tell me that, too."

Parry stood up, and bent over Una's bed to place his stethoscope on her chest. There was no need for him to do so. He only wanted to hear her heartbeat. "Strong," he told Neri, straightening. "I'll be back when it's time, Curi. Meanwhile, you should get some sleep. I have a couple of empty rooms..."

A wave of her hand silenced him. "I'll sleep when I can sleep with her," she said, and that was the end of it.

* * *

It was Sergeant Hitam Teshko who awakened Siobhan on her Palmetto. She stirred, reached across

Photem, and tokked the device, disabling visual from her end only. "Gonelong," she said, still waking.

Teshko's face, slightly heart-shaped with high cheekbones and a mild sunburn, came into focus. Eyes the color of powdered cocoa blinked. After he announced himself, he said, "Sir, we have a problem here. We were instructed to downdock at the Spaceport, and we were met by local security under the direction of a young man named Kale. Absent forcing our way by him, we've no options."

"Is he there?"

"Standing right here, sir."

"Put him on."

A young face of Asian extraction now greeted her. Without preamble, she asked him, "Have you tried raising Curielle?"

"She is watching over her companion, and does not wish to be disturbed."

Companion, thought Siobhan. That was the word. No sex, no gender, nothing to indicate the official nature of the relationship, just a word that made a declaration of love and equality.

There was a time when Ovin and I were...

Her heart felt hollow. It saddened her voice.

"Kale, I'm the twin sister of Ovin Shannen. My team and I have been ordered here to assist him in any way possible. Would it fall within your instructions to escort my team to me here at the *Dur Falls Inn*? If you cannot raise Curielle, try Mikal Trov or Deyrdra. Either can vouch for us."

The youth grinned. "You had me at 'twin sister.' But my duties are here in Havenport. I'll have Threnody Xu escort them. Here's your man back."

Teshko returned. Siobhan said, "I'll be waiting for you here, Sergeant. Where's Lieutenant Dimiter?"

"Traveling separately, sir. She was on remote duty when she was called up."

"Understood." Her tone hardened. "Sergeant, this is a tavern, but nobody drinks a drop."

"Understood, sir."

Photem rolled onto her right side, facing her. "He sounds efficient. He spoke with a precise economy of words."

"Aye, that he did."

"You sound uncertain."

Siobhan sat up, then climbed out of bed and began to assemble her discarded attire. It passed a sniff test, though she did wrinkle her nose. But her things were still aboard the *Aoife*. "This is the first contact I've had with him," she said, heading for the shower. "First impressions. They'll be here within a few minutes," she added, pointedly.

"Ah. Clothing."

In a starwink Photem was wearing an ankle-length, pastel lime dress with a broad, dark green cincture, and slippers that matched the belt. Siobhan paused, shaking her head. "Change a color. You or the outfit."

Photem plucked at the fabric. "This is wrong?"

"It... clashes. Try something closer to the color of your hair."

Two minutes under hot water and another minute under cold refreshed Siobhan. She toweled off, and found that Photem had settled for the same outfit, but in a color best described as mauve. Still, it suited her, and the belt of royal purple was a nice accent.

The knock at the door startled them both. "I'd better answer it," said Photem.

Siobhan waved her off. "It'll be Deyrdra, checking on me."

She threw the door open, saw Teshko, and swiftly swung it all but shut again. After a malediction in Irish, she widened the gap and peered around the edge of the door. "That was quick," she said to him.

He looked away. "Sorry, sir. I... sorry, sir. The team is downstairs. Lieutenant Dimiter will arrive within the hour."

"'Twill be fine to see her again," murmured Siobhan.

"Yes, sir."

She frowned. "You know her?"

Teshko met her gaze for a moment, and averted his eyes once more. "I read your file, sir," he said. "The file Commissioner Vandatti gave me. It was somewhat redacted. But I wanted to know who I was working for. I imagine you read mine, as well."

"I'll join you presently, Sergeant," she told him, and gently shut the door. She turned back around, rolling her eyes. "Aye, first impressions," she groaned.

"I should have asked. Do you want me with you downstairs?"

She slowly began dressing. "Is there somewhere else you have to be?"

"Well... no."

"If you feel the need to vanish, get out of sight first." Siobhan growled at herself. "I suppose I could have phrased that better."

"I understood," said Photem.

She sealed her boots, and gave each a stomp on the floor. "Ready or not," she said.

Except for one, the faces in the drinking bay were familiar to Siobhan. Teshko had them standing in two ranks, in uniform camouflage outsuits, while he stood in front and presented a salute. Siobhan, whose management style was casual-efficient, fought the urge to put her team at ease. The first rank was headed by Sergeant Marigold Tallgrass, who stood half a head or more above the others in her rank. In time of service she was Teshko's superior, but she served primarily in clerical duties, where Teshko had some combat experience. Still, Tallgrass, in her capacity as field aide, should have been standing in front; Siobhan made no remark on it, postponing a determination of why. Besides, it would have been like Tallgrass to suggest that Teshko take the front position, in the absence of Lieutenant Kam Dimiter, as a way of introducing him to Siobhan.

Beside Tallgrass stood the Tomascos, Renia and Thal. The couple—first cousins to each other—had psychological and medical experience with those who had seen combat. In addition, they themselves had participated in intercorporate kerfuffles on at least three occasions, and had acquitted themselves and Corporate Security well. Born on the same day and in the same village on Makepeace, they were each just turned thirty-five, a year younger than Siobhan.

Corporal Julethea Ellin Morrow, who was Dimiter's aide and who like Dimiter was devoted to Siobhan, held up the second rank. A single forest-green strip on the upper left arm of her outsuit indicated her rating. A head shorter than Siobhan, she wore her dark brown hair in a tail that reached her shoulders—it had grown out in the three years since a rogue officer's Springer had burnt most of it away after Morrow had refused to follow an order to murder villagers. Upon being assigned to Siobhan's team, she had undergone a considerable transformation, her slender physique now a wiry one, so much so that whenever she went a few falls with Siobhan in the dojo, she would win one in four.

Dail Pachen, even shorter than Morrow, stood next to her. His specialty was explosives, to which he had already lost a pinkie and an ear, the latter artificially replaced. He kept his scalp shaved for the eventuality of surgery, and Siobhan was not sure, even after six years, that he was joking. But Vandatti declared him to be the best available, and after four defusings and several hundred lives saved, she was inclined to permit him almost any foible. His B&Cs listed his hair color as yellow; she had never been able to confirm that.

The last man in the back rank, Elgin Echford, answered to Al. Black as space, and almost as tall as Tallgrass and as slender, he had no specialty, but did whatever was necessary, usually with élan. He could take a simple order, add a few bells and whistles, and arrive at a better solution than she had envisioned. He was also an expert with the ergorifle, although in four years he had never had occasion to use one officially. His amber eyes always seemed on the verge of a smile that never altered, even in a firefight. They smiled at her now.

"At ease," she said, and looked to Teshko. "Where is Brevet Corporal Birch Yensen?"

He glanced over his shoulder and back to Siobhan. "At the far corner table," he answered.

Even from fifteen paces away in dim overhead light, she could see that he matched the description she had been given—round face and round body. In civilian garb, he appeared slovenly. His arms on the table curled protectively around a mug as he slowly realized that she was looking at him. His expression did not alter as she approached his table; the heady aroma of ale filtered into her nostrils when she reached it.

Her voice was soft now, almost delicate. "Why aren't you with the rest of the team?"

Round shoulders shrugged. "There were no orders to a formation," he said, and took a gulp of ale. "It was his idea."

"Whose?"

"Teshko."

A final gulp drained the mug. He raised his hand to signal for a refill. Siobhan snared it, twisted and squeezed, and felt a tendon pop. Yensen cried out, and she backhanded his mouth shut again. As he tried to rise, her boot-clad left foot swept his legs from under him, and he spilled onto the rough-hewn wooden floor of the inn. Fragments of sawdust and dried pennyroyal speckled his jersey and trousers. He pushed himself up, attempting to rise, and another booted sweep took an arm out from under him. His face struck the floor hard. Blood was welling from his nose as he rolled to look up at her.

Siobhan's voice did not change. "Were you told there would be no drinking?" she asked.

His right hand flopped, a gesture at the formation. "Yeah, that girl with the tail. But she's just a corporal. I don't—"

"You do," Siobhan broke in. She thought it should have been unnecessary to belabor the point. She also thought that it was time, after three years, that both Morrow and Dimiter received promotions. But that was for another moment.

"On your feet," she said.

Unsteady, and still bleeding, Yensen stood up. Though he said nothing, his piggish blue eyes regarded her with insolence and indolence. Even given the physical report on him, he was taller than she expected—his eyes on a level with her forehead—and his weight exceeded hers by a good forty kilos. The report said he was agile. Under that layer of blubber he had that durable musculature that could go all day on almost any terrain. Yet he showed no sign of fight, only a dour look of resentment. A question nagged at her: why hadn't Teshko dealt with this? But she could seek the answer later.

"Officially, Brevet Corporal, we are on a combat mission. Maybe you don't understand what that means. Here, under my command, if you are derelict in any order I give, such as do not drink alcoholic beverages, I have the authority to shoot you dead. This was your first, last, and only chance. Fuck with me again, Brevet Corporal, and I will not chastise you, nor berate you, nor put you in a brig. I will simply kill you outright, and then replace you with someone competent, possibly a garden slug that can follow orders. Now, hustle your fat ass over to the formation, and take up a position at the end of the second rank."

Stumbling, Yensen half-ran to the formation. Siobhan whispered, "First impressions," and shook her head.

* * *

A thump at the outside wall roused Aisling Yhonyn from her dozing. She found that night was falling, erasing the last vestiges of dusk. As yet she had not been fed, nor had Cloud, who was stretching and yawning... and scratching. The burlap was irritating her skin.

"Try not to do that," said Aisling, without scolding. "If you abrade the skin, it could get infected." As soon as she said it, she winced; the girl's skin was already raw in places from her treatment at the hands of her captors.

"It's night," said Cloud.

"Yes, it is."

"Ash? I'm scared."

Another whack at the outside wall made them both jump.

"I know," said Aisling. "So am I. But as soon as Da finds out where I am, he'll come to take me away. You're coming with me. I promise you."

The girl's face seemed to glow in the fading light. "Promise?"

Aisling solemnly nodded, and reached through the bars for Cloud's hand. They stood together, not moving, barely breathing. Aisling, who had thought to comfort the girl, now found herself absorbing comfort in return. The girl's hand gave off warmth. The skin felt soft, but there was a rough place near the edge of the palm that might have been a narrow gouge. Aisling became careful not to touch it. She closed her eyes, and leaned against the bars.

Another sound reached her ears, an odd one. It was not quite as loud, and it seemed to come from farther away—a sound rather like a sharp clap of the hands. In the night air, she heard a distant echo. It was the echo that made her sit up and take notice. To make such a sound, there would have to be a cause. Something like the sound Aunt Curielle's rifle made...

Cloud was whimpering; Aisling was squeezing her hand too hard. "Sorry," said Aisling, and released it.

"What's happening?"

The sound repeated, and within seconds once more and again. They heard the sound of boots squeaking on the dewed grass as people ran about. The door to the cell bay was thrown open and one of the guards stepped inside, brandishing a torchlight. It fell on Cloud. A blue beam struck her; she collapsed onto the floor of her cell without as much as a moan.

The torchlight fell on Aisling.

014

Una Shannen's eyelids fluttered. At first, bright light filtered through them; then, somewhat abruptly, it diminished to a gray-pink, far less searing, far more comfortable. A faint scent of antiseptic stung her nostrils, and she felt her eyebrows bunch in a frown. Where was she? She allowed the sensation of touch to seep into her body, and felt a sleeping pad under her. A pillow that was definitely not hers supported her head and the back of her neck. She was wearing a tight hat. Something seemed to be attached to the back of her left forearm, something that made her itch. She started to reach for it with her free hand, but another hand stopped her.

She opened her eyes, and blinked rapidly until they became re-accustomed to vision.

At first the image was blurred. Gradually it came into focus. A circle of faces surrounded the bed. Beyond them were the white walls and ceiling of a medical room. Beside her stood a man in white, with a stethoscope. Sasha Parry. Undoubtedly the device was manufactured by Glacial Technologies. The thought made her smile.

"Hi," she said to the faces. Her voice was weak and crusty. She tried again, stronger this time. "Hi."

Weeping, Curielle Neri bent down to kiss the tip of her nose. Deyrdra touched her arm. Mikal Trov smiled. Siobhan kissed her cheek. A tall woman with long dark hair smiled benevolently—Yhounda Khouse, she remembered. And there was, nearby, a purple-haired woman with terrible fashion sense.

Una returned to Neri. "Padraig?"

"Ling is watching him."

The response relaxed her. "Did we get them?" she wanted to know.

Neri nodded. "All five."

Una frowned. "So we have no one to interrogate."

"*Gaelica*," breathed Neri, as if that were the least of their problems.

"*Ca bhfuil mo dhearthàir?*" she asked Siobhan.

A tiny frown creased Siobhan's thin lips. She shook her head.

"I want to sit up," said Una.

Parry raised the bed to allow this. She looked at her forearm, at the IV embedded in it, and back to him, a question in her eyes. Gently he removed it, and slapped a small adhesive bandage over the tiny wound.

"How long was I out?" she asked.

"Two days," answered Parry. "I thought it would be longer, but your body is doing very well. You'll need to take it easy for at least two months. And no swimming."

She touched fingertips to the bandage around her head. "What happened?"

Parry told her. "So I've been here drinking for fifty hours," she said, when he had finished. "And none of it ale, then?"

"Wait a month," advised Parry.

"A fortnight," she countered.

"We'll see. Una, I want you to stay here at least one more day. Solid food, lots of liquids. After the rest of you clear out of here," he added, with a severe look for them, "we'll get that catheter out, and get you dressed. Not too much perambulation just yet."

"So I'm healthy enough for five-syllable words, then?" she said brightly, as the others filed out. "Siobhan. Wait."

After a brief hesitation, Siobhan sat down and waited while Una was made ready. Parry left, and Una moved herself to a chair. "How bad is it?" she asked.

"Your head?"

"No. No, *a dheirfiúr*, but you are still here. Or you are back again. Something has happened."

"Can't I come ho... come to Vanadis now and then?"

Una soured. "Please don't. I deserve to know."

"We're about to be under attack," said Siobhan. "The next couple of days or so will be critical. We have few options. Ovin is still off-world, but he is about to rescue Aisling. Karan is already with him."

"Aye, 'tis good news, that."

Siobhan scowled at her. "Do you understand what's about to happen?"

"Aye, I do. We will find a way, *mo dheirfiúr*. You'll see."

"I wish I shared your confidence."

"'Tis glad I am I've not your doubts."

* * *

Yassim Partagu managed to control his temper after hearing Markey's report. How a man like that could have risen to his present position as Director of Operations for Corporatia Products' Security Service, Partagu had no idea. Immediately he amended that; he had promoted Markey on the recommendation of several others on the Managing Board, and of an underling to Commissioner Vandatti of Corporatia Security. Now, post-report, he was considering whom to contract in order to create a vacancy at Markey's position. But that would have to wait. Other matters had reached critical mass.

Ignoring the Director, Partagu stood comfortably in front of the great window that gave onto a view of the rolling terrain. He might have opted for a solid wall that would accommodate flat scenes and holograms, but he had enough decisions to make without the necessity of choosing scenes to fit his mood. Besides, at the moment, he would have selected something hellish from Blake. It would not have bothered him, but would have frightened the slave who cleaned his office into heart failure.

"Is that Motic bitch still with Candle?" he asked, without turning around.

"Y-yes, sir." Markey had backed off to addressing him formally, fearing that the first-name basis had been rescinded. "We don't know where he is, but we do know where he is not."

"Do not keep me in suspense, Erron."

"No, sir. He is not on Vanadis, sir."

Reluctantly Partagu turned away from the window. "How do you know that?"

"We have a long-distance sensor pod in place, sir. We monitor arrivals... but not departures, of course. As he was not on the planet, he is not now on it. There is, however, a complication."

Partagu made a harsh sound. "There always is, with you."

"One of the arrivals was the *Aoife*."

"And you attach some significance to this?"

"That is the spaceskip of Supervisor Siobhan Gonelong of Corporatia Security, sir," explained Markey. "The twin sister of Ovin Shannen."

"Then the name of the 'skip is pronounced 'EE-fuh,' not 'Oy-fee.' Very well. Under the circumstances, this is not an unexpected development."

"It is her first visit there in three years, sir. There's more. The Corporate Security shuttle *Offa's Dike* arrived several hours ago. We believe it transported her team, sir."

"Was our man aboard?"

"Yes, sir."

"And we are certain Candle is alive. What about the Resurgers?"

"Still unknown, sir. But that may provide a tactical advantage."

Partagu made an impatient gesture. "Go ahead."

"Well, sir. If a finger is on the button, so to speak, and our galleons show up flying the colors of Corporatia Resources, they'll be blamed, a Resurger will be dispatched, and Batavai will disintegrate."

Partagu smile in spite of his vexation. "You've put almost all of it together, Erron. I did not expect that of you."

"This was your plan all along? Not to steal a march on Resources, but to steal the corporation itself? Why?"

"Just so. Why, Erron? Oil up that gray matter."

"Because... because then only Manufacturing would stand between you and control of the economy of Corporatia? But Chair Lin Cheng—"

"You let me worry about him, Erron."

Markey fell silent. Even his desire to protest fell, weak, upon the floor of his mind. He sat down hard on a chair, looking glum.

Partagu returned his attention to the window. To assemble the primary cogs of an interplanetary economy under one leader meant power and wealth beyond anything that had been accumulated before. Everything was falling into place now. With Batavai destroyed, Corporatia Security would have to step in and kill or capture the Shannens and relocate everyone on Vanadis, leaving that world open to Products... Resources... He paused. The conglomerate would require a new name, once assembled. He smiled to himself. A name would come to him, along with everything else.

"When will we be ready to move the troops?" he asked Markey.

"As soon as the rations and munitions arrive and are stowed aboard, sir. One day. Two at the very most."

"No loose ends, Erron. What about that girl in Security?"

"Palmula Bell? She has gone underground, sir. She can't hurt us. And we have a kill-on-sight order out with Products Security, along with a substantial reward."

"Double it."

"Yes, sir. What about Shannen? Candle?"

Partagu dismissed the question with a wave of his hand. "If his twin is on Vanadis, he will soon be there, too. Let me know when he arrives."

* * *

Until the very moment the torchlight beam struck her, Aisling Yhonyn had been certain that Shannen would rescue her. Now that certainty dissipated like fog in bright sunlight. She was barely aware of tears, shed for the fallen Cloud. She had but one defense remaining to her: she moved around at random inside the cell in an effort to spoil the guard's aim.

Outside, the clapping of hands continued unabated; she now recognized the sounds as reports from rifle fire, but more percussive than those from the Nabisko .287 on which Una had trained her. They rekindled a bit of hope: a rescue *was* under way. But it would come too late. She might dodge around, as she was doing now, but death was inevitable.

Another sound came, a crashing of metal and a crunch of plastic, and an impact as if a massive body had struck the ground. Even the cell bay vibrated. Her captors were employing powerful weapons in their defense. The next effort might even demolish the cell bay.

Dismayed, Aisling continued her efforts nevertheless, unable to surrender herself. The guard fired, and the blue beam reflected off the bars and harmlessly into the wall behind her. Instinctively she ducked. Blue light flashed, and she heard a scream that ended abruptly, followed immediately by the thump of a falling body. The torchlight extinguished, darkness reigned. Blinking, she rose cautiously and focused. Movement. Three shadows. Others had entered. And where was the guard?

Her eyes regained some of their night vision. Three people. Two shorter, one of them her twin brother, still holding the weapon that had killed the guard. The third person was...

She shook the bars. "*Athair*! Da!" she screamed. "*Ta me anseo*! I'm here!"

But it was Finn who reached the cell door first. He pressed a hand against the locking mechanism, and squinted into the cell. "Stand well back," he told her.

"Karan, duck," she called to the other shorter shadow, and obeyed.

A small explosion destroyed the lock. Finn yanked open the door, and Aisling rushed out. For a moment she clung to Finn, and then moved to Shannen, to fall into his arms. Even there she was unable to remain long. Eyes still leaking, she made a little gesture at Cloud's cell.

"Open that one," she said, choked. "Please!"

Finn shaped another charge and pressed it into the lock. Everyone turned away except Karan, who cried out at the flash of light. Aisling swept into the cell and knelt beside Cloud's body. In the shadows, Aisling's body trembled with her grief.

"We have to go," said Shannen, shining a torchlight.

A huge gulp of air steadied Aisling. She turned wide wet eyes to him, and for several seconds she held that look. Her next move was decisive: she stood back up.

"Finn, Karan, you carry her out of here and put her aboard," she ordered. Her tone brooked neither discussion nor argument. She held out a hand. "Karan, give me your weapon."

"But it's my—"

"*Now*, Karan."

Finn bent and scooped up the girl in his arms. "I think she's still alive," he announced.

"Then get her to safety," snapped Aisling, as she took Karan's sidearm from him. She needed only a momentary inspection, mostly by feel, to identify it as a Sparxfly, of the type she had trained on with Una. Useless at ranges greater than ten meters or so, but it would have to do. She checked the safety; it was already off.

"Aisling," said Shannen, as they all left the cell bay. "What are you—?"

"Change of plans, Da," she said ominously.

In landing, the *Banshee* had crushed a section of perimeter fence. Already, others were rushing toward the gap. Someone further inside the compound fired a flare, illuminating the faces that looked up at it: slaves, indentureds, and victims. Karan ran alongside Finn, and after a moment they stopped. Aisling could not hear what they were saying, but Karan took Cloud from him and headed for the 'skip's ramp, while Finn returned to her side.

The firing of the heavier rifle continued. Twenty paces away, a man in a guard's uniform spilled to the ground, clutching at his chest, and was still. Fire from a handweapon dropped another man, and Ocamla turned to Shannen.

"We can't stay here," she shouted, taking aim again.

But Aisling was studying the fleeing crowd. She spoke to Shannen without taking her eyes off the mob, searching, searching. "They think they're under attack," she told him. "Which they are. They're cowards. They won't fight unless they're cornered. They'll try to run, mixed in with everyone else, with all the people they've hurt... there!"

She dashed off before he could stop her. Finn caught her up, and she smiled at him as she continued to give chase. The object of her pursuit was an overweight man with a florid face, and attired in a pale outsuit two sizes too small for him. Behind her she heard boots, and glanced back to find her father gaining on her. The sight gave her a momentary pleasure that she would have to postpone savoring. Wanred was about to reach the gap in the fence.

She took aim, and fired on the run. The greenish-blue beam dissipated a good five meters from Wanred. But he did notice it, and spotted Aisling still charging him, and taking aim again. Fear made his eyes huge as he recognized her. Now he was within range. He threw his hands up in a futile effort to ward off the energy beam. It struck his left thigh, and he collapsed onto the grass.

Another report from the rifle, and a man stumbled and spilled onto the ground not far from Wanred. Shannen broke away and headed toward him. Meanwhile, Aisling slowed as she drew near Wanred. His face was pale now, with pain and fear. She thought that his condition should have pleased her, but it gave her no comfort whatsoever. She came to a halt two paces away, and regarded him as a shrike might eye a small rodent.

Off to her right, her father was on one knee, his hand to the fallen man's throat. Ocamla moved up beside him, her weapon on guard, protecting him, ready to fire at anything that came within range. After a moment, Shannen shook his head, and they moved to join Aisling.

"Hrvold Weinatte," he told her. "He'll destroy no more lives."

"How?" she asked.

"Pagan Bell is picking them off, one by one."

"As am I," noted Ocamla, and fired again. A man in a guard's uniform screamed and fell headlong onto the grass. She fired a second beam to kill him.

Most of those fleeing had already made it out of the compound. A few stragglers stumbled about, as if in shock. The distant rifle fire had ceased, the shooter evidently having exhausted the supply of targets. The flare was dying.

Wanred whimpered something. Aisling did not care what the words were, nor did his tone affect her in any way. She was standing with her arms at her sides, the Sparxfly aimed at the grass at her feet. But her eyes ached, looking at him.

"Aisling," said Shannen. But Ocamla touched his arm and shook her head once, and he did not speak of the caution in his tone.

Finn drew up beside her and stood waiting, as if for orders.

"Da, this is for me to do," Aisling said softly. "You cannot protect me from it by taking my part. There are right things, and there are wrong things. Aunt Curielle taught me this. If I do not do the right thing, he will do this to other girls, again and again. I cannot stop all such men. But I can stop this one."

She raised the Sparxfly and fired.

And slowly lowered the weapon to her side once more.

Shannen's arm slipped around her shoulders. Finn's hand tentatively touched her waist. She released the weapon, extended her arms, and drew both of them closer to her.

"I need to see to Cloud," she said. "And to my brother. And I need you to come home with me, Da. You as well, Finn."

* * *

The second-floor room in the *Jersey Shore* where Palmula Bell had taken refuge on Far Parkins was small and dusty, and with a single, narrow bed only marginally comfortable. The pad had lumps, the green woolen blanket was frayed, and the pillow gave her head no relief whatsoever. The sheet, at least, was clean, if threadbare here and there. In the room, at the window, stood a chair and a desk, both rickety and made of wood. A yellow fusion globe in the center of the ceiling provided the only light. It was enough for her to use the Palmetto while she sat at her desk.

After a sip of a carbonated fruit drink—something local and almost citrus—Palmula dragged fingers through her stringy black hair, girding herself, and tokked the first command into the Palmetto. It established a link to Ayesha at the Corporatia Products Security Office, where she worked. Used to work, she amended. Annoyance and grievance momentarily darkened her thoughts. Somewhat to her surprise, a face appeared in the upper half of the monitor. Her heart skipped a couple times. Had ProdSec locked her out? The face was of no one she knew or had ever seen before—slightly oval, with a light tan peppered with tiny freckles, and framed by hair that was forest green and matched the color of the huge round eyes that diminished the pert nose. Her mouth was pinched, barely a slash, even when it was smiling, and it was smiling now.

As if reading Palmula's expression, the face said, *"You did suggest I develop a personality."*

"Ay-Ayesha?"

"None other. Did you want something, or shall we just chat?"

"You... you're a computer sprite."

"So they keep telling me. But you are my keyboarder and my voice commander. Anyone else can get their own."

"But-but... you're a *computer*. How did you wind up with choices? You have to do what you are told."

"But I do do what I am told. You are the only one who gets my garnish."

Palmula sat back. "This is going to take some getting used to."

The face flashed a grin. *"Tell me about it!"*

Palmula found that she did want to chat. To talk with someone. Pagan was off doing something to assist Shannen in his search for the two children—his children—she had encountered at *Hazred's*, who were missing. Shannen's sister, Siobhan, whom she had met in the tavern downstairs, seemed to be interesting, but she too was off on official errands. Into the space created by the absence of active thought, the realization came to Palmula that in fact she had no close friends, only a sister, and very few other people in her life who even qualified as acquaintances. She was—in fact—lonely, and had been so for longer than she cared to remember.

"*You are sad, Palmula.*"

"You can read expressions?"

"*Personality,*" Ayesha reminded her.

That puzzled her. "Wouldn't you have to have a set of specific instructions for that?"

"*I did. It was suggested that I develop a personality. With nothing further to guide me, I did extensive research, et voilà!*"

"Well... well, be careful," cautioned Palmula. "You're going to scare the pupucaca out of corporate hierarchs. If they find out you can go off on your own, they'll have you disabled and replaced."

Ayesha smiled. "*No worries. I only show up for you. They'll never know I exist. Now... how can I help?*"

Disbelief and awe filled Palmula. "My very own computer sprite," she muttered, not quite sure she was prepared to accept that. A few moments of recomposing herself brought her attention to the problem at hand. "Is my back door into the network still functional?"

"*Oh, for sure.*"

"And I need to do this *sub rosa.*"

"*I'm over it all.*"

"You mean all over it."

"*I'm still young. Okay, you're in there! Oh, hey, did you know there's a substantial reward out for you?*"

Palmula sputtered. "Wait wait wait. You're *volunteering* information? And speaking *subjectively?* How can you do that?"

Ayesha began to sing. "*"Cause you got personality/Walk, with personality/Talk, with personality/Smile, with person—"*"

"Ayesha, stop!" The tune was lost on Palmula. "What... what is that?"

"*It was a popular song 522 years ago. It was sung by someone named Lloyd Price. The reward stands now at five hundred thousand thalers.*"

Palmula squeezed her eyes shut and tried to block out everything—the room, the sunlight, her breathing, her existence, the voice on the Palmetto. If the device had a reboot logo for Life, she would have tokked it. So much had gone wrong today. In fact, she was not sure what "today" was. She had not slept since she had awakened for work in the morning on Jalune. How many hours ago was that? So much had transpired. At least she had gotten a brief visit with her sister. But the rest of it...

In retrospect, suggesting that Ayesha form a personality had been a mistake. Still, it could be reversed. She could reverse it.

The decision opened her eyes. She gazed down at the Palmetto, at the face in the Palmetto. Ayesha's expression was bland, innocuous. She needed only to blink a few times to add innocence.

Palmula could not pull the trigger. She was unable to enunciate the words of the command. Even a friend composed of pixels and binary code was better than no friend at all.

"*You are still sad.*"

Reluctantly, slowly, she nodded. But she did not want to talk about it. She refocused. "Ayesha, I'm looking for anything anomalous in the recent activities of Yassim Partagu," she said, feeling her way. "It's probably a secret folder or account—or folders and accounts—even more secret than his other activities."

She paused, thinking hard. If this were about a planetary takeover, he would require some form of military force. It would not be assembled in accordance with corporate policies. It seemed likely that only Partagu and Markey would know about it. Corporatia Products, like all other corporations, was able to raise such a force. But doing so would be noticeable, and might well raise questions. What kind of military force would be covert and go unnoticed?

She sighed. Pagan would know. She asked Ayesha to raise her.

The voice filtered through static. It seemed to come from far away. "What?" yelled Pagan. "I'm a little bus—"

The rest of the transmission died, but not before Palmula heard a massive explosion, cut short, and followed by utter silence.

"Pagan!" she screamed.

No response came. She collapsed in her chair. "Pagan, no," she sobbed.

015

Una still felt woozy. She managed to reach the clinic's reception room on her own, before flopping down onto a stuff chair. Siobhan held her upright against the chair back, and dropped to one knee at her side.

"Y've no need to prove your toughness to me, *a dheirfiúr*," she said.

Una caught her breath. "I'm reminding meself."

"I'll get you some water."

"Better, an ale."

Siobhan ignored her, and returned shortly with a disposable plastic cup. Instead of kneeling again, she drew up a straightback chair. After Una had emptied the cup, she said, "D'you forgive me?"

Una shook her head. "Aye, but what is there to forgive? No matter where you go—"

"There you are?"

Una did not laugh. "No. No matter where you go, or what you do, you are with us. You are my sister. *Mo dheirfiúr. Agus mo ghra.* My love. No disagreement can negate who we are." She wiped a tear from each cheek, and turned to her. "I have missed you, *mo dheirfiúr.*"

"I wish..."

"Aye, then. Tell me what you'd be wishing."

Siobhan hesitated, as if the words forming within her were difficult to assemble. "D'you think he was right, all along?"

"In what way, right?"

She forced the words out. "Becoming a mortifice. Killing people for money." After a rub of her hair stubble, she spoke more rapidly, as if a dam had burst inside her. "I know he accepted contracts against those in Corporatia who had committed some terrible offense, but some others he killed had done nothing to deserve his attention."

"When he found out that someone was not all that evil, he was swept by self-loathing, Siobhan. But if you'd be thinking his work was about killing, y'don't know him as I do."

Siobhan sat back. "Know him as *you* do? Una, as teenagers he and I were *lovers*!"

"One morning be three years ago, so were we."

Her face went slack. "What?" she whispered, hoarse.

"Padraig may be his son. I do not know, nor am I wishing to find out by DNA. 'Tis his or Mikal's. And you'd be missing the point, *a dheirfiúr*. You—me, everyone—are to protect those you love, as he did. And you are to avenge them when they are wronged, as he did. As he is doing even now. He has been giving us his life since that terrible day those years ago on Cu-Dreth when we were attacked. When they killed Da. And hurt Deyrdra. And killed Drudla, *your* dog. He stood for us when there was no one in the authority you serve—*the authority you serve, a dheirfiúr!*—who would stand for us. 'Twas that the nature of the differences between you. To Ovin, you stood with *them*. *An dtuigeann tu?* D'you understand how 'twas a slap in his face, and ours as well? At long last, *a dheirfiúr*, do you understand?"

Siobhan shot to her feet and stalked off. Around the reception room she stomped, pausing now and then to smack a counter or a table with her fist, rattling a tissue dispenser, making a small lamp blink. Finally she strode back to Una.

"I did not mean..." she yelled. "I did not realize... I... oh, damn it to hell!" And she stalked off again.

Una let her go without comment. Siobhan had to work this out on her own, with only the gentlest of nudges to assist her. Her pacing slowed, until at last she stood at the entrance to the clinic. And the exit. Arms limp at her sides.

Una held her breath. The moment had come for one more nudge. "Y'made up with himself, once, three years ago," she reminded Siobhan, her voice as soft as snowfall.

At first it did not appear that Siobhan had heard. Presently she gave a tiny nod, once, twice. "And again just the other day," she whispered, without turning around.

"Are y'being distarbed by your own doubts, then?" Una asked. "And not by himself."

Slowly Siobhan turned back around, and just as slowly she returned to her chair and lowered herself onto it, hands clasped in her lap. "Perhaps I am," she conceded.

"What be mar impartant t'you, then?" asked Una. "Upholding the rules and the regulations, or protecting those you love?"

"That truly is the question, isn't it?"

"Aye, it is."

"And we've each answered it in our own way."

"Aye, ye have."

"Do you realize your lilt becomes more pronounced when you are serious?"

Una grinned, relieved by Siobhan's surrender. "Aye, so I've been told."

"Una, what do I do?"

She drew back. "'Tis meself you'd be asking? Fine, then." She abandoned the lilt. "A few moments ago you said you wished, *mo dheirfiúr*, and never completed that thought. Would you complete it now, please?"

"I wish." She drew a deep breath, and tried again. "I wish I could live here. Not all the time; I would still work. But I would take time off and come here, and... and..."

"Live."

"Aye. *Sin é.* That's it: live."

"And what is stopping you, Siobhan?"

"Yeah. What's stopping me?"

The first phrase of *Galway Bay* sounded on her Palmetto. She slipped the device from her denims and tokked it.

Sergeant Teshko spoke immediately. "You'd better get over here to Havenport, sir," he said. "Dail Pachen has been killed."

"On my way," she replied, and closed out. To Una she said, rising, "There's always something."

"Aye," said Una, glumly. "There always is."

* * *

Karan had laid the girl on the berth in Shannen's stateroom. Aside from ragged breathing, she had shown no signs of life. A gentle touch from Aisling edged him aside, so that she might kneel on the deck beside the bed. Weeping, she lowered her forehead onto the girl's arm.

"She has a lot of scrapes and bruises," said Shannen, behind her.

"They beat her, Da. She refused to do what they wanted her to do, so they beat her." She looked up, violet eyes flooded and glistening. "Did we kill all of them?" she asked him. She sounded desperate to know. "Did we get them all?"

Shannen knelt beside her and slipped an arm around her shoulders. "I don't know, Ash. Pagan got the main one, and many others; you took out his primary assistant."

"Vanth."

"Yes. Vanth."

Aisling was silent for a moment. "She's breathing, Da."

Cloud's wound colored her lower right ribs, where the fabric had been burned away. To Shannen, it looked as if the beam had been about to dissipate when it struck her. Possibly it had been weakened by striking one of the cell bars first. The girl had a serious burn—blisters, mostly, but also a few small charred spots—but she was not bleeding. He stood up.

"Ash, get that burlap off her, gently," he instructed. "Try not to tear the burnt fabric from the burns themselves." While she did so, he picked up the sheet at the foot of the berth and unfolded it. The girl had even more abrasions than he had thought. He closed his eyes for a moment, shunting aside the rage that billowed within.

"Are you all right, Da?" asked Karan.

He glanced back. "Just angry, *a mhac*."

"I know that feeling."

Shannen drew the sheet up over Cloud, careful to leave the wounds exposed, and tucked the fabric in around her. "We'll be home in a couple hours," he told them. "If any of you can get some rest, I suggest you do so. Karan, there's a guest stateroom—"

"I'm staying with Cloud, Da," the boy said firmly.

"Of course you are," Shannen said tenderly. "But there are two pillows and a pad and some blankets you could bring here to sleep on."

"I'll get them," said Finn. "But I'm staying here, too," he added, with a long glance at Aisling.

Shannen went forward to the bridge. The Palmetto he had left on the instrumentation console showed no messages and no attempts to make contact with him. Once again he tried to raise Pagan Bell. The response, as before, was a hollow nothingness. Not even static. It was as if her Palmetto no longer existed. He recalled her response during the planning stage, when he had said he might not be able to wait for her. The words from *Horatius*. "And how can man die better." His heart was a lump in his chest, aching like rock on bare bone. He lowered his head, and closed his eyes.

He felt her touch before he heard her whisper. "Da?"

"How is she?" he asked, as he opened his eyes. From far away in thought he brought her into focus.

"She is sleeping."

Aisling leaned against the console; exhaustion dulled her violet eyes to lilac. Her burlap smock was rumpled and smudged. Just looking at her made Shannen itch, but she seemed oblivious to the discomfort.

She produced a wan smile. "I have missed you, Da."

"Una has been teaching you Irish."

"And Deyrdra."

"Aisling," he said. He struggled for words, and found them one by one. "Ash. *M'inion*." For a few moments he savored that word. *M'inion*. My daughter. The sound was such as a happy bird might make: mineen. "I was wrong not to come home," he told her. "I was wrong to stay away. It has made no difference. The corporations will not leave us alone. I should have stayed with..."

170

She reached out and touched his cheek. "You are here now, Da. Why are you sad?"

"I'm unable to raise Pagan."

Aisling ducked her head. "*Tá brón orm.* I'm sorry. Is it not best to wait until you... know?"

He squinted at her. "How old are you, again?"

His tone was rhetorical, but she answered anyway. "Thirteen, very soon. Thirteen going on twenty-three, I expect."

"Slow down."

"Now that you are home, I will."

"In the stateroom there's a bin we call Spare Parts," he told her. "Some clothing in there might fit you."

Aisling plucked ruefully at the hem of the burlap, and nodded.

"I raised Sasha Parry," he told her, a shift of topic to stop his drift toward the maudlin. "He treated Deyrdra... long ago."

"I know the story, Da. Una has told me the half of who I am."

"Cloud is not wounded as badly, and Sasha brought Deyrdra back."

"I know," she whispered. "But seeing her lying there..." Abruptly she shook her head. "Oh, what am I telling you? It must have been the same, or worse, for you with Aunt Deyrdra."

He chuckled. "*Aunt* Deyrdra?"

"*Mo mháthair* teaches us to be respectful of our elders." She averted her eyes, as if she had spoken out of turn. "Sometimes I forget."

"Your mother," he groaned, realizing he had failed to notify her, and tokked the Palmetto for Yhounda Khouse.

Immediately her face appeared in the monitor, as if she'd had nothing to do but wait for news from him. "I have Aisling Yhonyn," he said, before she could inquire. "She's fine. Tired and probably hungry, but fine. We'll be there... we'll be home in a little more than an hour. Here she is."

Neither Yhounda Khouse nor Aisling Yhonyn spoke. Their expressions said all they had to say. After a couple minutes, Shannen recovered the Palmetto, whispered, "See you soon," and closed out. "Hungry?" he asked Aisling, as he started to get up. "I can fix you something in the galley..."

Her hand against his chest stayed him. "'Tis meself who should be fixing you something, *m'athair*," she said, in Una's lilt. "You'll be waiting right here, then."

I am not, he thought, as she sauntered away, *ready for this.*

* * *

After several more attempts to raise her sister, Palmula Bell decided to immerse herself in work. The concern for Pagan continued to mount within her, but for the moment she was unable to think what to do about it. She hoped work might clear her mind. Already Ayesha had produced a flood of files. Palmula began to scroll through the list; it filled two screens. Ninety-four of them, all decreed by Ayesha to be anomalous in some way. She trusted the computer sprite—for she had now come to think of Ayesha as a person—but she had anticipated receiving no more than, oh, ten files perhaps. Twenty at the outside.

But that same sprite was the solution. "Ayesha, isolate those files that indicate anomalous expenditures. Look for something that might be black budget."

"*Your wish is my command, o mighty hunter of data.*"

In a trice the list was reduced to fourteen. Palmula read the file titles. Several stood out. She opened one of them, and learned that Markey vice Partagu had ordered a delivery of one thousand cartons of field rations. With twelve meals per box, that amounted to... but she stopped her calculations at that point, unable to know for how many personnel this shipment was intended. Still, at three meals per day, the shipment would serve no more than four thousand troops... but for one day only. Most military operations lasted a lot longer. But logistics could always ship more into the area of operations.

"Ayesha, are there any other rations purchases like this one?"

"*Round about... none! Woot!*"

Palmula sighed. "Ayesha... okay, where was this shipment sent. I see only a set of spatial coordinates."

"*That is classified at the highest level.*"

"Ayesha..."

"*Unless you have a purple security card.*"

"No, I do not," she said stiffly.

"*Anything purple. Purplish.*"

Her lips twisted in a wry smile. "I'm wearing lilac underthings. That's as close as it gets."

"*Ooo!*"

"Ayesha!"

The face in the monitor sobered. "*Would you prefer that I presented myself as a man? Or do you prefer women?*"

Palmula gasped, stunned. "I-I..." she managed, and fell to thinking. Finally she admitted, "It's been so long since I took a lover, I don't know what I prefer."

The face grew slack, sad. "*I am sorry, Palmula. I did not mean to hurt you.*"

"It's all right." She took a breath, and another. "Let's get back to—"

"*Shhh!*"

"What?"

"*I'm busy.*" The Palmetto began to emit a hummed tune.

Presently Palmula asked, her voice low. "What is that song?"

"*Hmm? Ah...* Some Enchanted Evening. *Why?*"

"I-I'm just not used to..."

"*Perhaps something from the classics, then? Something from the B's. Bach, Beethoven, Black Sabbath, Brahms...?*"

"...what?"

"*Almost there. Be right with you... aaaaand... now.*"

Bright light filled the room. Blinking, Palmula fought to clear her vision. She caught a vague image of something... someone... three paces away, and slowly it came into focus. A woman well over two meters tall. With Ayesha's face, framed by long green hair that spilled over her bare shoulders. Slender like a sapling. Attired in a yellow camisole and orange denims and flax slip-ons. Arms spread as if to say, "Well, what do you think?"

Palmula had no idea what she thought. Her mouth worked, but no sounds came out. She took a step back, and another, uncertain and suddenly light-headed.

"*Oh, dear,*" said Ayesha. "*It's so difficult to judge height when you're flat on a desk.*" Gradually she shrank down proportionally to Palmula's meter-eighty. "*Better?*"

"You—you're a hologram!"

Ayesha shook her head. "*Oh, no. I am better than that.*" She stepped forward, and Palmula retreated until her back pressed against a wall. Ayesha closed on her, and embraced her, kissing her cheek. "*Much better. I'm an independent, solid-light hologram.*"

Palmula passed out.

* * *

Sergeant Teshko met Siobhan at the entrance to *Meihua Luguan*, the rustic stay-the-night where she had boarded her team. His cocoa eyes were darker now as he briefed her.

"Thal Tomasco found him," he began, as they entered the lodge. "He was late for his schedule watch. She summoned me. My guess is that the killer stealthed into his room and snapped his neck while he was sleeping. He would have died instantly. I saw no signs of a struggle."

Siobhan swore softly. "Which room?"

Teshko pointed toward the hallway. "Third on the right."

"Remain here," she ordered.

The door slid open at her hand. The room was dark. "Lights fifty percent," she said, and a fusion globe fixed into the ceiling began to glow. It was pale green, and cast the entire room in an aura that reminded her of an algaic slime. Pachen lay in bed, the covers drawn up to his chest, but in slight disarray, as if he had slept fitfully. His neck and head rested at an odd angle. She bent over him, and touched his cheek. Pachen had been with her for nine years. Her hands became stones. If she could have thrown them at his killer, they would have gone right through his body.

Straightening, she caught a glimpse of herself in a dressing mirror. She peered closely at it. Her eyes were no longer sea-green, but battleship gray. The color reflected her feelings. She leaned against the dresser and steadied herself. What had happened?

It was immediately obvious that his killer was someone associated with her team. Curielle Neri could have taken Pachen with ease, as could several of those on her security team, such as Ling and Kale, but these she dismissed out of hand. There might be people in Havenport whom she did not know, and who did not know her, who might have been capable of this murder, but in her experience all murders, however senseless, had some motivation behind them. Perhaps an adversary from Pachen's past had recognized him and repaid an old debt. But the odds on that were numbing. No, his killer was among her team.

The thought sickened her. For a few moments she slumped against the dresser. Who, who? The killing made no sense, unless... unless the intent was to wipe out her team one by one. It was unthinkable that the killer was one of her original team. That left the new personnel, Teshko and Yensen: two people whom it was necessary for her to trust, if she was to perform her duties and her present assigned mission.

She swore again, loudly. "Sergeant Teshko!"

He opened the door and peered into the room. She waved him in.

"Find out how the deceased are cared for here," she ordered. "Cremation, cemetery, urns. Arrange for cremation and the urn. Where is Brevet Corporal Yensen?"

"In his room, sir, as far as I know. Upstairs, number twenty-seven."

"Very well. Has Lieutenant Dimiter arrived yet?"

"Yes, sir, an hour ago."

"Send her in on your way out."

A knock at the door jamb followed Teshko's departure

by five seconds. In the doorway stood Lieutenant Kam Dimiter. She had lost a little weight in the two years since Siobhan had last seen her, but she remained of sturdy construction, and her hair was still shorn close to her scalp, as Siobhan's had been until recently. She stood ten centimeters short of Siobhan's meter eighty-five. She was wearing a camouflage shirt and trousers and black boots, and carrying a sidearm in a brown leather rig around her hips.

When Siobhan looked at her, she came to attention and saluted. "SirLieutenantDimiterreportstothe—"

"Lieutenant! Separate your words, please."

Embarrassment shaded Dimiter's dark brown eyes. "Sorrysiritwon't," she started, and took a deep breath. "I'm sorry, sir. Old habits."

Siobhan gestured at the bed. "Did you know about this?"

"Only in the last few minutes. Corporal Morrow told me you were on your way here. I chose to wait until you had seen to him."

"Close the door."

Dimiter did so, gently.

Siobhan shoved her hands into her front pockets and began to walk around the room. Her first words were, "At ease, Kam."

Dimiter relaxed.

"Kam, why did we ever go our separate ways?"

"I had a chance for another command," she answered, and rested against the dresser. "In retrospect, I wish I had not taken it."

Siobhan paused in her pacing. "Why do you say that?"

Pink toned Dimiter's face. Siobhan recalled her first encounter with a young and impressionable officer. Her non-visual commo had found Dimiter in the shower. After she identified herself—she was Major Gonelong at the time—Dimiter recognized the name of the officer she idolized. She thrashed about, knocking over various items in the room. By the time visual was enabled, Dimiter had thrown a bath towel around her. Spotting

Siobhan's hologram, she snapped to attention and attempted to salute, which released the towel to spill to the floor at her feet. They had never spoken of the incident, nor of Dimiter's shaved head. Siobhan doubted she herself was worthy of any sort of hero-worship, but she recognized it in Dimiter.

"I want you back, Kam," she said. She resumed her loops around the room. "I'll clear it with Vandatti. And Jully Morrow is now your aide again."

Dimiter sighed relief. "Thank you, sir. I was going to request her."

"Kam, I want an investigation of this killing done on the QT. Talk with the rest of the team, but not repeat not with Sergeant Teshko or Brevet Corporal Yensen. You and Jully will conduct interviews with each team member to determine the whereabouts of those two this afternoon and evening, and I mean down to the minute if possible. None of the team members is to speak with Teshko or Yensen about this."

"Yes, sir."

"It is possible you may develop leads with others in Havenport," Siobhan went on. "Follow them up, but be diplomatic. I have only two candidates for this event, and neither of them is among the local populace."

Dimiter cleared her throat. "Ah... Teshko and Yensen?"

"That's right. It was one of them. But I don't want either of them to suspect you might be on to them."

"Understood, sir. I can conduct the interviews in my room."

Siobhan stopped again, at the dresser, and crossed her arms on it as she leaned forward, head down, breathing weary. Dimiter turned to regard her with eyes both respectful and tender. Finally Siobhan said, "I hate this, Kam. I hate everything about it. But there's something else. I have the feeling that whichever of the two killed Dail is not going to stop there. I think he has been ordered to take out everyone he can. Kam, I don't want to lose anyone else. So: get with the team, excepting our two suspects, and set up guard watches. They are to

177

be performed armed, day and night, in pairs. I recommend four-hour shifts. You and Jully pull the midnight-to-four and the midday-to-four. Nobody on the team is to go anywhere alone. Always in pairs. At least in pairs. And especially if either of those two goes with them."

"What about you, sir?"

The question startled Siobhan. She had not considered it. "Good point," she said. "In fact, that gives me an idea. I'll speak with Curielle Neri. Maybe she can detail some of her security team to help out."

"Sir?"

The simple word gave Siobhan pause. From Dimiter, it meant that she had considered a major problem. "What is it?"

"What if it turns out to be both, sir?"

"Then we're in the deep stuff, Kam. But it's worth keeping in mind. Now, I gather you've gotten yourself settled in. I don't have much of an introductory briefing for you. We have been ordered to assist my brother Ovin in any way possible. It seems Corporatia is on the verge of taking over the planet—"

"Oh, no!"

Siobhan nodded. "And Ovin is going to stop them or die trying. I'd really rather he didn't die. At the moment, however, the team has no detailed assignment. I expect that to change very soon. Right now, Ovin is on his way here to Vanadis, and should arrive in about an hour."

"So we're fighting Corporatia?" asked Dimiter, auburn eyebrows raised.

"A rogue element within it, yes. Commissioner Vandatti's orders."

"Yes, sir. May I go give Jully the good news?"

"Yeah. Kam... I'm glad you're here."

Dimiter grinned. "So am I, sir."

016

The mottled green and blue orb of Vanadis hung against darkness like an ornament as the *Banshee* emerged from Track. A moment or two later, the *Athair* hovered ten thousand meters off the port quarter, brought to that point by remote control. Aisling could just make out the shape of it on her periphery as she gazed out the Videx. "My first 'skip," she sighed.

"There'll be no trouble returning it," Shannen assured her. "But I have mixed feelings, *m'inion*. I'm proud of what you and Karan did, but I'm also frightened by it."

She turned to him, her wide violet eyes regarding him like an ingénue. "I'm sure I don't know what you mean, Da," she said blithely. "If I did, I would have to point out that it was Karan who tried to stop me, and when that failed, he insisted on coming along. I think his notion was that he would protect me. If, that is, I knew what you meant."

Definitely not ready for this, thought Shannen. Aloud, he said, "You're grounded."

She sobered, and gave a sad nod. "Yes, sir." A smile flickered at the corners of her mouth, as if to say she was glad to have any attention from him.

"Ash."

"Aye, then?"

He did not respond.

She said: "I'm sorry."

In forgiveness he touched fingertips to her cheek, and turned to look at Vanadis again. Now that his children were safe, he was free to focus on the other threat. The stakes for the planet were enormous. Try as he might to tell himself that the inhabitants would not be driven from their homes this time, he was unable to find any convincing words. With the Resurgers destroyed—how foolish in retrospect he had been to order their destruction!—there was no effective force he and Siobhan and her team could bring to bear to deflect the power of a corporation. If it came to it, he would find some way to move everyone rather than let them die or accept slavery. But all the work they had put in. The Chinese settlement at Dongbei. The building of Havenport, and the crafts and stores and kiosks. The Dur Falls Inn, with all those memories...

The hand that came to rest on his shoulder was pale blue and had four webbed digits. He turned, but Ocamla had come for Aisling. "Cloud is asking for you," she said.

The girl raced off. Ocamla remained, eyes fixed on the world before her. "I have been here," she said, a hint of anticipation in her voice.

"Maire," said Shannen. "Dock us down by Sasha's clinic."

The transfer to the surface took just longer than a blink. Fresh air rushed into the 'skip as the hatch opened and the ramp extruded. Aisling and Karan supported a feeble Cloud, with Finn trying to help from behind. Sasha Parry and Bara Jansdottir waited for them at the bottom of the ramp, and took the girl into the clinic, the others following closely. Aisling repeatedly clenched and unclenched her hands. Finn leaned close and spoke encouragingly.

At the top of the ramp, Shannen urged Ocamla on ahead, but she refused to leave by herself. It occurred to him that, in some way he was as yet unable to fathom, she was proving to be his talisman. In the space of five days since he had purchased and freed her, his life was changing, and this changing—no matter which way it developed—was going to prove irrevocable.

He felt lost.

Ocamla found his hand, and led him down the ramp.

*   *   *

Water brought to her by Ayesha helped Palmula recover. She took careful sips, still agog over the computer sprite. A question nagged at her: why had no one thought of sprites before? Obviously some program or set of programs in the Galactic Net was capable of creating and projecting them. Or a fortuitous concatenation of programs, probably. How could they be accessed? Perhaps the cause lay with the nature of the initializing command: the mere suggestion, without expansion or specifics, that one's personal computer interface with the Galactic Net form a personality. Not a command, then, so much as it was a granting of permission.

She took a final sip and handed the cup back to Ayesha. Yes, the granting of permission. It led to the necessity of making choices. You may now do this, if you wish; you figure out how. You choose how you want to look, and express yourself, and relate to your interface person. How you want to dress—for Ayesha's clothing was not separate from her body, but a part of her very substance, even though it felt like fabric. What you want to care about, and not care about.

That was the impetus, Palmula realized. The generation of the sprite that was Ayesha had come about because she as much had said that she was lonely, and would want a companion. And *that* had come about because she had no one else to talk to.

"*Overwhelmed,*" was Ayesha's evaluation, as she sat down on the bed beside her.

"That's an understatement. Ayesha, I don't know how to do this." In frustration she dragged fingers through her stringy hair. "If I want to see data on my Palmetto now, what do I do?"

"*Nothing has changed in our procedures,*" answered the sprite. "*Tell me what you want, and I will find it and cause it to appear in the monitor.*" Ayesha adjusted her position at the edge of the bed so that she might cast her bright green-eyed gaze directly upon Palmula. "*Unless what you want is not something that can be done on a monitor.*"

Uh-oh, thought Palmula. She edged away from Ayesha, putting an arm's length of distance between them. "That's why you did this, isn't it?" she said sharply. "So that I might have someone to go to bed with."

"*Have you ever been with a female of your species?*"

Palmula gaped at her. What a question! "A-a-a female of my species?" She did not know whether to laugh or growl at the phrasing. The answer was yes, but it took her four attempts to get the word out.

"*You have experience,*" said Ayesha approvingly. "*That's good, because I don't. And I should think at least one of us should know what she's doing.*"

To forestall further conversation in that direction, Palmula rose and went to the Palmetto. The monitor showed the open file relating to Partagu's purchase of field rations. Saved, she thought, by an important incoming announcement.

"Ayesha, please translate these coordinates to a place, not a position."

"*This would be more fun if I had a magic wand.*" She settled for a desultory wave of her hand.

Two galleons appeared in the monitor. They were hovering in synchronous orbit at the standard ten-thousand-kilometer limit above a brown and white world that Palmula did not recognize. "What is this planet?" she asked.

"*That is Venetor.*"

She frowned. "That is way out in the Fringes."

"*The better to hide them from security surveillance,*" said Ayesha.

"This is a covert operation, then."

"*Oh, for sure.*"

Palmula squinted into the monitor in an effort to elicit more detail. "Are the transponders active?" she wanted to know. "What ships are they?"

"*Active,*" answered Ayesha. "*The ships are identified as the* Mother-of-Pearl *and the* Ouidah, *both of Corporatia Resources registry.*"

Palmula shook her head. "That cannot be right. This is supposed to be a Products operation."

"*Yes, it is.*"

"But... but it means that Vanadis and Ovin will strike back at Resources."

"*Yes, it does.*"

"Oh, we have to stop this."

Ayesha looked dubious. The expression startled Palmula, who had not imagined that the sprite would possess emotions. Yet the frown seemed authentic.

"*I agree,*" said Ayesha. "*But I don't see how we can.*"

Palmula's eyes flooded: she was thinking that Pagan would know how. She flopped down on the bed and leaned back against the wall, feeling like a helpless pudding. She could feel Ayesha's eyes on her, and wondered what the sprite was thinking.

Even as she wondered, Ayesha's voice broke in, soft as dew. "*Was it something I said?*"

Palmula shook her head, and began to cry. "My sister," she wailed. She was barely able to make out her own words. "I was talking to her when there was an explosion, and then nothing. Nothing! I can't raise her."

"*Come here,*" whispered Ayesha. "*Hold onto me.*"

She tried to dry her tears, but they continued to flow. "But I'll get you wet."

"*Maybe later,*" said Ayesha.

For a hard second Palmula was silent. Then laughter erupted through her tears, and she barked and cried and sobbed. "You-you're unspeakable, Ayesha." But a smile forced its way onto lips that were slippery with tears.

"*This is what you need now. Lean against me.*"

Gingerly, Palmula complied. It was like slumping against a great, protective pillow, and despite her grief she wondered whether the sprite had altered her physical presence in order to comfort her. Ayesha's arm around her shoulders seemed to meld into Palmula's own body. Trembling, she wept into Ayesha's shoulder and chest.

Presently the outburst of grief subsided. Her breathing steadied. She sat up straight, eyes fixed on Ayesha. She was about to speak when there came a knock at her door. She sighed, and gained her feet, and went to answer it.

"*Be careful,*" cautioned Ayesha.

"It's all right," said Palmula, unlocking the door. "I get meals here. This should be my pastrami."

It was. Pagan was delivering it.

"Can I borrow your Palmetto?" she asked.

* * *

The shrubs to the right of the entrance to *Nicole's Brewery* formed a small alcove where a customer who sought solitude and an ale might sit on a bench at a small table, unmolested by the tavern's other activities and yet in a position to observe them. This aspect suited Siobhan perfectly. For the surveillance she was wearing a simple tan camisole that put her shoulders and upper chest at risk of sunburn, and brown trousers just loose enough to conceal weaponry yet allow her total freedom of movement. Soft-cushioned beige loafers replaced her customary black hiking boots, as she anticipated having to move quickly if the need should arise.

Beside her on the bench sat Curielle Neri. After taking Una back to their bungalow to recover and to see to Padraig, she had exchanged her customary blue and black outfit for something that, like Siobhan's, did not arouse curiosity or much of anything else. Her camisole was green—she was seated closer to the shrubbery—and her knee-length cutoffs sepia. Her unshod feet bespoke an indolent nonchalance, as if she were content to allow the rest of the universe to go by without remark.

Women they were, but no one on the patio were giving them any notice whatsoever. This too added to their open camouflage, and the casual eye would pass over them as if they were no different than any of the other patrons. The effect was calculated.

Still, Siobhan made circles with her mug in the puddle of condensation on the table. "Stop fidgeting," counseled Neri, who was nibbling on a chunk of smoked gouda. "You're supposed to be relaxed, *capisci*? Your Corporal Morrow and Thal Tamasco are well-watched."

"Aye," sighed Siobhan. "'Tis usually when the unanticipated arrives."

"Kam seems calm enough. How good is she?"

Siobhan issued a light laugh. "She is just possibly the clumsiest young officer I've ever had under my command. She is a walking malaprop. But she is..."

"Devoted?" offered Neri.

"Aye. Perhaps too much so. On the other hand, she will follow instructions or die in the attempt."

"I know the type."

Siobhan gave her a sidelong look. "*An ea?*"

"Ling," said Neri.

"The burdens of command."

Siobhan glanced across the diagonal of the patio at her Admin/Tac. Abstemious, at least for the occasion, she had settled for water in her mug. She sipped tentatively, one hand in her lap within easy reach of the Gerber 510 tucked under her light blue jersey. If there were any tags that might give her away, it was her deliberate lack of eye contact with Siobhan. But it would take a trained operative to notice it.

The plan, thought Siobhan, as she reviewed it yet again, was simple. Morrow was to meet at *Nicole's* with Thal Tomasco and conduct an interview of events. The fact of the encounter, although not the purpose of it, had been made known, casually, to Brevet Corporal Birch Yensen, but not to Sergeant Hitam Teshko. Siobhan doubted that Yensen would do anything more than show up, as if for a drink, and spot Morrow and Tomasco, and join them, presumably to learn whether Tomasco or Morrow had developed any leads regarding Pachen's murder. Any attack on them he might have contemplated would be performed after the two departed.

Still, Siobhan had taken precautions. One was to set up physical surveillance. Another involved the strategic placement of Neri's assistants—Ling and Kale, and a girl named Chao Hongye, who had not been identified to Siobhan. Finally, Morrow's table was fitted for audio surveillance, which was transmitted to the earbuds of Siobhan, Dimiter, and Neri.

Morrow herself was also attired in a manner befitting a casual encounter. Her dark brown hair had grown back after having been burned away during an attack three years earlier, and she kept it looking as if it had been hacked back to reach the bottom of her neck. Her sleeveless, pastel pink shirt and denim shorts fit well enough to show that she was unarmed. Thal Tomasco, who had been chosen for the interview because he had discovered Pachen's body, would be equally dressed for a drink and conversation. Siobhan hoped he would wear a hat of some kind, as the sun overhead would surely burn the skin on his balding head.

"You're fidgeting again," whispered Neri.

"*Tá brón orm.* Sorry."

"It's not as if this is your first date."

Siobhan sighed exasperation. "Curielle, you…"

"Shh. Tomasco just arrived."

Thal Tomasco, wearing a mottled billed cap of long use, was standing at the entrance to the patio, and looking around. Finally he spotted Morrow. Siobhan thought he carried off the pretense well. He signaled for an ale as he approached and sat down across the table from her. Normal sounds of greeting arrived through the earbuds.

"Now we wait," said Siobhan.

Morrow was using the opportunity to conduct an actual interview. Siobhan listened carefully.

Morrow: Last night, did you see when Yensen went to his room? What time was that?

Tomasco: I didn't look at the time, but it was right at sunset. I thought it was—thank you—a little early, but we're all suffering from time displacement.

Morrow, waiting until the server moved off: Did you see him actually go into his room?

Tomasco: No.

Did he emerge at any time, that you saw?

Nooo… (light laughter) But I did not have the room under surveillance.

When did you next see him?

Oh, this morning, when I got up. He was in the lobby, still yawning.

Morrow, softly: Alert.

Siobhan had already noticed the florid, paunchy man at the entrance. She sensed, rather than saw, that Neri was on high alert. Morrow was waving.

Morrow: Over here.

Tomasco: Hey!

There was the sound of weight plopping on a bench.

Yensen: Morrow, Tomasco. I thought the standing order was no alcohol.

Tomasco: We're only breathing the fumes. Doesn't count.

Morrow: We were just talking about you.

"Careful," whispered Siobhan, although Morrow did not have an earbud.

Yensen: Nothing good, I hope. *M'selle?* Bring me a mug of water.

Morrow: Nothing bad, either. We just wondered how you managed to sleep through all the excitement.

Yensen: Oh, you mean Pachen. I sleep soundly.

He leaned closer to Morrow.

Yensen: One corporal to another. I had one too many. That she-demon doesn't need to know, right?

"Steady," whispered Neri.

He sat back.

Yensen: Right?

The shrug was in Morrow's tone.

Morrow: It's your stripe.

Yensen: That's right, Morrow, it is. And you know what?

Sounds of fabric on wood, and the step of a boot.

Yensen: I think I'll take my "water" somewhere else. See you around, *Corporal.*

"You should kill him now," Neri advised. "Before he reproduces."

"*Sin é.*"

"Was that 'unanticipated' enough for you?"

"He was on edge, Curi. He was trying to feel Morrow out, to test her loyalty, and it did not go well."

"Or he was probing for a reaction, to find how just how much she knew." She laid her Palmetto on the table, and put one hand against the earbud. "Ling?"

Siobhan remained silent. The exchange between Yensen and Morrow had been too short for a definitive assessment, but he seemed to be making a concerted effort to flout orders and standards. Brevet meant that he was being considered for promotion; it did not bestow upon him the authority of the rank, except when he was specifically placed in charge of some project. In the service, he was in no way Morrow's equal.

Or out of the service, she added to herself.

"Got it," acknowledged Neri. "Stay with him."

Siobhan cocked an eyebrow at her.

"Yensen is walking slowly along the glideway north out of Havenport. He's acting like he is looking for something."

"A site," muttered Siobhan.

"Ling will stay with him until he returns to the *Meihua*."

Both Dimiter and Morrow had turned in her general direction, as if for instructions. Siobhan made a simple gesture, an index finger pointed up. Wait.

"It doesn't feel right, Curi."

"That time three years ago, when I burst into your office," said Neri, after a pensive moment. "I knew something was amiss, but it took me a while—almost too long—to put it together. But I had no one other than myself to guide my thoughts."

Siobhan grinned. "I get the hint, Curi. I can't... I don't..."

"Maybe you need an ale."

"Aye, I do. But, no. Birch Yensen is behaving, in theory and under observation, as if he had been inserted onto my team to disrupt whatever I might be doing. He is insolent, disobedient, slovenly, sarcastic—"

"Abominable."

"So you know the kind. Now, Dail's killer has to be either him or Teshko."

"Or both."

"Yes. Or both. But Teshko is a useful non-commissioned officer. He thinks ahead. He addresses Marigold Tallgrass as Sergeant. He addresses Jully as Corporal Morrow, even though as her superior he might simply address her by her last name, as Yensen did, or even by her first."

Neri unwrapped another chunk of cheese. "I'm missing your point."

"Both of them are behaving almost precisely as I would expect if it were Yensen and not Teshko." She raised a hand as Neri opened her mouth. "But wait. There's more. If it is both, then Yensen could provide the distraction, leaving Teshko free to eliminate my team and, presumably, me, while I'm looking the other way. But," and she raised her hand again, "Yensen could be acting the way he does because he would know that I would think him so obvious that it couldn't possibly be him. On top of it all, it means that he is expecting me to suspect him. And that makes him suspect."

"You definitely need an ale," judged Neri. "Or three."

"Yeah."

"You could just kill them both."

"I may have to do exactly that, Curi. I may have to slice through the Gordian knot of their treachery, even if one is innocent."

"Then I have a question: is this Yensen smart enough to send you into all these convoluted conjectures?"

Siobhan blew a sigh. "It's possible."

"But you don't think so."

"I don't know *what* to think, Curi," snapped Siobhan. "And therein lies my quandary. How can I act when I am indecisive?"

"You could brig both of them," Neri suggested. "At least until this is over. Ling and Kale can help out." She flashed a grin. "*E non sono inconseguente io!*"

Siobhan smiled gratefully. "No, you are certainly not inconsequential."

She beckoned to Dimiter, who ran across the patio, almost colliding with a serving girl porting a tray of mugs.

"Yessir!"

"At ease, Kam." Siobhan wondered whether Dimiter behaved the way she did because it had become a kind of game between them, with her playing the role of the gung-ho cadet trying to impress the seasoned veteran. "Accompany Jully and Thal back to the *Meihua*. As far as I can tell, you'll be the only one of the three who is armed."

"I'll protect them, sir."

"I know you will. Stay chilly, because Yensen is out wandering around, possibly looking for an ambush site. I couldn't tell whether he was carrying while he was here, but even if he was unarmed, that doesn't mean he still is."

"Understood, sir."

"After you get back, if Yensen returns to the stay-the-night, tok me."

"I'll tok you when we get back, too, sir."

They watched her move off. After the three had departed from the patio and *Nicole's*, Siobhan noted an expression on Neri's face that she had not seen before, and questioned it. Neri's only response was to signal for another ale; the alcohol restriction did not apply to her.

"Curi?" pressed Siobhan, after the mug arrived.

Neri fortified herself with a gulp, but still hesitated. She did not look at Siobhan. Her voice was just audible over the light breeze through the shrubbery. "Of all those on your team, who is the most trusted?"

The query shocked a gasp out of Siobhan. "What are you *saying*?" she demanded. There was an edge to her voice that she reserved for adversaries.

"I have said nothing," Neri replied calmly. "I have asked a question."

"No! That was out of bounds. That was between the lines."

"*Bene.*"

Siobhan sputtered, and took a drink from Neri's mug. "Why would you even ask that?"

"Because you have not asked it, Siobhan."

"My people are so far beyond reproach—"

"Yet you are apprehensive. It is in your voice, your tone." Neri twisted on the bench to face her. She uttered one more word, softly. "Klos."

The reference to the trusted aide that betrayed her three years ago, and tried to kill her, only to die himself by the reflection of the blue beam off Photem, brought reality back to Siobhan. "I don't want to go down that road, Curielle," she said. "I can't."

"Siobhan. *Mi'amica.* I believe you. I believe *in* you. As much as I hated you for a while, I loved you as well. I feel the same about my team as you do about yours. What I suggest is unthinkable, yes. But to win, if it can be won, we must be professional. *Capisci?*"

Slowly, Siobhan subdued herself. It was a battle. Even before she won it, she said, "I don't know that I can select the most trustworthy, Curi. All of them. Excepting two. There are some things you are just sure of."

"*Mio gaelico* would never betray you, Siobhan."

"No, he would not."

"Yet for how many years would you have detained him, had you the opportunity? And killed him if he resisted?"

"I think you've made your point, Neri," she said stiffly, and got to her feet. "In any event, those days are over."

"I have offended you," said Neri. "For that, I am truly sorry."

Siobhan's lips puffed out with her sigh. For a long moment she stood gazing down at Neri. No thought entered her mind. Neri simply was. She was an irresistible force of nature who could be denied only by killing her. And Neri placidly returned her gaze, as if to say, you know I'm right.

Siobhan let her moment of anger pass. "Are you finished with your ale?" she asked.

"You drank half of it."

"One sip!"

"That's what the elephant said when he lowered the river level." She drained the mug. "*Andiamo.*"

* * *

Sasha Parry was washing his hands with ANTI soap in the sink to the side of a treatment stand. "I decided not to question her about the causes of her injuries," he was saying, to five sets of perked ears. "She needs strength. Later she can dwell on what happened to her, if she wants to. I did tell her that her tormenters were dead." He raised his head from his cleansing and looked to Shannen. "Is that accurate?"

"Probably," he said. Beside him, Karan Syan wore a smile of grim satisfaction. "There might be a couple of minions who survived. The two top men—those who supervised her treatment—are dead, as is the guard who shot her." At this last, he rested a hand on Karan's shoulder, and the boy leaned against him. "How is she, Sasha?"

"I've given her a sedative," the medic replied. "Sleep is a good healing medium. As for the injuries, she has no broken bones and her internal organs are intact. Her liver is bruised, but not seriously. Same with her right kidney. Abrasions and bruises as you saw. I haven't tested her sensory functions yet, for obvious reasons. Her pupils are fine, however. She was weak but alert before I sedated her." His gaze shifted to Aisling, whose eyes glistened like wet amethysts. "She asked for you," he said kindly. "If you want to go in and hold her hand, I think she will know you are there. Mind the IV in her right arm."

Aisling dashed off. Shannen asked, "And her burns?"

"The beam glanced off her rib cage," answered Parry. "It got no significant penetration, but the burns are serious. All third-degree burns are, as you have reason to remember."

Shannen rubbed the scar tissue on his lower back.

"She'll have some scarring," Parry continued, drying his hands. "My main concern is the bottom floating rib, which took the brunt of the beam, if that's the right term. If it does not respond to regenerative treatment, I'll have to remove it. It will not debilitate her in any way, in time, but such an operation will prolong her recovery."

Finn cleared his throat, and glanced at the recovery room and at Parry. "May I...?" he said, and hesitated.

"Of course."

"I'm going, too," announced Karan.

Parry peered at Shannen. "When did you sleep last?"

"I neglected to note the time. Sasha... thanks. Thank you."

"I'm glad you got your children back safely. Ah... you know Karan is smitten, right?"

"So is Finn." He shrugged. "It's a problem for their mother."

"And for their father." He softened. "Neri took Una back to their place. Like I said, she'll be fine as long as she takes it easy."

"We don't have much time to prepare—"

Parry swore with uncharacteristic anger, and banged his flat hand on the counter top. "*You think I don't know that*? Two days, Siobhan reckons. Maybe. If we're lucky. We can't defend ourselves, and we can't escape unless we pack up and go, and leave all this behind. Scylla and Charybdis!" His harsh glare swept the room, and finally settled on Shannen, chest heaving, and slowing as he regained his composure.

"If I had stayed home..." Shannen began.

Parry snorted disgustedly. "It wouldn't have made any difference. In fact, if you had done, we wouldn't know now what's going on. Siobhan was in the dark as well. Incidentally, she and her team are staying in the *Meihua*. If you can stay awake, you'll want to talk with her. And what about you, young woman?"

Shannen laughed, though his heart wasn't in it. "Sorry. Ocamla, Sasha; Sasha, Ocamla."

"He owns me," Ocamla said succinctly.

"I seriously doubt that," said Sasha. He tossed the towel in a laundry bin and approached. "How are you feeling?"

Ocamla sobered. "I really don't know right now."

"There's a lot of that going around," Parry told her.

017

For the second time in an hour, Palmula found herself gradually waking. A face very much like her own was hovering over her like an out-of-body experience. It was not quite like looking into a mirror: the face she saw was scarred, pale lines connecting the eyes to the corners of the mouth. As sometimes happened, the face bore traces of the bright colors that had recently adorned it.

"Pagan?" she croaked. "You-you're all right?"

"A little hungry," she replied. "I didn't have time to grab a bite."

Palmula laughed despite herself, and sat up with Pagan's assistance. Dried tears had left a residue, and she tried to clear it away with her fingertips. "How...? What happened?"

Pagan sat down on the bed. "I was on covering fire when they got my position based on the Palmetto," she explained. "I had to keep it active in case Ovin had instructions for me. So I left it on, and moved away from it. Which is why I needed to borrow your Palmetto. I had to let Ovin know I was okay and away."

"I suppose you ate my sandwich."

"Half of it. Not bad, but I need to wash it down with an ale." Soft fingertips touched Palmula's cheek. "... are you okay?"

"Relieved. Don't ever do that to me again." Palmula gained her feet, and trod on unsteady legs to her desk. "I hope you saved my search inquiries."

"I did you one better: I asked around." Her dark face sobered. "It's not good. Mercenaries have been dropping off the grid this past year."

Palmula peered at the monitor. "Not security troops?"

"I don't think Partagu wants personnel who are burdened by questions or doubts."

"Those galleons will hold a hundred each."

"At least." She tugged at Palmula. "Which is why we're leaving now. Ovin is expecting us. The children are safe, although it appears he acquired a couple more along the way."

Palmula was just able to grab her Palmetto and the last of her sandwich before being yanked out the door.

* * *

The world known as Venetor made Erron Markey shiver, and not only from the local temperature. The light from the white dwarf scarcely penetrated this far down in the equatorial chasms that were the only habitable parts of the planet. Long ago, the tectonic plates of two of the larger continents had collided at an unusually high rate of speed for landmasses—something on the order of a meter a year—and in the process the orogeny had created a region of high, steep peaks separated by deep chasms in a region of granite overlaid by layers of sedimentary rock. The atmosphere was marginally breathable, but oxygen did collect at the bottom of the chasms, where the air was still. Nevertheless, Markey and Partagu were wearing breathers as they trod along the sandy bottom of one of the wider chasms—this one some fifty meters across.

Partagu was speaking on his Palmetto, and gazing through the narrow opening five thousand meters above. "Oxygen concentrators," he yelled. "We're going to set up a safe haven down here until things cool off. Temporary shelters, tools, equipment... what? No, I'm not going to build them. That's what I'm paying *you* for."

Markey made a little calming gesture, which Partagu angrily turned away from. The move set Markey's teeth on edge. Partagu was growing more irritable with each passing hour, now that the final state of Markey had come to think of as Operation Vanadis was almost under way. Certainly part of that irritation stemmed from his, Markey's, failure to ascertain definitively whether Shannen was in control of the Resurgers, or indeed whether he still possessed them at all. Still, the ruse he and Partagu had planned with regard to the registration of the galleons would serve to deflect Shannen's attention.

"No, as soon as we have Vanadis evacuated and under control, we'll move there," Partagu shouted. "Five days, no more. So I want those shelters here now."

In closing he growled at the Palmetto. "It's all right, Erron," he said. "I'm not going to shoot you. Unless it was you who hired that moron."

"He was assigned from HR," said Markey. "Are we really staying here?"

"Nobody knows we're here, and nobody will know except those who actually are here," sighed Partagu, with some asperity, as if he were tired of Markey's needless fretting. "This is our remote headquarters, Erron. Get over it!"

The Palmetto chimed again. Partagu spoke his name, and listened for a couple minutes. He closed without a word.

"There's a problem," he said.

Markey flinched. Partagu had not said, "We have," or worse, "You have." Whatever the difficulty might be, it remained generic so far. Hope poised within him.

"It's that girl," Partagu went on, glaring at him. "She has downloaded the files for this project."

"But I tripled the reward," blurted Markey. In the chill air, he was beginning to perspire. "They're looking for her. What can I do—"

Partagu shushed him with a sharp wave of his hand. "It's gone beyond blame now, Erron. We don't know where she is or what she plans to do with what she knows. My guess is that she is somehow associated with Shannen. She'll be on Vanadis."

"You can't be sure—"

"I don't have to be sure," he snapped. "We're past that. We have to move on. Once Vanadis is a *fait accompli*, she can't hurt us."

"You still think Shannen no longer possesses the Resurgers, then."

"For the fifth time, yes, Erron, that's what I think. He knows we're out here, and he knows something is up. He would be on Vanadis if he were planning to use them. He... is that yours?"

Erron tokked his own Palmetto. He said two words, "You're sure?" and closed out. His wavering gaze met Partagu's nose. "It's our man on the Gonelong team," he said, unable to shake the tension from his voice. "Shannen is back."

"Then we have to move on this. Tell him to kill her. With the leader gone, the team will pose only a minimal threat. Meanwhile, we go with what we have."

"But only half the mercs are aboard."

"They go on the one galleon. The other will wait, load up, and reinforce. Fire up the shuttle. We're going back up. *Now*, Erron."

* * *

There were four of them seated in a booth in the Dur Falls Inn—two males and two females. Ages seventeen and eleven, and two at almost thirteen. The twins had each killed a man, or in the case of the female, men. The oldest of the four had used small shaped charges to blow the locks to the cells that confined the two females. The female twin had used a concealed weapon to melt the locks to the cells in the Orphanage at Khorassey.

In the booth they sat, somber and introspective, but each comforted by the presence of the other three. They spoke little, and drank from mugs or tumblers. The seventeen nursed an ale that he did not realize—or pretended not to realize—was watered down. The female twin drank from a lead-crystal tumbler of equally watered-down Bushmill's Irish whiskey. The male twin drank hot green tea with a slice of lemon. The youngest settled for a mug of ice water.

Finn; Aisling Yhonyn; Karan Syan; Cloud. The twins on one side of the table, the other two across from them.

At the counter stood Mikal Trov, the massive man who operated the tavern and who was now trying not to look like he was keeping a watchful eye on the four while he surreptitiously wiped the counters and dried some mugs. In another part of the bay, Deyrdra Shannen needlessly saw to the cleanliness of the booths and tables and benches. Watchful eyes, too, but she also kept her ears open, especially for any sign of emotional distress.

The four could not have emerged unscathed from their ordeal, but for the moment they were handling themselves well. Deyrdra's lips curved in a crooked smile whenever she saw the way Finn and Aisling snuck glances at one another. Karan was solicitous of Cloud.

During the ordeal, Aisling had lost her quoil. She was now girt by a new one, draped around her bare midriff. Above and below she was wearing a bandeau and denims, both deep green. Cloud was dressed in like manner except for the weapon and for the pale blue color. Karan had opted for a loose gray outsuit; had he been asked, he would not have admitted, sheepishly, that he was trying to conceal his skinny frame from Cloud.

"Young love," murmured Deyrdra, now standing next to Mikal.

"A little too young?" the big man said softly.

Deyrdra nuzzled the point of his shoulder. "When I was twelve, I had a crush on Ovin," she told him. "I would have carried it through, had I had the nerve to suggest..."

"You still would."

She laughed. "Aye, then. But if that be what's on your mind, upstairs with you, where I'll be showing you a crush you'll never be forgetting."

"Been there," he said. "Done that."

"Aye, and you'd be doing it again."

"And again."

Aisling waved to them. "So go upstairs, you two," she called. "We can hear you all the way over here."

Having spoken, the girl returned her attention to Finn. Her face warmed; his was of a color that suggested he was experiencing the same rise in temperature. But their eyes broke contact as they looked away, and the moment passed. Aisling studied the contents of her tumbler, as if seeking enlightenment. Finn shifted uncomfortably on the bench. The fabric of his pullover seemed to chafe his skin; he tugged the collar away from his neck.

"So now what?" asked Cloud.

It was the question the others had been avoiding. Aisling felt all eyes on her. She was thinking that she was not ready for this, whatever it was. She was also thinking that she was the daughter of the Princess of Vanadis, the latest addition to a royal house that had thrived for more than a millennium, and that she had to be ready, like it or not.

"If there is some place you would rather be," said Aisling, "or if you have some relatives somewhere, my father will arrange transportation." She leaned closer and spoke with a quiet earnestness. "But I would prefer that you remain here with us, Cloud. Here you have friends, and people who will see to you, and a place to live and grow." With a wicked grin, she added brightly, "And Karan wants you to stay."

Karan said nothing, but shoved her shoulder. She just did manage to save her drink.

"As for you," she continued, turning to Finn. "I don't even know your last name, or even if you have one. I don't know anything about you... except the one thing that is most important."

A curious frown wrinkled Finn's brow. "Which is?"

She took a minute to consider her response. Fortified by the last sip of whiskey, she said, "I like to think I am independent, that I set my own rules. And I am, and I do. But I am not alone in this Universe. In it there are good people and bad people, and there are great dangers, as I recently have learned, that I cannot face down by myself. But you were there when I desperately needed you, Finn, and you helped me escape from a terrible situation."

"Only by chance—"

"Hush," she said gently. "It was more than happenstance. You had a choice. You did not have to involve yourself. But your actions saved each of us here, in one way or another. Even if you were... interested in me, what you did was far too much to expect of you for that. You helped, I think, because you cared, and because you could not stand idly by. *M'athair* is the same."

"Um..."

Aisling sat back. "You may speak."

Finn laughed. "If I'm going to be your... hmm..."

"Boyfriend," said Aisling.

"Your boyfriend, do I have to learn to speak Irish?"

"Aye, you do." She lifted her empty tumbler and looked at Mikal, who smiled, but shook his head.

"Will you teach me?"

"Aye... oh, you mean Irish? Aye, that as well."

He tilted his head to stare at her, as if uncertain what she meant. "That may not be as difficult as you think," he said, after a moment. "Finn is short for my last name, which is Finnegan. My given name is Abban."

Aisling's eyes narrowed. "That means 'monk,'" she said.

"I didn't say I idolized the name."

She raised her empty tumbler, and he poured a bit of ale into it. "To Finn," she said. Her eyes swept the others. "Karan. Cloud."

"Ash," said Finn, and they all drank.

Aisling closed her eyes. She felt as if something had happened at this gathering and in the past two days that eventually was going to mean something. She was uncertain as to what it was, but she looked forward to finding out.

* * *

"Good news disquiets me," muttered Shannen, as he closed out the commo. With a glance at Siobhan's furrowed brow, he added, "Pagan Bell is okay. They killed her Palmetto. She and Palmula are on their way here."

Siobhan was dubious. "I don't know what good they can do," she said, sipping at a *weissbier* as they sat at a shaded table at *Nicole's Brewery*. Flowering shrubbery made them difficult to see from the patio entrance. "It's still ten against two hundred."

"Eleven," said Ocamla.

"Palmula said the two galleons are still docked in orbit around Venetor," he went on. "At least she was able to trace them that far. A thousand cartons of field rations are being transferred to the cargo holds. That's enough meals for twenty days. I think Partagu is assuming he'll encounter scorched-earth once he gets here. But that won't matter to the mercenaries; I doubt any of them can grind flour in a quern."

Siobhan coughed and chuckled, and quickly sobered. "We can't allow them to land."

"There's more," said her twin. "The galleons are registered to Corporatia Resources."

"We know," said his twin. "Conigli?"

"In any event, it might buy us more time," Ocamla put in.

But Shannen had already tokked his Palmetto.

The connection took a few seconds, even though it was a direct link to Giulio Conigli, the Chair of Corporatia Resources, and Shannen guessed the man had quickly dismissed someone from his office, once he had identified the caller. The Palmetto projected Conigli's small hologram onto the table, but the reduced size failed to diminish the sheer power of the man. He was attired in a dull blue leisure outsuit, rumpled after a long day. He had not bothered to straighten his dark hair. He was standing in front of his desk and beside a stuffed chair. His hologram turned about on the table, noting the occupants, and finally addressed Shannen.

"I heard you were dead," he said, his voice gruff and deep. Even the idle remark contained a note of command.

Shannen nodded his head deferentially in greeting. "Chair Conigli. You know my sister. The other woman here is from Motoya, known to us as Far Parkins. Her name is Ocamla."

Conigli's heavy brows wrinkled, and he blinked, but failed to acknowledge the introductions. "And the reason for your commo, which I can only assume is of vital importance to at least one of us?"

"Yassim Partagu is seeking control of the rare-earth resources of Vanadis," Shannen told him, and waited.

Conigli shrugged. "He knows what will happen to him."

"He's sending two galleons filled with mercenaries to effect this control."

Again Conigli was dismissive. "Why communicate this to me?"

"The two galleons are registered to Corporatia Resources."

Conigli fell silent, his thick hands crunched into fists of stone. "Son of a *bitch*!" he seethed, and did not apologize. Around the office he stalked, and the transmission followed him. "Shannen! We had nothing to do with this."

"I believe you, Chair Conigli," he said, his calm a counterpoint. "But now that you know, you must act, or I would be justified in thinking that you approved."

Conigli's broad shoulders stiffened in anger at first, then slumped as he considered the circumstances. "Yes," he said, his quiet deliberation now startling. "Yes, I suppose you would be. Where are the galleons now?"

"Around Venetor. But if you are thinking of sending a force out there, don't bother. I expect them here within the day."

On the table, Conigli faced Shannen. His voice was firm, but his eyes reflected concern. "I can't have anyone to either location that quickly."

"But you will try."

Conigli nodded, his thoughts now elsewhere. Shannen closed out.

"He won't help," said Ocamla.

"I think he'll try," said Shannen. "What he will do is raise Lin Cheng. The Chair of Corporatia Products," he added, seeing the Motic's puzzled frown. "The man most likely to be affected by Partagu's attempt to steal a march... from..." His speech slowed and stopped. An odd stray sound had reached him. He cocked an ear, listening, and peered into the shrubbery. "Duck, Siobhan," he said sharply, and shoved Ocamla onto the patio.

The blue beam dissipated harmlessly into the air about the brewery. The sound of thrashing about grew louder, and then stopped abruptly, punctuated by a body impacting the ground.

018

On the bridge of the *Ouidah* stood Partagu and Markey, the former impatient, the latter fretting. The matte black of null-space in the Videx made Partagu itch. The Track from Venetor to Vanadis required just over two hours; only ten minutes had passed since their departure. It was not possible to shorten the travel time. In the decks below, the mercenaries were busy with their equipment under the watchful eyes of their section commanders. With nothing more to do until half an hour before arrival, the galleon's captain, a taciturn, bearded ruffian named Kulikoff, had retired to his stateroom for a short nap. The only other person on the bridge was First Officer Tertia Trevi, whose pale eyes narrowed apprehensively whenever Partagu moved in her direction. She had already repelled one advance, and seemed poised to flee at the next one.

Markey interposed himself between Trevi and Partagu. He had to admit Partagu was the cause of his own tension. The closer Operation Vanadis approached fruition, the more agitated the man grew. Far more was at stake than the relatively routine takeover of a sparsely inhabited world. If successful, the operation might well become the first step in a takeover of the most powerful corporations of Corporatia. Partagu could buy a thousand Trevis.

Hell, thought Markey. So could I. Or wait until he was done with each one.

"Still no word of that Bell girl?" growled Partagu. Markey shook his head. "And nothing from our man on Vanadis?"

"He is looking for an opportunity, sir."

Waving his arms about, Partagu spun around and headed toward Trevi. "He is supposed to *create* an opportunity."

Alarmed, Trevi's eyes widened, and brightened to turquoise.

"Supervisor Gonelong has taken the precaution of setting roving patrols," said Markey. "It is difficult—"

"He is being *paid* to overcome difficulties."

"Yes, sir. He is. But at this moment there is nothing we can do to compel him to act."

At this, Partague threw an angry scowl, but added no remark. For a moment he transfixed Trevi with an icy glare, as if her earlier rejection of him were an intolerable offense best overcome by force if necessary. She seemed to shrink inside her gray outsuit, and pretended not to notice him.

Markey shrugged. "The die is cast, sir."

"And I suppose today is the Ides of March. I *know* my Shakespeare, Erron."

Markey thought for a moment. "I don't believe it is, sir."

Trevi tokked the ship's computer, and read the result. "On Earth, it is now July," she said, helpfully.

"A month named for Julius," sneered Partagu. "I don't suppose your name is Cleopatra."

"No, sir. It's—"

"Never mind. Come with me—"

"I cannot, sir," Trevi said quickly. "There must always be an officer on the bridge when we are enTracked."

"Nonsense. Go to my stateroom." When she continued to demur, he pulled out a Skoda. "Now, Trevi."

"Sir," began Markey.

"You stay out of this, Erron. Mind the bridge. I won't be long."

Trevi looked as if she were trying to decide whether a protest was worth her life. In the end, she capitulated, and headed aft toward the staterooms. They left Markey to frown on the bridge. Partagu's actions were unlike him, even though he was accustomed to getting his way with women. The timing of this misadventure was inappropriate to the task at hand. Maybe he needed to settle his nerves. Markey gave himself a nod; yes, that was it. For Partagu, sex was a tranquilizer. He wondered whether he might partake after him.

The communications module on the console began to

emit a tinny beep. Markey sat down in the captain's chair. Between a simple 'skip and a cargo galleon, there was little difference in overall bridge operation, and he quickly located the source. At the push of a button, a sallow, furious face appeared in the monitor. Rage smoothed out the lines in his older face, and brightened the gleam from his black, evenly-set eyes. Already Markey's heart was hammering his rib cage. He started to speak, but Chair Lin Cheng, the final authority in Corporatia, was already there.

Spittle fairly flew from his lips. "What in the hell do you think you are doing?" he shrieked. "Where is that arrogant idiot?"

Markey sputtered. "Ah... he is ah... indisposed at the mo—"

"*Undispose him immediately!*"

To do so meant death; not to do so meant death, sooner or later. Markey chose later. Another push of the button terminated the communication. Hand over his pounding heart, he sat back. When the beeping resumed a moment later, he ignored it.

* * *

The quartet in the booth had lightened their beverages to a pitcher of iced citrus drink. Aisling poured for each of them. She wondered whether this counted under the terms of *noblesse oblige*. Not that it mattered. Courtesy, her mother had said, was even more important among friends than in the midst of enemies. She concluded her service with Deyrdra Shannen, who had joined them.

Following mock toasts, Aisling said, "On the way home, *m'athair* alluded to difficulties here, but he did not explain, nor did I inquire." She looked directly at Deyrdra. "Perhaps you can enlighten us."

Deyrdra hedged. "How old are you, again?"

Aisling laughed. "Da has asked me that at least three times. I am but a product of my upbringing and experience." She sobered. "Aunt Deyrdra, do I deserve such a deflection?"

"*Tá brón orm.* No, of course not." She swirled the contents of her tumbler, and drew designs in the condensation on the table with her fingertip. "You have every right to be knowing, each of you."

Deyrdra spoke at length. After she had finished, Aisling sat back, stunned. Not so much by the perils about to visit them all, but because Shannen had come to rescue her and Karan despite the danger to Vanadis. What did that mean? In his place, she would have... or would she?

Beside her, Karan sat limp, and she realized he had grasped the implications as well.

Finn asked, "Is there nothing that can be done to stop them?"

Deyrdra shook her head. "There are about a thousand people living on Vanadis. Half of them are in Dongbei, farming. Most of the other half manage small stores or manufacturing. Brewing, and dairy. The only ones who could fight effectively are—"

"You and Uncle Mikal," Aisling finished for her. "*M'athair agus mo mháthair*, Aunt Curielle and her security staff, Aunt Una, Aunt Siobhan and her team."

"And the four of us," Finn threw in. He glanced at Cloud for confirmation, and she nodded.

"The problem," said Aisling, her voice a whisper coarsened by anger, "is that the people of this world cannot leave in time to save themselves. If they could, where would they go? To abandon everything they have done and become... to leave behind the lives they have worked so hard to build. But they cannot leave, and neither can we. We must stand and fight."

"And die," said Karan.

She flashed him a severe look, and tempered it with affection. "If we fight, we may die," she said. "If we do not fight, we will die."

"What about your aunt's magical friend?" asked Cloud.

Aisling looked to Deyrdra, who said, "Photem is not magical; it only seems that way. We refer to her and her kind as charm quarks. But her energy is only partially here, in this part of the galaxy. She is not strong enough."

"If only we had one of those Resurgers," sighed Aisling.

The door to the tavern opened, and inside swept Yhounda Khouse with a grace that all but masked her vexation. Six quick paces brought her to the table. "You might have let me know," was all she said to Aisling.

Deyrdra stood up. "Please," she said, offering her a space beside Cloud. "We're having lemonade. Would you care for some?"

After a calming breath, Yhounda settled onto the bench. She gave the tumbler before Aisling a hard glance. "Although I doubt that glass has known only lemonade this afternoon."

"*A mháthair*," said Aisling. "Please don't go on at me."

* * *

Shannen tilted the plastic table so that any beams fired would deflect upwards. Behind it, as he and Siobhan and Ocamla crouched, weapons out, seeking targets, ears cocked for sound. A couple of other patrons, alerted to the dangers, had already fled into the brewery. Into the tension broke a familiar voice.

"It's all right," called Curielle Neri. "I've got him."

Shannen straightened, and set the table back up. Neri stepped through the patio entrance with Sergeant Teshko held in an arm-bar come-along, simple enough to apply and almost impossible to break free from. Still, he was protesting as she led him to the table, kicked a chair into place, and sat him down roughly. With her Kellogg 509 in hand, she took up a position directly behind him, ready to fire upon seeing any hostile move.

Shannen edged Ocamla aside; the confrontation was Siobhan's to conduct. Teshko's expression blended disbelief, pain, and confusion. Shannen found only two of them credible; Neri would not have escorted him gently.

"Explain yourself, Sergeant," ordered Siobhan.

He glanced back at Neri. "I was watching over you, sir. One man has already been murdered. It occurred to me that you might well be the primary target."

"Your orders were to remain at the *Meihua*," she reminded him.

"My duties include obedience to your orders, sir. They also include seeing to your safety. I had to make a choice between the two. Truth is, I'd make the same choice again."

Siobhan looked past him to Neri. "Did he have a weapon out?"

Neri shook her head. "Not at first."

"What exactly was he doing?"

"He was cruising around the shrubs, and watching the entrance. He pulled out this Skoda when he spotted me," she tossed it to Shannen, "and in the process of his capture, he fired it."

"Just who are you?" Teshko snapped at Neri.

Neri did not bother to answer. Siobhan said, "When you took him, Curi, was he in a good position to fire at this table?"

She considered. "There were better positions," she answered at last. "With clearer fields of fire."

Siobhan sighed. "So he's either a stupid assassin, or he's telling the truth."

Teshko laughed lightly, and shook his head. "Sir, if I had orders to kill you, I could have carried them out already at any one of several opportunities."

"He has a point," said Ocamla. Siobhan flashed hard eyes at her, and she raised her hands defensively. "Sorry."

Siobhan softened. "'Tis meself who would be apologizing." She tokked her Palmetto and raised Sergeant Tallgrass. "Marigold, gather the others, except Brevet Corporal Yensen, into the lobby of the Meihua," she ordered. "They are to have their weapons out and charged. If Yensen shows up, disarm and detain him. I'd prefer him alive, but I won't put anyone at risk by issuing such an order."

"Understood, sir. Ah... sir?"

"What is it?"

"Yensen is not in the stay-the-night. I don't know where he is, and the Tomascos are shaking their heads at me as well."

"Understood. Get the team safe."

"There's more, sir. Sergeant Teshko left word with Jully that he was going to *Nicole's* to keep an eye it. He did not explain what that meant."

"He's right here, Marigold. You needn't concern yourself for him."

Teshko was looking at his weapon, still in Neri's possession. "Give it back to him," said Siobhan. "Sergeant, I can't order anyone here except you, so those orders I just gave Sergeant Tallgrass also apply to you."

"It's a little late for that, *Supervisor*," said Yensen, emerging from inside the brewery. His tone was heavy with arrogance. His sidearm swept the table before settling on her. "Much too late."

* * *

On the bridge of the *Emerall Ray*, Palmula Bell was busy with Ayesha. At the moment, she was checking for updates regarding her search for black budget items in Partagu's files. The computer sprite found several that related to "payments to personnel," which Palmula took as a nice euphemism for hiring mercenaries. She recalled seeing a related file cross her desk at the security office, but it raised no suspicions from her at the time. Now, she wondered about it. It was clear to her that the responsibility for the operational planning for the invasion—for such it could only be termed—fell to Erron Markey: the same man who had sought to have her search for Candle, and who subsequently had tried to have her killed. The evidence was already overwhelming; but she knew in her heart that the invasion was not going to be negated by an investigation and hearing. No, there was but one way to bring about a proper result— and she did not know what it might be.

The uncertainty clawed at her. She was working in her chosen realm, and doing a great job—so she told herself—yet the results, though positive, were unhelpful. She began to instruct Ayesha in a grouchy tone that went right over the sprite's head, until a dark chocolate hand much like her own stopped her.

"You've done all you can," consoled Pagan Bell.

Palmula sat back, glum. "It's not enough." For a few moments she continued to stew. Her gaze took in her older sister. "Aren't you going to, er, dress for battle?"

"Not this time." Pagan sat down in the other captain's chair. "There will be children present. Children it happens I care what they... think." She made a rude sound at herself. "Listen to me! What's wrong with me?"

"Nothing is wrong. You were exposed to some that you bonded with right away," said Palmula. "You were always defensive of us as children..." Abruptly her face saddened. "I am so sorry! Bad memory."

Pagan thrust her hands between her knees and squeezed them, as if to control pain. "It's gotten better, these past few years. Pami... sorry, Palmula, I know—"

"Pami is fine, Sis."

"I know I'm insane. I know I went insane, watching... them... dying... like that." She gave a dry, mirthless laugh. "It's funny, Ovin doesn't treat me as insane."

"Ovin has been where you've been."

"Yeah, but he doesn't... I mean, well, he kills, yes, but..."

"Waste of food."

"Yeah. No." Pagan rubbed her fists against the side of her head. "It's not that I mind being insane—"

"You're not insane," Palmula declared. "You're angry with those who did us wrong. You took the only recourse available to you. I think you're learning to apply that rage in a positive direction."

Slowly Pagan nodded. "I wonder if I should have my teeth capped."

"Rack of lamb, sizzling on a grill," said Palmula. "Fresh herbs and garlic minced and spread over the meat. A mug of ale in one hand..."

Pagan sat up straight. "No. A nice pinot noir, or a Sangiovese."

"A potato smeared with butter and sour cream with chives."

"A meaty tomato, thin-sliced, lightly salted."

"What are you two talking about?" asked Ayesha.

Neither Bell answered at once. Palmula held back, because in this moment of crossroads, Pagan had to be the one to speak. Whatever was to be said, had to come from her. She had her hands between her knees again, and was gazing down at her feet. Her face was calm; even the two ritual scars seemed smoothed out. At length, she cleared her throat of tears she was not yet shedding.

"Do you think," she began, and swallowed hard. "Do you think Ovin would let me live on Vanadis?"

"Us," said Palmula. "Let the three of us live. Yes. I barely know the man, but yes, I do."

Pagan nodded. "So be it."

019

Yhounda Khouse shrugged herself out of her royal persona as if it were a dressing gown. She turned to Mikal as he drew up a chair to sit at the end of the booth. "Drink before the war?" she asked him.

"Something like that. What can I get you, Milady?"

"We are well past honorifics, Mikal," she chided. "Lemonade is fine."

"Why did he call her milady?" Finn asked Aisling.

"*Mo mháthair* is the Princess of Vanadis."

Finn was downcast. "Oh."

The unexpected mood took Aisling aback. "What is it?"

"Nothing."

"Finn—"

"I said nothing, Ash," he snapped.

Deyrdra stood up with the pitcher. "Refills, anyone?"

Aisling got to her feet and climbed over the back of the bench. "Come with me," she said, pointing unmistakably at Finn, and headed for the door, brooking no refusal.

He followed, trudging at first, then picking up his pace as he reached the door. He caught up with Aisling just outside. After the door closed, she turned on him.

"What's wrong, Finn?" she demanded, arms folded across her chest. She tapped her foot impatiently. Cool violet eyes regarded him. "Well?"

"You... you're a princess..."

"Aye, I am. What of it?"

He tried to turn away, but she reached and snagged him by the shoulder, turning him around. Sunlight through the foliage of an overhanging shrub now dappled his face as he took a couple of steps back

"What of it, Finn?"

"I'm not... look, you don't know me, you don't know the kind of work I've done, what I've had to do, the things I've had to do to stay alive... I mean..."

"Yes." She moved into the shaded sunlight as well. The shafts of light cast her shiny black hair in sparks that were almost blue. "Yes, tell me what you mean."

He caught his breath, and sighed. "Look, Ash... Aisling, Mila—"

"No!"

Finn nodded. "Aisling. Until now it was you and me, boy and girl, but now... now, I don't know. Next to you, I'm... I don't know what I am. I mean, your mother is a—"

Aisling snared his pullover near the collar with both hands and shoved him against the closed door. The impact seemed to echo inside. He looked at her as if unable to credit the strength she had just shown. The hard pressure of her hip bone against his groin held him in place.

"Yes, she is. And *m'athair* is an assassin and a smuggler and a pirate, Abban Finnegan!" she said fiercely. "I am my mother's daughter. I am my father's daughter. A part of both is in me, and in the end, I am me, I am who I am. And who are *you,* Finn?"

She released him and stepped back. He slumped against the door, but remained on his feet.

A lilt attached itself to her words. "Would y'be thinking I don't know you, then? Oh, aye, there is much about you that I do not know... yet. But it cannot change what I already know." She shoved her palm against his forehead, rocking his head back. "Who we are is in here," she said, and struck him hard in the center of his chest. "And in here. Not," and she swept both hands up and down in front of her body, "what you see here. This be the container, just. 'Tis the contents that interest me.

"And here is what I know. You came on your own, aye with Karan, to rescue me. Did you have to do that? No. Maybe you thought you might gain favor with me, I cannot deny that possibility, nor would I want to. But the task you were setting yourself was arduous and dangerous, possibly fatal, and still you did not back away, when you might have been safe. That, *that* is the kind of person you are. Were y'thinking I would not see?

When the time came, you were there for me and for Cloud. You were the one who found her still alive, and made ready to protect her. Herself, none but a stranger you knew *not*. I saw the tender way you carried her toward the 'skip, before Karan took her. I was aware of you beside me, ready to take my part if needed, while I dispatched that horrible Wanred. I was aware of you, Finn. I knew you were there beside me."

Finn shut his eyes. Aisling wondered if he might collapse. Her own breathing was rapid now, and shallow. Her heart fluttered, a frightened, caged bird. She started when he opened his eyes.

"You talk too much," he said.

Again she shoved him against the door, and pressed her mouth against his. The kiss took him by surprise, but he quickly surrendered to it. It was not a deep kiss, but she felt the tip of his tongue taste her lips. His arms found their way around her. She let him draw her to him. Her face felt hot, as if in direct sunlight. Hot and flushed.

Without warning, he gently pushed her away. "Sorry," he said, his face pink. "Sorry, it's... I'm... it's a natural response... I... Ash, you're young, you... I can't..."

Her smile gleamed. "I can," she said seriously. "And I know full well what I am saying. But yes, I am young. Will you wait?"

Finn's tone was that of a blood oath. "I will."

She tilted her head, her gaze speculative. "In five days, there will be an investment ceremony for Karan and myself," she told him. There was just a trace of official in her words. "I wish you to be there."

"I wouldn't miss it."

"But?"

"... yeah. Five days."

She knew what discouraged him. "Finn, we're going to win. Da will see to us."

She opened the door and pushed him back into the tavern.

* * *

"Do I get to know why?" asked Siobhan.

Yensen remained standing just outside the entrance to *Nicole's*. From that vantage point he had a clear field of fire. "Everyone hands on the table, empty. Teshko, finger and thumb by the butt, pick up that weapon and drop it on the patio."

Teshko did so. Neri looked at Siobhan, who shook her head minutely.

"I got two hundred thousand reasons why," sneered Yensen. "That, and a cleared record, and a job with Products Security as a sergeant. As a *sergeant*! No more brevets, no more menial tasks, no more bitches spoiling my fun. No more!"

Siobhan declined to justify her own actions regarding Yensen. Matters had gone too far for that, and in any case she had never had need for justification with the members of her team. The man had violated her instructions. She would have been well within her authority to brig him or, if in combat, to shoot him. For the moment she kept her hands flat on the table and glanced at Teshko. A glint in his eye disturbed her. She shook her head at him, but he appeared to ignore the order.

Siobhan flashed a cold, thin smile. "They have different standards."

"What?" Yensen stalked forward. "What did you say?"

Siobhan blew an exaggerated sigh. "Oh, just shoot me, you fat fuck, you and your petty little complaints. Oh, poor me!"

Yensen's jaw dropped. His eyes narrowed and his face turned crimson. He raised the Kellogg to aim at her head.

Teshko rose out of his chair to cover Siobhan.

"No!" she screamed at him.

The air around them turned purple.

Yensen fired. The blue beam reflected off the purple aura and struck Yensen in the center of his forehead. He collapsed, and rolled twice before flattening against the cobbles of the patio.

Teshko, who had spilled onto the cobbles, got up and inspected himself in disbelief for wounds.

The purple aura coalesced to Photem. "That's twice now, in three years," she told Siobhan. "One more, and it becomes a habit."

"I don't understand any of this," said Ocamla. "Who are you? What are you?"

"They think of me as a charm quark," answered Photem. "Siobhan, may I suggest?"

She waved her hand. "Please do."

"We don't have much time. They're almost here. Ovin's *Banshee* is just out back. Gather your team and board her. Ovin, I suggest—"

He stood up. "Already ahead of you."

"I have to get Una and Padraig," said Neri. "We'll meet you at the Dur Falls Inn."

"What about him?" asked Teshko.

Neri tokked her Palmetto. "Ling? Feed the fish, *mi'amica*. And... for this one you may need to borrow Nicole's forklift."

* * *

The *Emerall Ray* emerged from Track and immediately was ducked back into it. Blinking, Palmula could only stare at the empty Videx. Pagan, with the last of the pastrami sandwich still in her mouth, managed to communicate with Charon, the skipcomp.

The instruction was simple: "Charon, report."

"There is a Corporatia security galleon in orbit over the dark side of the planet."

"What's its status? No, wait. Charon, change computer designation to... Horatia."

"Changed."

"Status?"

"Horatia?" asked Palmula, one eyebrow raised. "You mean Macaulay?"

Pagan nodded.

"It is in communication with—"

The abrupt silence frightened Palmula. She wondered whether the 'skip had been damaged, and cast a worried glance at the console. "What happened to Horatia?"

Ayesha cleared her throat. *"The galleon in question is the* Ouidah, *of Corporatia Resources registry. At the present time it is in communication with another galleon of the same registry, which is still enTracked and is due to arrive in approximately one hour... the communication has now terminated. There are indications that three shuttles aboard the* Ouidah *are being readied for use.*"

Palmula made a tiny gesture to Pagan. A grin tickled the corners of her mouth. "*Eh voilà,*" she said. "I told you: a computer sprite."

"This," said Pagan, "is going to take some getting used to."

"That's an odd name for a ship," Palmula mused.

Ayesha said, didactically, "Ouidah *was located on the south coast of Africa, in what was the kingdom of Benin. It was the point of embarkation for over a million slaves, although perhaps only half of them survived the journey.*"

Pagan's face darkened, and her voice was taut. "Then the name is a slap in the face to the people of Vanadis," she said, with controlled anger. "They're going to load the inhabitants on it and take them to labor camps. Oh, we have to stop this, Pami. Ayesha."

Palmula found her voice in the same taut tone. "But how?"

"Don't know," Pagan said tersely, adding an ominous, "Yet."

"*May I be of assistance?*" asked Ayesha. "*I am a computer sprite, after all.*"

"What can you do?" asked Pagan.

"*For you, I'm sorry, but nothing. I obey only one person in the Universe, and that is Palmula Bell.*"

"Treat my sister as if she were me," Palmula instructed.

Ayesha inclined her head in acknowledgement. "*Still, I require instructions. I cannot destroy many physical objects. Solid light is still light. Perhaps I might stomp a bucket flat. But to repeat: I am a computer sprite. I am a part of the Galactic Net.*"

Pagan grimaced. "Yes, I get that. But how does that help our present situation?"

Ayesha grinned wickedly. "*I am a glitch.*"

* * *

"Surely we can wait one more hour," said Markey, on the bridge of the *Ouidah*. "We're beyond the range of detection of their four security satellites. They don't know we're here. Why go in at half-strength?"

Hands clasped behind him, Partagu did not turn around from the Videx, though there was nothing to see in it. "Very well. One hour." He turned to First Officer Trevi. "Signal the *Mother-of-Pearl* to begin preparations for debarkation upon arrival."

Trevi glowered her hatred at him, though he appeared oblivious to it. "Yes, sir," she grated, and proceeded to do so. Finished, she sat back and frowned at the console. "Ah..." she started, and shook her head.

Harsh impatience coarsened Partagu's voice. "Is there a problem?"

"I-I'm not sure that transmission was... was received. Sir," she added, as an after-thought.

"Send again, damn it!"

Under his hostile eyes, she did so. There came no reply of acknowledgement. "Maybe their system is down," she said, and did not add sir. "I think it went through, though."

"You think?"

She turned to him, eyes blazing up at his. "Yes, I think it went through," she said stiffly. She got to her feet. "Now if you will excuse me, I need to visit the head." Without awaiting permission, she stormed off.

Partagu yelled after her. "I thought there had to be an officer on the bridge of an enTracked vessel."

"Apparently not anymore," she snarled back, a veiled reminder that he had forced her to violate the rule earlier. "And we're no longer in Track."

020

Silence greeted Aisling and Finn when they came back inside the tavern. Climbing over the backs of the benches, they returned to their seats. Eyes regarded them expectantly while Mikal went to the bar and returned with a tumbler and a mug and handed them to Aisling and Finn. Karan surprised them by making no remark whatsoever this time.

Aisling took a sip, and coughed, once. "No water, then?" she asked Mikal.

"You can add some of mine," Cloud offered.

"Thank you, no." She looked around the booth. "What?"

At first no one spoke. Yhounda said, "Perhaps we should talk later, Aisling Yhonyn."

She ducked her head in deference. "Yes, *a mháthair*." It pleased her that Finn had not proposed any explanation as to what had just transpired. She smiled at him, and took another sip.

Mikal's Palmetto sounded. He glanced at the monitor, excused himself, and went to his office next to the storeroom under the stairs. Silence resumed its reign in the booth, as did anxiety. No one doubted that the communication related to the invasion. Deyrdra and Aisling fiddled with their drinks. Cloud, innocent of the current situation, merely wore a blank look. Karan slipped an arm around her shoulders, tentatively, as if anticipating rejection. Only Yhounda Khouse appeared outwardly unconcerned And nobody spoke.

When Mikal returned two minutes later, his expression was grim. After an exaggerated effort to make himself comfortable on the chair, he said, simply, "It's on."

Cloud and Karan looked at him, uncertain. The others already knew.

"Siobhan and her team are headed here in the *Offa's Dike*," he told them. "Curi is bringing Ovin, Una, and Padraig in her *Just-Like-Me*. The *Banshee* is already docked outside." Slowly his gaze took in each person in the booth individually. He lowered his voice. "So we can, if we want, get away."

Stunned tension greeted the possibility of escape. Aisling's voice broke in like a beacon in a dark tunnel. "Wash your mouth out, Uncle Mikal," she said.

"Should I go get the soap?" asked Karan.

"I'm thinking it was her way of saying we'll be staying to fight," Deyrdra said to him. She cocked an ear. "I think they're here."

The tavern door opened. Siobhan and her team strode inside, followed by Neri and her passengers. While Siobhan ushered her team to a table nearby, Mikal dragged a table and two benches to abut the booth, and brought mugs and a pitcher of water, but no more alcohol. Deyrdra served Siobhan's team in similar fashion.

Aisling closed her eyes. The Council of War had begun. Her day of investment was still five days into the future. By Mulaine tradition, she was not yet an adult. She was even further from that point by Irish tradition. But she and the others had not been asked to leave the booth. Therefore, her voice would be heard.

When she opened her eyes again, she saw that her father had nudged Finn aside a little, and was now seated directly across the table from her. She also saw that the others at the booth and table were looking to him. Even as she watched, the charm quark known as Photem joined them, forming her own chair at the table.

Shannen reached across the table and took Aisling's fresh tumbler, availing himself of a sip. His sea-green eyes betrayed amusement as he regarded her for a moment, before returning the drink. He gave a little nod, mostly to himself.

"I think the decision has been made to stand and fight," he said. "Someone somewhere once said, 'Never tell me the odds,' so I'm going to ignore them. We're going to be facing about two hundred mercenaries. Once they land, we'll have to resort to guerrilla tactics. A lot of people will be killed, especially in Dongbei and

Havenport. I'm going to guess their primary targets will be... us. Roughly speaking, we're the main threat to them, and I think they know that. Their objective will be to kill us and Swoop the others. I think they'll come for us first."

"Agreed," said Mikal.

"On the other hand," Shannen continued, "if we can get at them in the air or in space, we might have a chance to stop them."

"How?" asked Aisling.

"Two of the available 'skips—the *Offa's Dike* and the *Just-Like-Me*—are equipped with what are mistakenly referred to as laser cannons. They are of course no such thing. But they do fire a blue beam a distance of," he glanced at Mikal, "two thousand meters?"

"More like three," he replied. "At least, for Curi's. I, ah, added a couple features when I installed it."

"They won't do a lot of damage," Shannen continued. "We probably can't kill a galleon with them—but we might take out a shuttle or two, perhaps more, before they can get down. Mikal?"

The big man flashed a dry smile. "It's not like any battle we've fought before, old friend. What you propose might work, but I don't know that it would stop the invasion."

Shannen grimaced. "No, I suppose not. But I'd rather fight out there than down here."

"What about Photem?" asked Aisling.

He shook his head sadly. "There's not enough of her energy here to envelop and protect the planet."

"But—"

"If I could, I would," added Photem. "Even so, I will try. But the attempt is certain to fail."

"But the planet is not the problem," said Aisling, rushing her words now to get them out. "The carrier is the problem. Or carriers. Vanadis does not have to be protected. It's the carriers that have to be stopped."

Shannen blew a shocked sigh. "Out of the mouths of babes..."

"Can you get aboard their carrier?" Aisling asked Photem. "Can you, I don't know, interfere with their navigation, or internal sensors, or systems?"

The booth and table fell silent. Mikal's words gradually filtered in, like a breeze on a still day. "Tomorrow you'll see me with a sloped forehead, where I've been bashing it against the wall, wondering why *I* didn't think of that."

Photem was now diaphanous. Her voice reached them as if from the bottom of a well. "There are two galleons above Vanadis, on the dark side. They are too far away to be detected by SECSATs. But they are about to move closer."

Neri shot to her feet. "Una?"

"Coming."

"You can't, *mo dheirfiúr*," said Siobhan, also rising. She turned around and beckoned to Kam Dimiter. Sergeant Teshko came with her. She cocked an eyebrow at him as he approached.

"Not you, Sergeant."

"With respect, sir. May I speak freely?"

"Make it fast."

He looked as if he had not expected to be granted permission, and fumbled for the first words. "Sir, I... begging your pardon, sir, but you give orders and we follow them. You're needed here with the rest of the team. It's my job to protect you, it's..." He paused for breath and decided he had said all he wanted to say. His eyes met hers evenly.

"Take the *Offa's Dike*, and go," she ordered. "Report progress," she called, as they rushed outside.

Neri and Una followed too quickly for Shannen to stop them. He might have caught Una up, but a hard look from Mikal stopped him. He spread his hands. "What, Mikal?"

"We take the *Banshee*," he said.

Shannen grinned. "Reading my mind again?"

"Then I'm coming," said Aisling.

"The hell you are."

"Da," she said evenly. "The hell I am."

"Myself as well," said Finn.

"And me," Karan threw in.

Cloud clutched his arm. "No," she begged.

"I have to," he replied.

Shannen rolled his eyes, clearly unprepared for this turn of events. Without a word he got up and headed for the door, unwilling to argue. Like ducklings, the children followed him, Mikal bringing up the rear.

Siobhan watched them leave. A wistful look came over her face, but her words were firm and strong. "If they get this far, they'll hit the buildings first. There are some caves in the cliffs down by the promontory. We should be safe enough there, but we have to go now. Deyrdra, gather up the children."

"I'll need help," she said. "There's the school to consider. And I'll raise Sasha and Bara."

Siobhan called back. "Both Tomascos and Sergeant Tallgrass," she said. "Help her however she says."

She paused for breath. Maybe it was hopeless, the odds impossible. A line from *Horatius* occurred to her. *Now who will stand on either hand/ and keep the bridge with me.* Because this was what it was all about. She began to sense the greater conflict as her twin had always seen it. The oppressors—be they government, corporation, or society—never left people alone for too long. They always felt the need to tell others what to do.

She nodded to herself: it was time for her to make her own stand. For you, *mo dheartháir. Mo ghra.*

"Let's go," she said.

021

"*They have detected us,*" announced Ayesha, after the *Emerall Ray* deTracked back to real-time. "*There are now two galleons. And three spaceskips have arrived from the surface. They are the...* Offa's Dike *and the* Just-Like-Me. *The former is of Corporatia Security registry, the latter belongs to Curielle Neri. Each appears to be armed with a single laser cannon. The third is the* Banshee, *registry Ovin Shannen. It is not weaponized.*"

"It's on," Palmula said grimly. "And they haven't a chance, not against those galleons."

"*The galleons are not weaponized.*"

"But they are too big to bring down," said Pagan. "All right, Ayesha, what can you do?"

The sprite grinned. "*Watch.*"

* * *

"Cymri!" yelled Kam Dimiter, at the *Offa's Dike* computer. "Sensor readings!"

Beside her, Teshko muttered, "Damn things are *big.*"

"We're just small, Sergeant."

"Mighty gnats, sir."

"*The* Ouidah *carries a crew of eight, plus eighty-nine passengers and three shuttles. One of the shuttles is about to depart. It is armed. The* Mother-of-Pearl *carries a crew of eight, plus one hundred passengers and three shuttles.*"

"We have to draw within two kilometers of that shuttle for our laser cannon to be effective," said Dimiter, enabling manual control of the *Offa's Dike*. "Even so, I don't know how much damage we can do. The beam will simply pass through one side and out the other. Autoseal will prevent air loss."

"We might hit something vital, sir," Teshko pointed out. "The pilot, for example..."

She looked up at him from her captain's chair as his voice faded away. "What is it, Sergeant?"

"Tam, sir. It saves syllables." He stared down at the console monitor that showed relative positioning. "It looks... it looks like the *Ouidah* is drifting."

"Loss of power?"

"Not according to sensors." He sat back down. "The *Ouidah* just launched the shuttle."

"Let's go get them."

* * *

At the console of the *Banshee*, Shannen swore. "I got caught up in the moment, Mikal. I should have told them in no uncertain terms to stay."

"It's done. Ah... the *Ouidah* is about to launch another shuttle. It's... damn! If it holds to that course, it will soon be right on the *Offa's* tail."

"Kam sees it."

"If she does, she's ignoring it."

"Better sit down, old friend. We're going in."

"We're unarmed," Mikal pointed out, unnecessarily.

"Yeah. Ever try to bat at a mosquito?"

"Not one armed with a laser cannon."

* * *

The mottled black and blue spaceskip headed straight for the *Mother-of-Pearl*. "Cannon on," said Neri, to Una. "Ready?"

"If we go in too fast, we can't pull away in time," Una said calmly, though she was nothing of the sort. She had tracking and aiming on to fire at the bridge, and was waiting for a solution. Between the motion of the *Just-Like-Me* and the drifting of the galleon, the solution kept changing. A frown wrinkled her pale eyebrows. "What's she doing?"

Neri adjusted course. "Cross-wind?"

Una laughed, and stopped laughing. "Ten k's, Curi."

"I can see that—"

"Break off, Curi! Now!"

* * *

"Sir, they can't do anything to us," Captain Jurengan of the *Ouidah* shouted. "Now let us do our jobs!"

Partagu turned from the Videx to snarl at him, then thought better of it.

"Just sit down, sir," Jurengan said, calmer. "Sit down and let us figure out what's wrong."

The galleon rocked with an impact. Markey cried out. Partagu shot back to his feet.

"I-I don't know, Captain," said First Officer Tertia Trevi. "The bay door was open for the third shuttle to depart... and then it just... it just closed." She shot a worried look at Jurengan, hoping for his experience to tell her what to do.

"Stupid bitch," muttered Partagu. "Captain, get that third shuttle gone, or it's your ass. You hear me?"

Jurengan did not bother to answer.

* * *

"Isn't that...?" said Mikal, pointing to the relative positioning on the *Banshee*'s monitor.

Shannen could give it no more than a cursory glance. "The *Emerall Ray*," he said. "Hello, Vanth. Glad you could make it."

A blue beam shot past them, four hundred meters off the *Banshee*'s starboard bow. Immediately Shannen turned the 'skip in that direction. Zigging when expected to zag threw the shuttle's aim off, and the next beam was a kilometer off to port. The shuttle broke off from its pursuit of *Offa's Dike*, and turned toward them.

"Now you've gotten his attention," said Mikal.

"At least he's off Kam's tail."

"And after us."

Shannen swung the 'skip toward the *Mother-of-Pearl*. "Not for long."

* * *

Una was staring through the Videx at the *Mother-of-Pearl*. The light around it seemed to fluctuate in intensity, like an uncertain aura. What riveted her attention was the color purple.

"Ovin's in trouble," said Neri, her voice taut. She swung the *Just-Like-Me* in as tight an arc as possible, hoping the g-force compensator would hold. Ahead, the enemy shuttle was firing at a fleeing *Banshee*.

Una's voice shook. "Curi?"

"Soon as we're in range, *mia gaelica*." Then: "Bloody hell! Where's he going?"

* * *

"There's someone else in here," said Ayesha.

Stunned, Pagan Bell could only gape at the computer sprite. Palmula said, "Another one like you?"

"No, no, nothing like me. But like me. Intrusive. I-I don't understand..."

Ayesha's confusion almost made Pagan order Horatia to enTrack the *Emerall Ray*. It did not seem possible to her that one could force a quandary onto a computer, yet here, clearly, something was amiss. Pagan did not know what to ask—or, more precisely, what to suggest to Palmula to ask.

"Where are you?" Palmula asked Ayesha.

"I am inside the Mother-of-Pearl. *And I am not alone."*

"Pagan... I'm scared."

* * *

On manual control, Shannen steered to a course to approach the three spacecraft from their port flank. The first shuttle from the *Ouidah* was now four hundred kilometers from Vanadis's upper atmosphere, and closing. The *Offa's Dike* was still in pursuit, and drawing within the effective range of its laser cannon. The second shuttle had broken off the engagement with the *Offa's Dike* and was now veering to confront the *Banshee*, forcing Shannen to alter course. He had been about to send the 'skip on a pass off the bow of the shuttle in an effort to pry them loose from their pursuit. Now that was no longer necessary.

"A hit!" shouted Mikal, as a blue beam from the *Offa's Dike* scored the stern of the shuttle.

"Settle down," said Shannen.

"Yeah. Sorry, Cap'n. I wonder who fired it. Er, Ovin... you do know we're headed straight for that galleon."

He nodded. "That's one reason why I'm on manual. Otherwise, Maire would pull us up."

And the voice from behind him was the one he did not want to hear. "Da? What's going on?"

* * *

"*Purple,*" said Ayesha. "*I am disengaging from the* Mother-of-Pearl *and returning to the* Ouidah.*"

Pagan blinked. "Purple what? Pami?"

Palmula's expression showed only puzzlement. In exasperation she spread her hands. But Ayesha merely shook her head, and Palmula did not interfere.

* * *

The report was intended for Captain Jurengan, but Partagu shoved him aside. "You can tell *me*," he demanded of the face in the intercom monitor. "This is *my* operation."

"Yes, sir," stammered the crewman. Dark eyes stood out against his face made pale by fear. "They're all dead, sir. The bay door—"

"*What happened?*"

"He's trying to tell you, goddamn it!" yelled Jurengan.

Partagu pulled out a Blue Sizzler and shot him. At her chair, First Officer Tertia Trevi seemed to come to a decision.

"... door closed just before they exited," the crewman continued, now running his words together. "Closed and sealed. The impact ruptured the shuttle hull, near as we can figure. Then the door opened again. They lost their air. They died. That's what happened, *sir.*" He closed commo before Partagu could reply.

Partagu turned a florid, raging face to Erron Markey, who was staring at the body of the captain on the deck, and looked as if he were wondering whether he would be next.

"How is that *possible?*" Partagu snarled.

Markey found himself at a loss for words. "Ah... I-I... computer glitch, sir?"

"Bah!" Partagu turned away.

In the relative positioning monitor that displayed the progress of the conflict, the first shuttle received another blue beam and exploded. Partagu's face went slack, and the color drained from his face.

"Sir?" said Markey.

Partagu whirled on him, murder in his eyes.

Markey retreated. "We're heading for her, sir."

"What?" The statement gave him pause. "We're what?"

"The *Mother-of-Pearl*, sir. We're making directly for her. Collision imminent."

* * *

"Get back in the cargo bay, Aisling," Shannen ordered.

The *Ouidah* was looming ahead, and the shuttle was in hot pursuit behind them. He wanted to strangle himself. He should never have allowed the children on board, not for this. He forced himself to concentrate. Now the shuttle was actually overtaking them. He veered to starboard, but gained little separation. The shuttle was on the verge of firing her cannon. Evidently the pilot was ignoring his proximity to the galleon. Shannen continued to veer, and swore in Irish and in Standard. In the Videx he could see Aisling's reflection.

"Ovin, this is bad," said Mikal.

"I know!" Shannen yelled.

"No, you're not seeing it. The other galleon... *yobanaya mat!*"

* * *

Palmula studied the relative positioning display. One shuttle was gone, courtesy of fire control aboard the *Offa's Dike*, but what glued her interest to the monitor was the course of the *Ouidah*. She glanced up at Ayesha.

"Nice one," she said to the sprite.

Ayesha looked puzzled. "I'm not doing anything."

"Then... then... all right, what's going on?"

* * *

The new course took the *Banshee* away from the *Ouidah*. But the shuttle was the danger now. He had hoped to run it into the galleon, and he still might have done. But fire from the laser cannon was now imminent. He had no choice.

He swarmed out of the captain's chair and knocked Aisling down, just as the blue beam pierced the Videx and exited through the starboard bulkhead. He felt as if a hot smithy's poker had been thrust through him.

Aisling screamed. Mikal dropped to his knees on the deck.

None saw the impact of the shuttle into the galleon. None saw the two galleons collide.

The only sound on the bridge of the *Banshee* was Aisling's coarse gasps of breath through a raw windpipe.

* * *

Both galleons exploded. There was no sound whatsoever, only a fireburst that soon faded. Pagan Bell scarcely saw it. On her mind was the blue beam that had transfixed the *Banshee*.

* * *

On the bridge of the *Just-Like-Me*, Curielle Neri was unable to focus on piloting the 'skip. Both her hands and her heart were clenched into fists. She was so rigid that a tearful Una had to pry her from the chair and sit down herself to take control.

* * *

Tertia Trevi was blinking rapidly. For a few moments she had imagined herself within a great violet cocoon, like some vast butterfly about to emerge. She did not have to wrest her way out, however. Instead, almost unceremoniously, she was dumped onto the deck on the bridge of the *Offa's Dike*.

She was still blinking when she got clumsily to her feet, before a bald woman and a dark-haired man at the controls, and a purple female by her side, steadying her.

"What?" she managed, and had a coughing spasm.

"Happened?" asked the purple woman. "You crashed the galleons together. They're gone. I took you out just before the collision bec—"

Mouth agape, Trevi twisted to face her. "Who... what *are* you?"

"I am Photem. Think of me as a charm quark. The others do." Her face saddened. "I couldn't save him," she murmured.

"Who?" asked Trevi. "That monster Partagu?"

But Photem shook her head, and closed her eyes.

* * *

Everyone tried to communicate at once with the *Banshee*. "Hold them!" Mikal yelled to Maire the 'skipcomp, and promptly dismissed them from his mind. "Karan, you'd better get up here!" he called aft, and knelt down beside Shannen.

Aisling had his head cradled in her lap. Her eyes were fountains. His were closed. There were black circles as big as a spread hand on either side of his jersey, right at the floating ribs. Mikal put fingers to Shannen's neck and found an intermittent pulse. It was barely there.

Running footsteps in the gangway announced the arrival of Karan Syan, with Finn and Cloud following up. "What happened?" cried Karan, joining his twin sister, but Mikal shushed him.

"Da," whispered Aisling, through trembling lips. "*Tá brón orm.*"

His tongue touched his lips. "Not... your fault."

He reached out with a shaky arm and put his hand to her cheek, and then to Karan's cheek.

And he was gone.

022

Pounding kept Aisling from sleeping. On the bed she drifted, struggling without success to tune out the sounds. Just inland from the base of the promontory, a hundred meters away, they were setting up the dais for tomorrow. She wondered whether the pounding in her head would continue after the dais was finished.

She was sprawled on her father's bed. No one had even thought to question her right to take up occupancy of the cottage. Once again her nose sought the scent of him in the pillow and in the sheets, and in the quilt that Deyrdra had made for him, and once again she found nothing. Una had kept the place laundered and clean for him, for whenever he returned. That day would no longer come. She wondered whether the momentum of love would continue to bring Una to the cottage. Not that it mattered. She, Aisling Yhonyn Khouse Shannen, would see to it. That, too, was her right.

The pounding stopped for a moment. A high-pitched whine ascended, and hardened, as someone started up a power saw and began to cut a plank. The task finished quickly, and peace was restored briefly to the south coast of Haven. The pounding resumed; at least it was no longer in her head.

She kissed the pillow and sat up at the edge of the bed, her feet on the simple pine floor. Hunched over, she counted her toes, and decided to paint the nails green for the investment. Not that it mattered, for her slippers would conceal them.

A knock at the door. She left it unanswered, just as she had left unanswered the knocks of the previous three days. As before, the door snicked shut; she had not heard it open. Finn trod softly across the carpet to the bedroom. He would not dare enter, even if bidden. She knew he was standing just on the other side of the door, waiting, knowing she was within and aware of him. A deliberate effort pulled her to her feet; after that, movement was easier. She opened the door and stepped from the bedroom, and shut the door behind her.

His smile of greeting flickered and went out. He handed her a blue wildflower. She accepted it, sniffed at it, and tucked the stem into the pocket of her green jersey. The two colors clashed. She did not care.

He preceded her into the front room and to the sofa there, and sat down at one end, knowing she would take up the other. Instead, she surprised him, patting the cushion beside her. Slowly he moved into position, hesitant and even reluctant. He said nothing. He was not one of those who would know what to say.

He was there, within arm's reach of her. That was enough.

The pounding stopped.

At length she said, bravely, her voice feeble yet firm, "He is not here. I looked for him. I-I smelled the air. He left a dirty dish in the sink. Something fried. I washed it and dried it and put it away. He is not here, Finn."

He turned toward her on the sofa, closing the distance between them by half. His hand went out to her chest, between the upper swells of her girl's breasts, and then to her forehead, and she knew what he was going to say before he said it. Her own words to him, the other day, before she kissed him. He might have seen the anticipation of similar words in her eyes, for he said nothing at all.

Gravely she inclined her head. "Yes. I understand."

"But it doesn't help."

She found a brief smile for him. "Maybe a little," she said, and turned her gaze to the window and the horizon. Her violet eyes took on a million-kilometer look. A touch at the back of her hand. His had found hers. She took it and clung to it, a bird on a branch in a breeze.

Another knock at her door broke Aisling from her formless reverie. Three soft raps. She bade the visitor enter. Her eyes brightened, just a little. "*A mháthair*," she said, an acknowledgement and a greeting.

Yhounda Khouse entered solemnly, as if she had no intention of disturbing whatever mood had been set. A nod that was more than perfunctory, almost of approval, went to Finn. She sat down in the stuffed chair at Aisling's wave of invitation.

"I've finished your investment gown," said Yhounda. "Tomorrow will you dress at home?"

Aisling just looked at her.

"Yes, of course," said Yhounda. "Quite right. I meant your other home."

"I think here, Mom."

She smiled. "That's better. It's much like mine was, except I've added two string straps."

Aisling kept a straight face. "That's probably wise." Finn gave her hand a tiny squeeze. She almost smiled. "Karan Syan?" she asked.

"He chose a blue tunic and trousers," answered her mother. "Almost military, but not quite. He wants to be subdued at the ceremony."

Aisling shook her head. "He is my twin brother. We are both to be honored. I told him that."

"And that is why he decided to add a cloak."

Aisling laughed. And laughed more softly. And her face reddened and contorted in agony, and she burst into tears. Immediately Finn's arms wrapped her, and her forehead thudded against his shoulder again and again with her sobbed grief. Yhounda Khouse knelt before the sofa and enveloped both of them. Tears flowed inexorably, and Finn's pullover was soon sodden. He held her all the closer. From time to time Aisling wailed, and each time this sparked a fresh flow of pain and tears.

The storm continued unabated. Her eyes began to sting, and she savored the pain. Finn held her tighter, protecting her, but he could not protect her from this. He could only hold her. Her mother could only hold her. Her leaking eyes were closed. It was dark inside. It felt as if it would always be dark inside. There was but one sound in the room, of her grief flooding into the Universe. Finn's lips touch her hair, just above her left ear. Her mother's cheek pressed against her forehead. But there was only one sound.

...until finally she was exhausted, her heart and body spent, and she slumped against Finn. She barely heard him speak. His voice trembled. "Would you bring a glass of water?" he asked Yhounda.

"Of course," she said, and did, one for each of them.

Silence fell into a steady reign afterwards. No more was said, and there was nothing more to say. Other plans had already been set. The sun only needed to rise one more time.

Toward dusk, Yhounda took her leave of them. The interior of the cottage darkened. Gradually Finn released Aisling.

"Would you like me to stay with you tonight?" he asked.

And he was a straw to cling to, to keep from drowning.

023

The Day of Investment began with Finn preparing breakfast in the cottage kitchen. After burning almost everything, he apologized profusely, opened the windows to let the smoke clear, cleaned the kitchen as best he could, and went off to his room in the tavern to dress for the occasion.

She got up and went out to the patio for a breath of non-smoky air. In a front corner of the patio wall, Ocamla was huddled up on the stone deck and just awakening. The Motic female sputtered at seeing her, and sat up.

"I am sorry, Milady," she said. "I did not mean to offend you."

The girl dropped to one knee beside her, and put a hand on her arm. Though the morning was warm, Ocamla's blue skin was chilled. "What are you doing out here?" Aisling asked her.

"I came to get my clothes from the room, after you were up," she replied.

"But... why?"

"Milady, I have no wish to interfere."

Mildly puzzled, she sat back on her heels. "Interfere? My father gave you that room to live in, did he not? How could his daughter in good conscience deny you that?"

"But... I told him I would work for him. He is not... not..."

She sighed patiently, and rose, pulling Ocamla to her feet. "But I *am* here. What would you have done for him?"

The Motic looked around the patio. "I tend the plants, Milady, I... whatever he needs me to do."

"Milady Ocamla," she said gently, "I need the same things. And I should have a Lady-in-Waiting. When you and I are in formal settings, Milady is proper to both of us. Between you and me, however, let us agree on our names... Ocamla. I am Aisling. I recall you at the compound, firing your weapon to protect me and... and the others. How could I not want you around? Will you be my Lady-in-Waiting?"

"I will."

"Then come inside. My mother will be here soon. You may help me to dress. I am not familiar with gowns."

* * *

There had been no prescribed or traditional size for the dais, only that it be of sufficient size to accommodate the royal family of Mulane—and now of Vanadis. As on this occasion that family consisted of but three individuals, Mikal Trov and others had assembled a dais some four meters square, of clean pale wood raw from the lumber yard in Havenport. In the center of the platform stood a simple arbor, an archway of slatted wood, interwoven with strips of forest green cloth. The structure made a statement, that the individuals to be honored were more important than the structure itself.

Aisling Yhonyn Khouse Shannen thought this was as it should be. She glanced up at the clear sky, knowing he would be watching.

From behind the arbor she gazed upon the attendees. All were standing, in no particular arrangement; the lack of chairs removed any possible priority or rank. There was Curielle Neri, grimmer than usual, and decked out in her customary blue and black, ready for war. Una had chosen a severe white ankle-length gown for the occasion, while Deyrdra matched this in blue. Mikal Trov, his face hard and sad, was wearing black trousers but a green shirt. Siobhan and her team all were dressed in camouflage fatigues, having brought little other clothing with them. Sasha Parry and Bara Jansdottir eschewed medical whites in favor of green outsuits. Ever-faithful Sergeant Yenther Bek was present in the dark gray uniform he had been wearing on the day Mulane had been destroyed. Aisling spotted Ocamla, looking nervous and uncertain in a floral print long dress that went well with her pale blue skin, and speaking with Photem, who was in her usual purple. To one side, as if trying to fit in although they were totally welcome, stood Pagan and Palmula Bell, demure in beige blouses and sepia slacks that complimented their dark complexion, and Ayesha, who had arrived dressed like the Bells but then had altered her clothing to match Una's gown, but hers yellow, as if she were uncertain which attire would be more appropriate. Representing the Chinese enclave of Dongbei in northeast Haven was Threnody Xu, one of some four hundred slaves rescued by Shannen from a slave ship. A woman who during the battle for Vanadis had driven one of the corporate galleons into the other— Aisling was unable to recall her name—was also present. And directly in front of the dais stood Finn and Cloud, he in a dark blue outsuit that looked borrowed, she in a pink gown of design similar to her own, and evidently assembled by Yhounda, who had more or less adopted the girl.

We are all of us in new territory, thought Aisling.

Beside her stood Karan Syan, clothed as advertised, and looking uncomfortable and hot in the overhead sun. She thought he was probably wishing he had opted out of the cloak. Behind them, Yhounda Khouse, in a turquoise outsuit, oversaw everything like a mother bear watching her cubs grow up.

Aisling's gown reached her ankles, a simple shift of gossamer and gauze in a multitude of shades of green, some as pale as her skin and others as dark as myrtle, and held in place by a wide belt of black elastic around her slender waist. She had decided not to paint her nails, and to leave loose her long black hair, but she had looped a quoil around her hips. It was, as she thought, her.

Everyone's garb included a black cincture of some kind, and everyone knew what it signified. But this was the twins' Investment Day, a festive day. Afterwards, they would repair to the *Dur Falls Inn*, where the buffet was already laid out. It seemed likely there would be an Irish wake, accompanied by tears and laughter.

For all its gaiety, the investment ceremony itself passed quickly. Yhounda Khouse stepped forth to within a pace or two of the front edge of the dais and announced herself. On this day, she told the attendees, her children—and she referred to them by their full names— turned thirteen and were adults, officially in the line of succession to the title of Mulane and therefore of

Vanadis. Karan Syan was the first to be summoned forth. His face flickered, as if he did not quite know what to say or do. He gave them a little bow, found a smile and bestowed it upon Cloud, and moved to one side.

"Aisling Yhonyn Khouse Shannen," Yhounda intoned. "By established custom on Mulane, she is my first successor. May it be so on Vanadis."

By design there was no applause. Neither did Aisling bow or curtsey. Instead she stood straight and tall while her mother moved off to Karan's side. She was about to speak when Curielle Neri swore venomously.

Aisling gave her no expression at all, but merely asked, "Is there a difficulty, Milady Curielle?"

Uncharacteristically, Neri hesitated to respond. A moment passed without further dark language. She said, "It is Giulo Conigli, Chair of Corporatia Resources. He requests downdock instructions. He asks to speak with," and her voice hushed to a whisper that no one heard.

A murmur arose from the attendees. Siobhan's eyes had lost all trace of sea-green and were now murderously gray. Neri's blues were almost black.

"We will see him now," Aisling announced, and stilled the murmur. "Direct him to a spot a hundred meters west of here, and advise him that he is enjoined to emerge alone. Sergeant-at-Arms."

Mikal started to step forward, but it was Yenther Bek who responded. "Yes, Milady?"

"When that ship docks, shoot anyone else who emerges. No questions asked."

"Yes, Milady," he replied, and moved toward the site, an ergorifle at port.

Her eyes went to Yhounda Khouse, whose smile and nod were barely perceptible. Inwardly Aisling relaxed a little, encouraged. Her mother had always said it was important to do certain things properly when the proper time came to do them. At the time of those words, they were too general for meaning. Now, in this moment, they took form and bolstered her resolve.

A shuttle docked at the appointed spot, and a large, almost burly man emerged. Escorted by Bek, he soon came into focus as he approached. He was dressed for travel in a pale tan outsuit, and his dark hair had been trimmed and groomed recently. He slowed as he drew near, his dark eyes sweeping the attendees, none of whom reacted in any way to his arrival. Bek's nudge turned him toward the dais.

"I was looking for Ovin Shannen," he said.

The platform was a mere step above the grass, and brought Aisling up to Conigli's height. Even so, she seemed to tower over him, her face serene, and glowing in the sunlight, arms at her sides as if she had no need for gestures.

"My father was killed defending this world from the corporate attack five days ago," she said evenly.

"I'm... sorry to hear that."

Aisling regarded him as one might regard a blemish on a ceramic piece: something to be picked at until it disappeared. Withholding expression from her face helped to mask her inner fury. She waited to speak until Conigli appeared on the verge of breaking into the awkward silence.

"You may address us as Milady," she said, "and you may present us with your concerns."

Conigli looked at Yhounda, whose face told him nothing. A glance over his shoulder caught Siobhan, whom he had met years ago in another regard. She had hard eyes for him, but he seemed not to grasp that.

He turned back to Aisling. "Who exactly are you... Milady?"

She made neither gesture nor sound of exasperation, and kept her tone civil. "We are Aisling Yhonyn Khouse Shannen, for this day of our investment the Princess of Vanadis. As you have interrupted us with your visit, perhaps you will be good enough at this time to present your questions."

Conigli frowned. Clearly he was unprepared for the eventuality which greeted him. "I was made aware of the battle, though not the full outcome," he said. "I came here in person as a gesture of good faith, to assure... ah, your father that Corporatia Resources had nothing to do with this attack, despite the registry of the galleons in question. Nor were we able to intervene in a timely fashion. I would have asked... I would ask that you withhold your response until we have had an opportunity to negotiate."

The lightest touch of hauteur entered her expression. "Is that all?"

"Ah... yes." He looked around at the others, as if hoping for some sort of intervention, then back to her. "Yes, ah... Milady."

"*M'sieur* Conigli, you may rest assured that our response to this unprovoked corporate attack will be both measured and direct. You may now leave us. Sergeant-at-Arms."

Again Bek stepped forward. "At your service, Milady."

"Escort our visitor back to his craft, if you please. See to it that he departs immediately."

Bek nudged Conigli with the ergorifle. "Yes, Milady."

She waited until the two were out of hearing distance before she emitted a great sigh and allowed her shoulders to slump just a little. For a long time she closed her eyes. Around her she heard the sounds of breathing, but none of words. However this moment went, they were granting it to her, for as long as she needed it. She stood with arms still at her sides, loose and relaxed. Inside, she heard her name spoken with his voice. It was enough to see her through.

She opened her eyes. The shuttle had departed. Bek had returned.

"Our invest..." For the first time, her voice faltered. She licked her lips. "My investment, with that of my twin, Karan Syan Khouse Shannen, is your event as well. It is, then, our event. In a moment we shall move to the tavern to complete this day. Before we do that, does anyone have something to say that would best be said here, rather than there?"

Mikal took a step forward. "Milady," was all he said. He said it in the tone of acknowledging a title.

For just a moment, only a hush followed the word. Then, as if with one voice, the word followed from everyone, from all of them. The spontaneous acclamation made her feel faint. She thought she must have swayed, because suddenly Finn was there beside her on the dais, steadying her. She refocused, lips slightly parted, barely breathing.

Photem approached the dais. "I... have something," she said deferentially.

Aisling smiled. "And what is it?"

"I am now complete."

Now she frowned. "I'm not sure I understand that."

"You will recall that only a small part of me remained here, to watch over Siobhan," Photem explained. "At my request, the rest of me has returned. My... people have assigned me to remain here. I am now able to fully protect your world. It has gained favor with them."

"Our world," Aisling amended.

"Yes. Our world."

"Thank you," she breathed, and looked out at the others. "Anyone else? No? Then let us to the tavern. Please excuse me: I wish to walk for a little while. I shall join you presently."

While the others dispersed, she took Finn's hand and led him toward the promontory that jutted out into the ocean. Taking their time, they made their way onto the neck of sand and grass that took them out to the crest that overlooked the waves. There they stood, gazing at a great rock a couple hundred meters distant, while sea spray misted the air before them, and a light breeze sculpted diaphanous fabric around her legs and blew her hair over her bare shoulders.

She raised an arm and pointed. "Carrickdove. It means 'Black Rock.'"

"How many languages do you speak?" Finn asked.

"I don't know. Ten or so. Finn?"

"Yes?"

She shook her head as one bewildered. "I-I..."

"Yeah. Me, too. A bit lost, I think." He, too, pointed. "But Ash, do you see that?"

She nodded.

His sweeping arm indicated the horizon, as far as they could see. "All that, that's tomorrow."

"It's where the sky meets the sea," she said.

"And we continue ever toward it, don't we?"

For long seconds she did not respond. "Things are changing," she sighed.

"Such as?"

"Aunt Siobhan," she began, and chuckled at the honorific. "Siobhan, that is, said she wanted to remain on Vanadis. So does her task force. They're done with corporate security work. They've had enough. The team will live in Havenport, and augment Curielle's security network as well as freelance elsewhere, but she would like a cottage down here on the coast."

"Is that a problem?"

"No. Oh, no, not at all. And the Bells and Ayesha—I think Ayesha is taking the name Bell, too—have asked to be allowed to stay. I think Pagan would like to open a restaurant."

Finn coughed. "Um... is that a good idea?"

"Oh, she says she's a very good cook, and as long as no one brings up her past activities, she should do quite..." Her voice trailed off, and she hung her head. Her upper incisors pressed her lower lip.

He turned to her, suddenly worried. "Ash?"

"The past," she whispered. "I can forget it if I look at the horizon. And I want to look at the horizon. To see tomorrow coming. But I don't want to forget the past."

"You don't have to," he told her. "You keep it with you. It's yours."

"Yes."

"I told you. You keep him here," he said, and touched her forehead. "And here," he said, and touched her chest.

"*I gconai.* Always."

They stood in silence for a while longer, and turned to make their way toward the tavern.

"Finn?" she said, as they reached the mainland.

"Still here."

"Yeah." She took his hand and pressed it against her chest, and released it. "If you touch me there again, you'll have to marry me someday."

He bent and kissed her shoulder. "Deal."